Scream
My Name

Scream
My Name

KIMBERLY KAYE TERRY

APHRODISIA

KENSINGTON BOOKS
http://www.kensingtonbooks.com

APHRODISIA BOOKS are published by

Kensington Publishing Corp.
850 Third Avenue
New York, NY 10022

ISBN-13: 978-0-7582-2875-8
ISBN-10: 0-7582-2875-9

First Kensington Trade Paperback Printing: April 2009

10 9 8 7 6 5 4 3 2 1

Printed in the United States of America

Scream
My Name

Leila

I

_____

"You're on the line with Carmelicious—what's on your mind?" The smooth, husky-timbered voice poured like milk chocolate into Leila's Jeep.

Leila uttered a mild curse, coming to a near halt in the bumper-to-bumper traffic on I-35N, due to an accident further up the highway.

Damn.

Just her luck. Of _course_ there would be an accident, when she needed—desperately needed—to make good time.

Her eyes darted to the flashing numbers on the clock on her dashboard. She couldn't be late for the appointment she had scheduled with the investor. Too much was riding on this meeting.

She blew out a frustrated breath of air, smoothed one of her locs behind her ear, and turned up the volume on the radio.

"Yeah, yeah—hey, Carmelicious, this is your boy, Andre."

"Hello, Andre, I'm listening . . . what's on your mind?"

"Well, now see, this is my first time listenin' to your show, and girl, I don't know what you women are thinkin' saying it's a man's *job* to take care of the financial end and whatnot of a relationship! Y'all done got it twisted!"

"Oh, yeah, Andre? And how have we 'done got it . . . *twisted?*'" There was only a small change in inflection in her softly accented southern voice, a change Leila knew good and well boded ill for the hapless caller—one he was too dense to pick up on.

Andre continued, "Yeah, that's right, this is the new millennium and last time I checked, it was women who started all this equal rights stuff way back in the day. If y'all want equal rights on jobs and thangs, why stop there? Why get all hot around the collar if a man expects the woman to chip in, you know, to—"

"Earn her keep, Andre?" Carmelicious smoothly supplied.

"Yeah! You know what I'm sayin', girl! That's it, that's it! *Earn her keep!* Ain't nothin' for free these days, is what I'm sayin'. So, if a woman expects a man to do for her, well now she damn sure needs to do somethin' for him. Remember that song from back in the day: 'If you do for me, I'll do for you?' Yeah, that's what time it is!"

"And just what is she supposed to *do* for him?" Carmelicious asked, and despite her frustration, Leila smiled at the DJ's oh-so-innocent voice.

"Like that last caller, asking if it's wrong for a woman to want a man to take her out to a five-star restaurant—to wine and dine her. Hell, yeah, there's something wrong wit it! Women been gettin' a free ride for too *long!* Why a man gotta bleed his pockets dry to show a woman a good time in order to get a little sniff of that kitty cat? See here, I can make that cat purr, baby, I can make it purr . . . *grooowwl* . . . you hear me?" Andre asked, warming to his topic, now on a *roll.*

"Uh huh, I hear you, Andre, I hear you! You're even giving Carmelicious sound effects! So no, I ain't mad at you! Go on, Andre."

The caller laughed, foolishly encouraged by Carmelicious's

antics as she egged him on further, thinking she was on board with his craziness. Leila shook her head and inched along in the mad rush-hour traffic, checking the clock on her dashboard, for the third time in the last five minutes.

She had less than twenty minutes to get to her appointment with the investor.

Or with the man she *hoped* would be an investor. God, she needed some serious cash pouring in right about now if she planned on landing a lucrative account with a local fundraising group, catering all their special events, including all their deliciously lucrative political dinners. Leila visualized her near future with a nearly orgasmic shudder of anticipation.

Landing the account would mean bumping up Aunt Sadie's Café, and its new catering side to the next level. Taking Aunt Sadie's to a higher level would mean she could stop working night and day at the café, and hire more people to work for her. She'd be able to enjoy life for the first time in years.

She didn't know the last time she'd gone out and had fun, just a day of shopping without worrying about a check not clearing, or charging one credit card to pay another, robbing Peter to pay Paul. And then there was Mary, with her hand out constantly, asking where her money was. She'd be able to stop playing a juggling act with her food distributors in order to get the supplies she needed to run her business.

And the latest bit of information, that a land developer wanted to buy out the entire two blocks of land where Aunt Sadie's Café had resided for forty years, along with the other small neighboring businesses, was a headache she most definitely didn't need.

Just the thought of her last exchange with Brandan Walters created an instant knot of tension at the back of her head. Damn him.

Leila blew a tired breath of air, and blindly reached for the ever ready bottle of Motrin in the middle of her console near the gear shift.

She couldn't let Aunt Sadie's fold, and she was damned if she'd sell it out to the highest bidder. That was *not* going to happen. She had to make Aunt Sadie's a success; it was all she had left of her great-aunt.

The memories of the two of them working side by side for years, from the time she was a small child and then came to live with Sadie were ones Leila cherished, and no amount of money would lure her into selling the property.

She'd worked day in and day out at the business, along with her small, overworked staff, in order keep the business afloat after Aunt Sadie died. Leila had let things slide then, but felt guilty when she'd climbed out of her grief long enough to see what had happened to the business. She became more determined than ever to see it successful.

And damn if she was going to allow another greedy, self-absorbed conglomeration steal her dreams for the café.

Her great-aunt, the indomitable Aunt Sadie the café was named for, started the business forty years ago, and had lovingly created such delicious meals that the small diner had grown and prospered. When Leila graduated from culinary school, she'd joined her great-aunt, and the two expanded the café to include a catering business.

Her great-aunt was not only a great chef, but was also an astute businesswoman. Leila had been excited about their new ideas, and the pair began to make plans for expansion. They started talks with the shop owner next door, Mr. Gomez, who was ready to retire, about buying his shop. Plans included remodeling the café and adding to the menu some of the more exotic dishes that Leila had become expert at creating, as well as teaching their small staff some of the culinary skills she'd learned in school.

All of that had come to a screeching halt when Sadie had suffered a stroke. After her stroke, she'd had rehab, and although she had to take it easier, she'd rebounded and joined Leila back in the business. Then, everything had been going fine until her great-aunt had suffered more back-to-back strokes that had ultimately proved fatal.

Leila had been lost without Sadie.

Her great-aunt had raised her from infancy after her parents died in a car accident. Sadie had been the only mother, the only family, she'd ever known. Without her, Leila was alone and grief stricken, and the business had suffered.

It had taken reading one of her aunt's old notes she'd found folded in her favorite Bible while clearing out the old dusty attic, to finally allow the pain of her loss to be relieved.

Sadie had always had some quip, always said the right thing at the right time to make Leila feel better. Leila had been going through her things when she'd found her personal black Bible, and opening it, she found a letter Sadie had written to her. In the note she'd written a simple passage that had allowed the tears to flow from Leila's eyes, the pent-up emotions she'd held in check for so long to have free reign, and in doing so, her healing had begun.

Leila, baby, you've been my joy. Without you my life would not have been as rich or as blessed as it has been. Now I know you're probably sad, crying, and carrying on, girl . . . stop those tears. I still want my grandbabies and won't no man want to look at you all red in the face, eyes all swollen, snot running down your nose, if you keep on with all that!

Through her tears, Leila had laughed out loud at Sadie's words. Swallowing her tears and wiping her face with the back of her sleeve, she'd continued reading.

There is "a time to weep and a time to laugh; a time to mourn and a time to dance." I'm not going to quote the rest, because I raised you right and I know you know the passage. Baby, the best thing you can do for your auntie is live and enjoy your life, make Aunt Sadie's all we knew it could be, and find a good man! You do all that, and know that your mama—cause you know you're like my very own baby, the child of my heart—is smiling down at you, happy that her baby is living her life the way I taught her to. And don't forget my grandbabies!

By the end of the note, the tears had gradually come to an end, and Leila was smiling. She'd groaned and laughed when she read the last line, carefully refolded the note, and tucked it back into the worn old Bible, determined to honor her great-aunt's request.

"All except that last line," Leila murmured out loud as she maneuvered in the heavy traffic. "I don't see that happening anytime soon. Auntie Sadie, I need a man for that, and the ones I've come across lately definitely don't bring out any maternal longings in me."

When she noticed the traffic easing, she sighed in relief, downshifted her gears, and switched lanes, seeing her exit coming up ahead.

"Hell, I once took a woman to a lake for a good time with a sack lunch and a smile, and when it was time to get down with it . . . let's just say that the young lady was nice and wet . . . and not from the lake, if you catchin' what I'm throwin' you, girl," the caller Andre guffawed, still on the air with Carmelicious.

Leila put her thoughts of Aunt Sadie and the woes of her business out of her mind, a small grin stretching her mouth as she listened to Carmelicious's caller.

"Oh, *God* . . . no, he didn't," Leila groaned, her attention divided between the hellacious traffic and the nut job on the radio who didn't know Carmelicious was about to serve him his balls on the proverbial platter.

"Oh, yeah, Andre, I do indeed get what you throwing me, playa," the disc jockey laughed lightly. "Tell me more." Carmelicious encouraged the man, her voice still low, sexy, and totally in control.

As though what the caller was saying didn't bother her in the least.

As though she wasn't about to lower the boom. As though she wasn't seconds away from *letting him have it.*

"You're about to get schooled, dude," Leila murmured out loud. The traffic eased and she pressed her foot on the accelerator and shifted the gear stick, finally able to pass the accident, and sped along the highway.

The man didn't know what he had coming, had no idea what he'd gotten himself into. Leila picked up the remote and tapped one of her short nail tips on the small button to raise the volume on her car radio.

"What would you call a nice time? *Hmmm . . .* why don't you tell Carmelicious about this park date, about what you did *to get her all nice and wet.* Hmmm? I'm listening, Boo." Her voice practically oozed sugar and sweetness as she handed poor Andre the rope to hang himself.

And she called him Boo.

Leila made a *tsk* sound and shook her head.

Whenever Carmelicious called one of the hapless males that called into the show Boo, it wasn't an endearment.

This was going to get ugly.

Leila reached down and moved the lever on the side of the seat, and eased herself back. Might as well get comfortable and watch—or listen, as the case may be—to the upcoming train wreck. She lightly rested her hands on her Jeep Cherokee's leathered-covered steering wheel, and relaxed.

"Okay, well . . . after I picked her up, I noticed she was all dressed up, real fancy like, you know?"

"I could imagine," Carmelicious said.

"Yeah, well, uh, then," Andre paused, hesitant, no longer feeling so confident. But he plowed through anyway: "I told her, I said, 'Girl, you might as well change clothes now. Where we're going don't require all that fancy stuff you got on.' Told her there was a change in plans. I was taking her to the lake for a nice moonlit picnic."

"And she was okay with that, Andre? The change in plans, I mean?"

"Yeah, she was cool. Got real excited in fact. So we got to the lake and swam for a while. At first she acted all sididy when the lake I took her to didn't have nobody there. Hell, I thought she'd 'preciate that it was so cozy, with nobody around, just me and her."

"Maybe she was expecting something a little less . . . destitute?" Carmelicious piped in, and if the man had had any sense he would have noticed that her smooth voice had a distinctly sharp edge to it.

He didn't.

Instead, he went on as though he was the wronged party.

"Desti-what? Anyways, I spread out a blanket. It was kind of itchy, was one of my green army blankets, so I made sure I put my T-shirt on top of the spot she was sitting so she wouldn't get itchy."

He went on to explain how when the time came for him to make his *move,* after they'd eaten the authentic Philly steak sandwiches he'd bought back from Austin from the barbeque joint his cousin Melford owned, the young lady refused him.

"Come talkin' 'bout how she don't roll like that! I told her ass she better roll like somethin' cause I didn't go all the way to Austin for them sammiches for nothing!" The more he got into his story of how she was unappreciative of his moonlit picnic at the abandoned lake, the more animated his voice was, the more boisterous he became, until he became downright indignant.

"Umm, hmmm," Carmelicious replied.

"I was 'bout ready to take her unappreciating ass home when she stripped out of her clothes. And oooh wee! Girly had it going on! Apple Bottoms all the way, if you know what I'm sayin'!" He chuckled. "Well, you know, I thought it was time to make that move, yanno? I mean, it was time to get down to the dirty, dirty!" Andre's voice, as he was now fully into his story, was high-pitched. So much so that Leila had to adjust the volume on her radio.

"So after she gets all wet, swimming and whatnot, it's time for Andre to show baby girl how I make a girl wet. Don't need no water, no swimmin', the only strokin' she'd be gettin' was from Daddy Long Stroke, if you get what I'm sayin'." He laughed again at his lame attempt at witticism.

There was a full five second pause after he spoke.

"You still there, Carmelicious?" he asked.

"Yeah, I'm here, Boo."

"Oh. Okay. So what you think about all that?"

"Do you really want to know what I think about you and your Philly steak *sammiches,* your cheap-ass dating practices, and your *Daddy Long Strokes?* I think you need to buy a clue, sweetheart. Now. Do not walk. Do not amble. Do not skip. Run. Run to your nearest clue dealer, barefoot and naked if you need to, and buy your ass a clue. If you *really* want to get a woman nice and wet, treat her with respect. Dignity. Take her to a restaurant where you don't talk into the head of a big-ass clown to take your order. Pull out her chair. Compliment her if she's looking fly when you pick her up for a date instead of telling her to change clothes. If she needs you to help her out, not just with the financial, but with whatever, if you call yourself her man, *do it*. Hell, take out the trash for her without her having to ask your rusty ass. See, Boo, that's what really gets us women *nice and wet."*

With that, a very loud dial tone hummed, before Carmelicious continued. "Maybe I should change the name of the show to *Nice and Wet*. What do you all think?" the DJ laughed. "Alright now, ladies, after educating the latest booga boo for the day, it's time for your honey-colored, self-proclai*iii*med doctor of *love and 'lationships*—and yeah, y'all know I stole that line from Babyface—to roll out!"

Leila, still chuckling over the latest "booga boo" that Carmelicious ministered the long hand of justice to, eased over into the next lane. The road had cleared and she was finally able to pick up speed and maneuver out of the early morning rush.

"I'll catch you all tomorrow. Now it's time for Mr. Clancy O'Neil to take over and start your workday off right with the R&B that gets your heart thumping, your feet tapping, and your booty *moving* . . . on your number one smooth R&B station, from yesterday and today, the one the only KLJS. But I'll see you here bright and early Monday morning. Now it's time for Mr. Clancy O'Neil to take over and start your Friday workday. And ladies, if you run across a man with a greasy-assed sack lunch with a Philly steak sammich and a smile . . . run, *do not walk*, in the opposite direction from that fool as fast as your two feet will carry you! Your girl is out of here for the day, but remember Carmelicious's three S's: always play it sexy, smart, and safe. Y'all be good, but if you can't be good, be delicious in your naughty!"

When Carmelicious said her trademark closure and a Queen Latifah oldie, "Ladies First," came pouring out of the speakers, Leila adjusted the volume on her remote, seeing her exit coming up soon.

She quickly swerved in front of the SUV in the next lane with an apologetic wave so she could make the turn, and exited. When a horn blasted her, she glanced over her shoulder and cringed when she saw the oversize vehicle behind her narrowly miss being hit by a much smaller car riding its bumper.

As Leila rode along the exit, she bit her bottom lip in worry when she saw the vehicles trying to avoid a collision. She reached the light and strained her neck to see the two cars, but was unable to.

Sending a silent prayer upward that she hadn't unintentionally caused a fender bender, she sped through the intersection as soon as the light turned green, checking the time on the dash, her heart racing, hoping she hadn't missed the appointment with the investor.

2

Leila found a space to park in the underground lot, grabbed her briefcase, jumped out of her car, and wearing three-inch heeled black boots, she sprinted as best she could across the cement floor of the garage. When she came to the elevator, she quickly stabbed a short manicured nail on the elevator button, hoping against hope that with the repeated jabs, the elevator would get there sooner.

No such luck.

Impatiently, she checked her diamond-chip antique watch—one of the pieces of jewelry she'd inherited from her great-aunt and uttered a small curse under her breath.

When the elevator doors finally opened, she briskly walked inside and fumbled in her purse to retrieve the slip of paper with the floor for the offices she needed to go to. Pressing the lobby floor button, she waited as the slumbering elevator rose, thinking she could have simply walked up the flight of stairs and arrived there sooner.

When she'd spoken to Jacob Swabb's assistant, she'd been told she'd have to get a pass from security before they'd allow her to go to their offices.

Once the laboring elevator reached the lobby, she walked across the tiled floor, the heels on her boots echoing a loud click, click, click across the tiles, toward the main elevator.

Within seconds of pressing the UP arrow key, the elevator doors opened smoothly and Leila breathed a sigh of relief.

"Miss, I'll need to see some identification, please." Leila glanced around and sighed as she spotted an older uniformed man with an obvious limp slowly ambling toward her.

She forced a smile on her face as she fumbled in her purse for the necessary ID.

Afterwards, she turned away before his voice halted her. "Who you comin' to visit, Ms. James?" he inquired, hoisting his already high-waist pants farther up his body, his hand coming to rest on the nightstick holstered to his wide hips.

"I've got an appointment with Jacob Swabb," she dutifully supplied.

"You'll have to come this way to sign in, young lady." The old man nodded his head toward the kiosk desk where another guard, at least ten years older than he, sat in one of the upright chairs.

Damn, just what she needed. A geriatric watchdog to make her even later than she was.

She walked alongside the limping old man, and in her side vision, sized him up.

She could take him down. Easily.

Her stilettos added three inches to her already impressive five foot, nine inch frame, making the top of the old guard's head reach to about the midpoint of her breasts.

One feign to the left and a swift reverse mad dash to the right. Yep.

That's all it would take.

Old man, you're going down, she thought.

She could reach the elevator, be inside, and on her way up before the old man knew what hit him.

"Lee Lee, God don't like ugly . . ."

Guiltily, Leila hung her head at her mean thoughts as she imagined Aunt Sadie bringing her to task just as she'd done so many times when she was alive.

After what felt like forever, the guard pulled out a large black book and Leila waited impatiently as he fumbled with his glasses before scanning the book.

"Hmmm." He looked away from the book and glanced at Leila over the tops of his bifocals. "You sure you have an appointment with Mr. Swabb?"

"Yes! Please, I don't have time for this. Mr. Swabb is waiting for me!" Leila took a deep breath and forced herself to lower her voice at his bushy, white upraised brows.

"Well, looks like you gone have to wait. 'Cause see here, if you had an appointment with Mr. Swabb, you already missed that boat, honey," he said in a slow and easy southern drawl before shutting the book definitively.

"Wha . . . *what* are you talking about?" she asked, dread pooling in her gut.

"Mr. Swabb had a meetin' to attend. Left 'bout fifteen minutes ago, he did. Ain't that right, Charlie?" he asked the guard sitting next to him.

Without glancing away from the paper, the old man nodded his head and said, "Yep. That's about right, Charlie,"

"Both of your names are Charlie?" Leila asked, momentarily distracted.

"Yep. Makes it easier that way," Charlie number one replied, nodding his head vigorously up and down, his mouth doing some strange movement around his teeth, as though he were chewing on something.

Leila quickly forgot the strangeness of the matching names, and didn't bother to question the oddness of his statement.

What was she going to do now?

"Whaccha gone do now?"

With irritation, she glanced at the old man as he mirrored her exact thoughts.

"Hey, Charlie, how's it going?" a deep masculine baritone voice, asked and Leila turned as both old men began grinning.

She turned her head to see what—or who—had made Charlie number two turn away from his paper, and both Charlies' wrinkled faces split in identical Cheshire Cat grins.

Oh, my. No wonder, Leila thought as soon as she caught the visual of the man coming their way.

Her breath caught in her throat and everything feminine inside her cried out in welcome as well.

Leila had always prided herself on the fact that she was no wilting flower, no damsel in distress. She was a strong, capable, independent businesswoman on her own who didn't need or want a man to complete her.

She was educated, talented, and had her own business. Even though she was fast approaching the big three-oh, and hadn't had a date in longer than she wanted to think about, she was more than happy with her life. On her own.

But . . . well, *damn*.

She didn't know the last time she'd been presented with a fine piece of manhood like the one coming her way.

Even from a distance she could tell the man was built like a Mack truck, all broad shoulders tapering down to a trim waist and, as her eyes traveled down the rest of his body, legs so thick they looked like they could choke the heck out of a horse.

Her gaze traveled back up the length of his body. He wore a broad Stetson on his head, shadowing his eyes, but as he drew nearer she could see a finely chiseled nose, a sensual mouth with a slight crinkle in the corner as though he was used to smiling, and a strong square chin with a deep dimple in the center.

At her height, and with her penchant for wearing heels three inches or higher, even while at work in the café, she was used to being eye level with most men. Usually she had the advantage, and many had to look up to her to see her face.

But not with this one.

As he stood in front of the kiosk, his eyes—startling they

were so vividly blue—ran over her in a lazy appraisal and Leila felt an instant awareness arc between them. She felt off kilter, strange, as he gazed at her.

The old guards exchanged remarks, and when the blue-eyed man turned away from her, she let out a small whoosh of air, unaware that she'd even been holding her breath.

Lord, what a man.

A man's man, her great-aunt would say about this one, Leila thought in reluctant appreciation and agreement.

As he greeted the guards, Leila's admiring glance traveled back over him, from his trouser-clad thick legs, over his muscular tight butt she thought she could bounce a quarter off of, over the shirt tucked into his lean waist, and over his thick chest and broad shoulders . . . until her eyes met his bright-eyed gaze. He tipped his hat in a small silent salute.

Embarrassed to be caught so obviously ogling him, Leila pulled herself up short and glanced away.

"Mr. Walters! How you doin' today?" Charlie number one asked.

"Nothing much new, fellas. Another day, another dollar," he returned in a deep, lazy baritone.

The kind of voice that brought to mind long hot summer days, with her perched on top of an old fence, watching him rope cattle with sweat glistening off his hard bare chest, tight jeans firmly molding his even tighter hind end, wearing the Stetson perched down low . . .

As her imagination took flight, Leila felt a chill wash over her skin. She crisscrossed her arms over her chest, running her hands over the back of her arms at her unexpected yet very vivid imagery.

Her body's reaction to his sexy baritone, along with her overly active imagination, was as immediate as it was undeniable. Her nipples beaded against her bra, her stomach clenched, and she had to run her tongue over lips, despite the sheen of gloss she'd swiped over them.

Embarrassed at herself, although no one knew what she was thinking, she cringed. She didn't know when the last time the sound of a man's voice got her so hot and bothered.

But she knew good and well it wasn't only his voice, as sexy as it was, that had her body acting like a cat in heat.

She slid her glance over his big body, standing so close to hers, and felt warmth radiating from him, reaching out to her like some kind of heat-seeking missile.

He turned to face her and removed his hat, running one big hand through the dark, thick strands.

His hair, a dark rich sable, was cut low in the back, and the front was slightly longer, long enough to form deep waves.

One corner of his mouth hitched upward as he looked at her, and as if she had no control over her own lips, Leila felt them return the smile.

His smile widened, showing his canines, and Leila was reminded of a hunter on the prowl. She shivered when goose bumps sprinkled over her arms.

His gaze roved the length of her body, starting at the point of her high heel boots, and slowly traveled up to her hips in the slim-fitting short black leather skirt, to the indenture of her waist, before he stopped at the fullness of her breasts pressing against her blouse.

When his hot gaze centered directly on her breasts, she felt her nipples tighten and poke past the flimsy protection of her bra, pressing hot, hard, and thick against the silk of her blouse.

And obviously very visible.

She saw his swift intake of breath as his eyes flew to hers. For one moment, the two of them were enveloped in a silent, sensual cocoon, hyperaware of each other as everything else around them faded away to nothingness.

Leila's breath caught and her mouth became dry.

Their attraction was unexpected. Instant. Combustible.

"Got a busy day planned, Mr. Walters?" Leila heard one of the Charlies ask, as though from a distance.

When the man turned his head away from her, with what looked like reluctance, she closed her eyes briefly and blew out a breath of air, feeling as though she'd just been slammed with a semitruck and had been holding her breath for hours, instead of the few seconds their exchange had been.

"And I've told you both, my name is Brandan. Mr. Walters was my daddy," he replied with an easy smile.

The men spoke briefly and the sensual fog she'd been wrapped in slowly cleared.

Walters. Brandan Walters.

Damn, why did that name sound so familiar? Leila worried it over in her mind until realization dawned.

Sanchez, Walters and Reed.

Her eyes widened and her heart slammed against her chest as she glanced back over the man . . . Brandan Walters . . . as he casually spoke to the two Charlies.

Sanchez, Walters and Reed was the name on the letterhead at the top of the legal papers she'd been receiving over the last two months from the corporation trying to buy out the block of downtown businesses where her restaurant was located.

The same corporation she was hell-bent on fighting. The same corporation that was *just* as hell-bent on acquiring her property to capitalize on the city's downtown revitalization project.

Their plans were to build a set of high-end condominiums that would compliment the city's plans for building an exclusive shopping district, hoping to attract wealthier patrons to the downtown area.

Her eyes narrowed as she stared a hole in the back of his head.

This was the same man she'd been involved with in heated,

sometimes down-and-dirty notes and emails over the last two months.

The same man she'd also decided it was high time she met face-to-face, once their heated exchanges had reached the point where she was dreaming of the unknown man at night.

Embarrassed, confused, and thinking there was something seriously wrong with her when she'd woken just this morning with her hands buried in her cooch after having a wet dream about a man she not only loathed, but had never met. The time for some lovin' was long overdue if he began to invade her dreams at night.

Leila felt incredibly stupid at that moment. In her excitement over meeting the investor, it hadn't dawned on her that his address was the same as that of Sanchez, Walters and Reed's.

She narrowed her eyes and glanced at him leaning casually against the kiosk talking to the old guards, her mind at work, furiously trying to figure how she could use this time to her advantage.

"I'd better head on up to the office, gentlemen." His words brought her mind to a spinning halt.

Yes.

He turned to her and smiled. "Have a nice day, ma'am," he said, nodding his head, a glint in his bright blue eyes. He paused as though waiting for something.

She simply nodded her head in return and murmured some good wishes. God, what could she do? What could she say to prolong the moment? She had to think of something, and quick, in order to use this time.

Aunt Sadie's Café depended on it.

She felt his hesitation, as though he wanted to say something to her, when Charlie number one spoke.

"Sir, I believe a young lady headed up to your offices a bit ago, said she had an appointment with you? Isn't that right, Charlie?" he asked, scratching his head and turning to Charlie number two who sagely nodded his head, his attention focused on the newspaper.

Damn those Charlies!

"Thanks for the heads-up, guys. Guess I'd better go then," he said, and with one final look her way, left, his long legs taking him away from them.

Then he walked away, cheerfully whistling, no doubt thinking of some other poor woman's dreams he was going to demolish. Leila grit her teeth.

She shoved out of her mind the fact that he'd invaded her dreams the night before, before she'd ever met him. And now that she'd met him in the flesh . . .

She shook her head. No time for those thoughts.

She unconsciously began to drum her fingers on the kiosk and stared at his broad, retreating back before her lips stretched into a wide smile.

"Anything else we can do for ya, Miss?" Charlie number one asked, a frown on his aged face as he stared down at her.

"No. Thank you, men, for your help. I'll just call next week and reschedule with Mr. Swabb." With a nod in their direction she quickly walked away.

Leila turned as though walking toward the exit. She glanced over her shoulder and once the old men were no longer looking in her way, she quickly reversed her steps and walked briskly toward the closing elevator.

"I'll tell you what I'm going to do now," she murmured and stepped inside the elevator. "I'm going to pay Mr. Brandan Walters a little visit."

3

After Brandan entered his inner office, he casually tossed his Stetson in a nearby chair.

He sat down in the oversize leather chair behind his desk, picked up the phone, and buzzed his assistant.

"Judith, what do I have scheduled for this afternoon?" he asked.

"Why don't I bring in your calendar when I bring your coffee, Mr. Walters?" she asked, and Brandan agreed.

Today was Friday, the last Friday of the month, and he wanted to break away early if possible so he could make it to Austin before the rush hour traffic hit.

He had a full weekend ahead and the past few weeks he hadn't had the chance to get away, kick back with a beautiful woman, and leave business behind.

This weekend he had plans with a beautiful hot blonde he'd met the previous week, and he wanted to spend the entire weekend letting her prove she could do all the things her body promised it could deliver.

Damn, it had been too long since he'd been with a woman.

By choice. He'd been restless lately, and although he'd had plenty of opportunities, he'd declined the many offers thrown his way, much to his partners' amusement.

Damian told him he needed to stop "ho-ing" around, settle down, and find the right woman. And after he'd stopped laughing at *that* thought, Mateo accused him of being in a sexual slump, and claimed the cure wasn't abstinence—as their happily married partner, Damian claimed—but the exact opposite. His advise was to go out and saturate himself with women, all the while laughing at Damian's assertions of true love and commitment to one woman.

Whatever the answer, he needed . . . something, he thought. Something that would ease away the tension that had been steadily growing the longer he went without a woman.

If he thought about it, the last time he'd been with a woman had been shortly before he'd started communications with Leila James, the owner of one of the properties he and his partners were trying to buy.

Just the thought of the woman, and her sharp little emails—emails that had started off professional, telling him she had no plans to sell her property, but had grown progressively sharp—provoked him.

A reluctant laugh burst from his mouth when he thought of their last exchange. She'd emailed him with her usual in-your-face attitude, and he'd shot back an answer, telling her they'd simply build around her and her little shop. He even referred to Dr. Seuss's tale of the two stubborn creatures who refused to see logic, oblivious to the fact that the world went on, with or without their assent.

Well . . . she then called back, and left a blistering message on his voicemail, basically calling him a money hungry, no sex-life having dirt bag whose only aspiration in life was to trump on small business owners' dreams.

She'd told him that if he had had a life, he'd have better

things to do with his time than harass her. He'd definitely have better things to do than to read Dr. Seuss. Instead of screwing around with her, he'd be out getting screwed by a woman.

"Damn," he muttered, and shook his head. "Hell, maybe there's some truth to that," he murmured out loud.

It had gotten to where he looked forward to their exchanges, and if a few days went by and he'd not heard from her, he'd shoot her an email.

Always polite, to the point ... with just a bit of bite. She seemed to like it that way, he thought with a laugh. More than once he'd contemplated calling her and inviting her out to have a drink where they could talk about the issue, but had refrained from doing so.

He had an image of what she looked like, how she would be, firmly in his mind. He wasn't ready to chance that the reality, and his fantasy of her might be nothing alike. The conversations, emails though they were, had been the most engaging conversations he'd had with a woman in too long a time.

Thinking back, her voice, low, smoky, deep, and sexy as hell, had turned him on more than any of his recent dates had. He had to admit to a certain anticipation if and when they ever met.

As he waited for Judith to appear, his thoughts left Leila James and went to the woman in the lobby. He smiled, the edges of his lips pulling up in a purely masculine way.

She'd immediately caught his attention the minute he'd entered the lobby and laid eyes on her long leggy body.

Even from the back he could see her agitation as she spoke with the Charlies.

Brandan chuckled. Hell, anybody not familiar with the Charlies would get agitated with the pair and their antics.

He'd checked her out, starting at the tips of the sexy stiletto-heeled boots on her feet that added at least three inches to her already impressive height. His gaze had then traveled up the length of her long shapely legs—legs that had instantly wrought images of being wrapped around his waist—to her softly rounded hips, past the sexy indentation of her waist, and onward to small, perfectly rounded breasts pressed tightly together, highlighting the soft swell of her dark honey-colored cleavage.

She had the most striking face he'd ever seen. Bold features, full sensual lips, light brown eyes with a ring of gold around her irises, tilted up slightly at the corners, giving her a mischievous look.

High sculpted cheekbones, and a small nose with the slightest hint of a dimple at the end, completed the picture of bold, unabashed beauty.

She'd had her long hair in what looked like upswept dreadlocs, yet several had defiantly escaped the sophisticated updo, and for a moment, Brandan had wanted to wrap his fist around the errant locs and pull her to him.

"Mmmm," Brandan smiled.

The memory alone was enough to make a man forget his responsibilities and hunt out the sexy, statuesque beauty.

Damn.

It didn't help matters when he'd caught her large, sleepy eyes roaming over him, head to toe. Just as he had been checking out every fine inch out of her.

They hadn't exchanged a word.

Hadn't needed to.

They'd been caught in some strange cocoon of their own until one of the Charlies had interrupted. He could still feel the aftereffects.

Hot. Charged. Electric.

Judith, his assistant, walked in his opened door with a steaming cup of coffee in one hand, and balancing his calendar in the other, effectively dousing the directions his thoughts were taking him regarding the woman downstairs, and their strange, sexually-charged encounter.

"I have your calendar and coffee, Mr. Walters."

She placed the mug of coffee in front of him and sat down in the chair facing his desk, her half lenses perched on the end of her nose as she glanced over his calendar.

Judith was old school, and when it came to organizing Brandan's calendar, had a tendency to forget such things as spreadsheets and Microsoft Excel.

Neither did she deem it professional to take him up on his many requests for her to call him by his first name. She was all business, from the top of her neatly coiled hair, to the conservative three-piece suit, to the bottom of her appropriately-heeled navy blue pumps.

"Thanks, Judith," he replied before taking a drink of the coffee she'd sweetened perfectly to his taste.

"Umm . . . perfect," he murmured, and was rewarded for his praise with a minute uplift of her thin lips in what he *thought* was a smile.

"Thank you, Mr. Walters," she replied, and sat very straight on her chair, her legs close together as she perched on the edge of the leather chair.

The way she sat always reminded him of a tiny bird preparing for flight at any moment.

She even looked like a bird, Brandan thought, surreptitiously running his eyes over her small, frail-looking form.

At six feet, six inches tall, he was used to towering over most women, and many men. Judith couldn't be much taller than five feet, as the tip of her neatly coifed chignon barely reached his midsection. He always felt like a giant next to the small woman.

Although he'd instructed her on her first day working for him five years ago that business attire around the office was casual, Judith continued to wear variations of the same business suit she wore today: dark blue skirt and matching jacket, dress shirt, and sensible shoes.

Nothing like the beauty in the lobby, he thought, his mind again going back to the woman he'd encountered.

"Ahem . . . are you ready, Mr. Walters?"

Brandan shook his head and felt his cheeks warm. Damn. Caught daydreaming like some schoolboy with a crush.

"Sorry about that, Judith. Just thinking about the downtown project," he said, though he could have sworn he saw her brow rise as though she could read his thoughts and knew he hadn't exactly had his mind on acquiring the new commercial property.

He adjusted himself in his chair before he gave Judith his full attention, firmly putting the woman from the lobby out of his mind.

"Yes, well, shall we go over your calendar, sir?"

Leila furtively looked up and down the long hallway, making sure no one saw her. She felt a bit crazy, knowing she was acting way over the top.

One would think she was attempting to break into Harry Winston's to steal the Hope Diamond the way she was acting.

She checked her watch. It was close to lunch.

After her duck into the elevator to avoid the two Charlies' watchful eyes, her triumph had been short-lived when she realized she didn't know which floor held the offices of Sanchez, Walters and Reed. She'd had to do a retreat and regroup, trying to figure how she could find out without going back to the lobby and risk running into either Charlie.

So, she'd done it the hard way.

Thankfully, it was past time that most people used the elevators, after most were settled into their offices, and not yet time for the mass exodus of lunch.

So she'd pressed each button—all thirteen of them—gotten out, and checked each glass door. Most had the name of the company displayed, and only a few times did she actually have to go inside the doors to find out. It was on her sixth try, that it finally hit her: Just ask one of the receptionists which floor held Walters's business.

She cursed Brandan Walters, mentally blaming him for her unusual denseness, particularly when she found out he was on the top floor.

The penthouse.

Figures, Leila thought with a curl of her upper lip.

That accomplished, she'd thanked God there was no special key to access the top floor.

Now here she was acting like a cat burglar as she crept down the long hallway, her heels sinking into the thick, plush carpet. At the end of the hall a large glass door with a small discrete plaque proclaimed itself to be the office of Sanchez, Walters and Reed.

What was she going to do now?

In her mental figurings and planning, she hadn't exactly thought of just *what* she was going to do once she reached his office, only that she had to seize the opportunity quickly.

Opportunity for what? that unwanted voice of reason asked. What was she going to do? Storm inside, demand that Brandan see her, and once he did, he'd listen to what she had to say and abandon his plans to buy her out?

Fat chance.

She'd once tried to make an appointment with one of his partners, but to no avail. The man hadn't even had the decency to return any of her calls.

And then she'd gotten a passive aggressive note from Brandan Walters, explaining that she was the lone owner holding up progress, and it had been on between them, at that point.

The two of them had gone back and forth, first in letters, and then in emails. She'd not gone the route of demanding a face-to-face conference, hadn't even called him. Call it pride or whatever, but she wasn't up for being ignored again.

But then he'd likened her to a Dr. Seuss character, and she'd lost it. She called him and had gotten his voicemail. She hadn't even been aware of what she said to him, she'd been so angry. But she was *sure* it was something that would have had her great-aunt, had she still been alive, washing her mouth out with lye soap.

Although, in his emails, Brandan hadn't made her feel ignored at all. Truth be told, she had begun to look forward to their emails, his always professional, yet she felt his humor coming through on several occasions.

Particularly when she all but called the man a lowlife, an unscrupulous hustler, out to make that almighty dollar by any means necessary.

Okay, so maybe she'd gone a *tad* too far on that one. But Aunt Sadie's meant everything to her. It wasn't about the money. The money they'd offered had now doubled, and the initial offer had been lucrative. She knew some of her neighbors weren't exactly pleased with her.

Yesterday she'd caught several of them going to Ms. Mayflower's shop late at night. She knew the woman had never really liked Aunt Sadie because of an old rivalry over some man long forgotten. Her great-aunt had been a beautiful woman and had never settled down with one man, but always had some handsome man calling on her.

But no matter what, she knew her great-aunt never messed around with another woman's "leftovers," as her aunt had laughingly once put it. So whatever beef Ms. Mayflower had with Sadie, it had been one-sided at best.

As soon as the offer had come from Sanchez, Walters and Reed, Ms. Mayflower had been the first one to jump on board. When it became known that Leila was against the buyout, that had seemed to spur the old lady on to start a campaign against her.

Leila shrugged it off, putting it to the back on her mind so she could concentrate on the here and now. She straightened her back, and purposely strode toward the door.

She'd figure out a game plan once she was inside.

4

"I would like to get out of here early today, Judith."

Brandan placed his balled fist at the small of his back and massaged his aching joints. He grimaced when the knot refused to loosen.

"Can I get you something for that?"

Brandan swiftly removed his hands from his back at her inquisition.

"No. I'm fine. Just a few kinks I can walk out." He feigned nonchalance when he took a faulty step and stumbled before he quickly righted himself.

Actually his back hurt like a son of a bitch.

The ever efficient Judith opened one of the drawers of her desk and withdrew two pills, holding them out in the palm of her hand.

He was so used to playing off the pain, he automatically said no when asked if he was hurting. Judith, of course, knew better. Gratefully, he accepted the pills and swallowed them without the benefit of water.

"Thanks, Judith."

"Well, let's see, after the meeting with the partners, that's it for your day. You don't have anything pressing that can't wait until Monday," she replied after he nodded in gratitude. "They should be here any moment," she finished.

"Good," he replied, and just as he glanced at the large face dial on his Rolex, his door opened and both of his partners, Mateo Sanchez and Damian Reed, walked inside.

"Right on time, gentlemen. Let's go in my office," he said after greeting both men.

He'd known Mateo since high school, and the pair had met Damian while playing college football at Texas A&M, and the three men had become friends.

Brandan and Damian had been drafted right after their senior year to the same NFL team, while Mateo hadn't.

Instead, after completing his bachelor's and master's degree in business, Mateo had returned to San Antonio and gone into business with his father, a wealthy local who was a residential and commercial real estate owner, with holdings spread throughout Texas.

Damian had played ball for several years, traded from the team he and Brandan had gotten drafted to originally, yet they all kept in touch with one another and remained friends. When Brandan had gotten injured was no longer able to play, and been forced to retire, Mateo had approached him about going into business together.

Damian followed soon after he'd retired due to an injury as well, and the men went into the commercial real estate business together.

By aggressively learning the market, paying close attention to real estate trends, anticipating up-and-coming commercial hot spots, and buying land before it was desirable in urban and downtown areas in various cities, they'd soon become one of the top commercial real estate companies in the state.

Mateo had grown up with money, while Brandan and Damian

hadn't, both having earned football scholarships to attend college.

Damian had grown up in a middle class home with both of his parents and a slew of younger sisters. Mateo had taken an instant liking to Damian, and the two had become close, nearly as close as brothers.

Brandan had grown up alone with just his mother, and nine times out of ten, unless he was in a football game, his mother had been too busy working to give him much attention. Had it not been for one of the ranchers his mother worked for as a cook, he would have never been able to attend the football camps as a teen that had helped him earn a scholarship for college.

When Brandan hadn't had a place to go on spring breaks, knowing that it wasn't really an option for him to stay with his mother once he'd graduated high school and was no longer a child, instead of staying around the dormitories, Damian had invited him to go home with him.

At first he'd been apprehensive about going home with Damian. He'd heard many stories about Damian's father, who, from the pictures he'd seen, was his twin in looks as well as size, running off any man who looked twice at any of his daughters.

He'd been told many stories about Damian's close-knit family, he being the only boy with five sisters, and a father who was hell-bent on keeping his daughters away from any man between the ages of eighteen and eighty.

Now, Mateo, first checking to see if anything was on the seat, lifted the tail of his suit jacket, fanning it away from his body so he wouldn't sit on it.

After he sat, he brushed away imaginary lint from his gabardine slacks and matching suit jacket, and adjusted the gold diamond-studded cuff links on his shirt.

Mateo was the most fastidious straight man Brandan had ever met.

Every pleat on his pants was pressed to perfection, his shirts were always crisp, and although the office was casual, like Judith, Mateo chose more formal business attire than either he or Damian.

He walked into the office looking like he was ready for a damn formal event in near military precision.

He was like that in everything he did. From his personal attire, to the car he drove—a sleek metallic gray Aston Martin Vanquish—to the women he dated.

All were beautiful and unattainable for the average Joe . . . expensive and perfect.

"So, is everything a go with the Miller project?" Damian asked, interrupting his thoughts.

Although their main interest was seeking out potential lucrative land to sell later, when interest in the area was hot, they were involved in projects where they were investors in the new development as well.

At Brandan's request, they'd become investors in a city youth center project, located near the downtown area.

"It's a go. Demolition is set for next month. The architects' plans were approved and the first rising will be in late spring. Just got the report from Bronsons," Brandan replied, referring to the architectural firm that was responsible for the building plans.

The center would be private, but because the city was involved, something Brandan himself had made sure of, scholarships on a sliding scale would be available to those who couldn't afford the annual dues.

"How's it going with the Santiago block?" Damian asked, referring to their latest project. "Any word yet on the tenants? How many have agreed?"

"Let's see, I have it somewhere. Let me check," Brandan replied and opened the black leather-bound notebook in his hand, flipping through it until he'd found the page he was looking for.

Though he really didn't need to check. The project details, as well as Leila James, were firmly entrenched in his mind.

"It's all good. Just waiting for one last tenant."

"Same woman who sent us the letter protesting us 'destroying her livelihood?'" Mateo asked and laughed.

"Yeah," Brandan said, and ran a hand through his hair in frustration. "Leila James. Owner of Aunt Sadie's Café. In fact, she's taking it up a notch. Says she going to fight us. Going to the city's Hall of Historical Records to stop us from buying the land."

"How in hell is she going to do that?" Mateo asked, his good humor rapidly disintegrating.

"She says there's some tree on her property that has historical significance."

"Damn, if it's not one thing, it's something else. She's the only one holding out on us, and holding up the project. The other owners were more than happy to sell and get five times what their businesses were worth!" he replied, a frown creasing his brow as he glanced over the document. "What the hell does she want? You'd think she'd be happy to get it off her hands. Didn't she inherit it or something?"

"Let me see it," Damian asked. With a sigh of disgust, Mateo handed the document over.

Just the mention of the woman—Leila James—caused conflicting emotions for Brandan. He'd been the one "assigned" to deal with her. Over the course of the last few months, the woman had raised his blood pressure to soaring levels. He didn't know what would happen if he were to actually come face-to-face with the woman, but it was something that admittedly—embarrassingly—he inexplicably got hard just thinking about.

Damn. Yeah, he needed a woman.

"I'll contact her again," was all he said to his partners.

"So that's it, right?"

"You got plans?" Damian asked, handing the document back to Brandan.

"Yeah. A date," Brandan replied absentmindedly, and placed the document back in its file.

"With who, Serena?"

"No, broke it off a few weeks ago with her."

"This makes what? The third new woman in as many weeks, amigo?" Mateo replied with an easy laugh.

"And the problem with that is . . . ?"

They all laughed. Brandan knew he wasn't known to keep dating one woman much longer than a few months, but even for him, this was a lot.

"Looking for Ms. Right?" Mateo asked, and a small smile lifted one corner of his mouth.

"About as much as you are."

"Yeah . . . *right.*"

"You guys never know, stranger things have happened. The right woman could come along, and you'll be trading your sports cars for minivans with built-in TVs to keep the kiddies occupied while you take a road trip to Disneyland," Damian laughingly warned.

A look of indescribable horror flashed across Mateo's face, and Brandan barked out a laugh, only to have Damian turn to him.

"What are you laughing at? Out of the two of you, I'd lay my kids' college fund that you're the first one to be picking out a beige tricked-out minivan!"

"Yeah, well, I don't think Wanda would like you losing your kids' tuition money on that one. I like the single life just fine."

"Man, not every woman is the same."

When his friend turned his dark-eyed gaze toward him, Brandan felt the slightest bit of discomfort, as though Damian was looking right through him.

He knew Damian was referring to his mother and their uncomfortable relationship. "The right woman comes along and man, it's like *BAM*, that's all she wrote. Tagged and bagged . . . the rest is history."

"That would have to be one hell of a woman. And one big-ass bag," Brandan replied nonchalantly.

Before Damian could respond, the office door flung open abruptly.

"Miss, I'm sorry, but you don't have an appointment! You can't just go in there—"

"I'm sorry Mr. Walters—gentlemen—I thought she'd left after I told her you were unavailable. I went to the restroom but when I came back, she was going inside! I tried to stop her but she—"

Surprised, all three men stared, each with varying expressions on their face, as a beautiful, tall, determined-looking woman stood towering behind Brandan's small, very flustered assistant.

"Look, miss, I've told you—"

"No, that's fine, Judith. She can come in. In fact, why don't you head out for the day. I'll lock up," he said, never taking his eyes off the woman who'd moved from behind Judith, and was now watching all of them with an air of majestic expectancy. As though she had every right to barge into his office without notice.

It was the woman from the lobby.

Brandan barely noticed when Judith reluctantly took her leave. He saw both of his partners staring at the woman with just as much interest as he, and when he noticed a sly-ass grin cross Mateo's face, something in him wanted to knock the man's teeth down his throat.

He turned to the woman and asked, "We have an appointment, Ms . . . ?"

5

Okay, so now that she'd barged inside, she had to do something.

She thought Brandan was alone, even though his assistant told her he was busy. After she'd come up earlier and had seen the amount of traffic going in and out of his office, she'd decided to retreat and figure out some sort of game plan.

So instead of going to his office, she'd left instead, done a bit of window shopping, absentmindedly strolling around the busy midtown area, her mind working through the puzzle of saving her restaurant.

She'd returned after a hour or so, wanting to catch him before he left for the day. She still didn't exactly know what she was going to say to him.

Now she stood in the room, with three very interested pair of eyes staring at her, each with varying expressions on their faces.

As Judith firmly closed the door behind her, Leila in turn glanced at each of the men in the room.

She vaguely remembered the assistant telling her that Mr. Walters was leaving after the meeting with his partners. At the time, her only thought had been to catch him before he left for the weekend.

Leila quickly ran an assessing eye over each of them, her natural ability to sum up a man quickly coming to her aid.

Like Brandan, the two other men in the room were large, although neither had the breadth of shoulders and sheer overall intense masculine presence that Brandan did.

These were his partners, she assumed, and the one lounging in the chair closest to Brandan was probably Mateo Sanchez. His olive-colored skin and dark wavy hair suggested that he was.

His eyes, nearly black, ran over her in a lazy, very sexual manner, a look she was quite used to. And though he was gorgeous, with his dark coloring, classic features, and olive-colored complexion set off to perfection against this designer suit—Armani if her guess was correct—his obvious interest didn't do a thing for her.

She turned her gaze to the third man occupying the room. He too was large, muscled, and one fine specimen of manhood as well. His skin was the color of bitter milk chocolate, and his features were bold, with lips full and luscious, her personal favorite. The kind of lips that devoured a woman in one fatal swoop. The kind of lips a woman would be crazy *not* to want to devour her.

He must be Damian Reed, the third partner in their firm. Whereas Sanchez's gaze was openly interested, openly sexual in his appraisal, this man's was much more subtle, as though he appreciated the way she looked, but that was about it.

Leila wasn't conceited, but she had a mirror, had grown up with them in fact, so she was quite aware she was attractive. She just didn't allow it to define her.

So yes, in his dark-eyed gaze she saw male appreciation, but that was all she detected. A quick look at his left hand, with its gleaming gold band, told her the reason.

Although that never stopped half the men she knew from checking out a woman, this one simply gave her the impression that he was curious as to who she was, not that he wanted to get in her panties.

And the eyes told it all. Leila had been taught by her great-aunt that a person's eyes never lied. Sanchez's eyes told her he was a player. This man's eyes told her he wasn't.

After her quick assessment, she turned to Brandan. And though this was the first time they'd met in person, she felt as though she *knew* him.

The look in his bright blue eyes shot electric awareness her way, just as she'd experienced downstairs in the lobby, straight to her gut. The same sparks she'd been feeling from the first time they'd exchanged communication, before she'd ever met the man.

She shivered, cleared her throat, and spoke. "I, uh . . . I thought I'd come by . . . so that we could continue our business discussion," she said, clearing her throat again.

She hoped to God he wouldn't embarrass her by asking what the hell she was talking about. She held her breath.

As soon as she spoke, she saw his eyes narrow, a frown creasing his forehead. Her heart sank straight to her toes and her gut clenched, preparing for him to bust her out.

He surprised her.

"Absolutely. I agree," he said, and Leila almost sank to the floor in relief.

Some of the nervous flutters in her stomach calmed, and she inhaled a small, quick breath and sent a quiet "thank you" heavenward. "Why don't you come in, have a seat. My partners and I were just finishing up for the day."

Leila felt like crossing her arms over her chest in feminine protection against his looks, as he leisurely glanced her over as she stood stiffly in the doorway.

The two stared at each other, the attraction she felt down-stairs hitting her again. She tried to ignore it, reminding herself she was on a mission here—not to get laid, but to save her busi-ness.

"I thought you had plans, Brandan. I'd be happy to sit in for you with Ms.—"

Leila reluctantly moved her eyes away from Brandan Wal-ters and surveyed the man who was watching the exchange with interested dark brown eyes.

"James," she replied. "Leila James," she said, noticing all three men sitting up further in their chairs.

She waited for recognition to set in. The wait wasn't long.

"Would that be the same Leila James who owns Aunt Sadie's Café?"

Leila turned to the tall, handsome black man who asked the question, and mentally braced herself to remain calm, stiffening her spine when she noted how the atmosphere in the room sub-tly changed from idly curious to hostile in five seconds flat.

"Yes," she replied.

"Didn't know you had a meeting planned with Ms. James," the one she assumed was Sanchez casually replied, but Leila wasn't fooled.

"We're done here, right gentlemen?" Brandan asked, turn-ing to his partners with expectancy. "Ms. James and I have din-ner plans."

Her head whipped around, surprised. A fiery spark of aware-ness arced wildly between them as he waited to see if she'd dis-pute his words. When she only slightly nodded her head, he turned to his partners in satisfaction.

Although both Mateo and Damian rose to their feet, it was Mateo who, with a slightly raised dark brow, asked, "I thought you had plans of a different sort tonight, amigo. Weren't they with Selena?" He snapped two fingers and "tsked" himself before continuing. "Sorry amigo, that would be Angela, wouldn't it? Serena was last week, si?" he blithely continued.

He strolled toward Leila with his hand outstretched and a small half grin on his face.

Brandan wanted to knock his gleaming-ass teeth down his throat, anger washing over him in crimson waves.

She allowed Mateo to grasp her hand with both of his. He lifted it to his lips and kissed the back of her hand.

Brandan's jealousy eased when he caught her withdrawal and the fleeting flash of irritation cross her face before she schooled her expression, and gave his partner a tight smile.

Yes. This was the woman he had come to know through their emails. The kind of woman who, if given the right provocation, would not tolerate such liberties from a man she didn't know.

"Why don't you allow me to take you to dinner instead? I'm more than willing to listen to whatever . . . proposition you have in mind," Mateo murmured, and when he released her hand, Leila resisted the very tempting desire to wipe her hand on her skirt.

Everyone's attention was on Brandan, and Leila was fascinated by the slight flush that colored his cheeks.

He walked over to Mateo and, although the two men were of similar height, Brandan seemed, at that moment, to tower over his partner as he stood glowering at him.

"That won't be necessary, *amigo*, I can make arrangements to reschedule my other . . . appointment," he said, subtly maneuvering his body so that he stood closer to Leila.

Leila looked at both men, biting the inside of her cheek, working this new puzzle in her mind.

By any means necessary.

That was her motto when it came to saving Aunt Sadie's.

She glanced toward the other partner, as he too came sauntering her way, a look of supreme amusement on his dark hand-some face.

"Whichever one of my partners you decide to discuss your situation with, Ms. James, I'm sure you'll make the right choice."

Leila tried to discern a deeper meaning in his words from his facial expression, but with that cryptic answer, he wished them all a good weekend and left the office, leaving Leila alone with two men, both of whom wanted, for their own reasons, to take her out to dinner.

She bit back a smile.

Things were looking up for her and Aunt Sadie's, she thought, hiding her smile of satisfaction as she glanced at each man in turn.

6

"Beautiful. I've never been here before," Leila said as Mateo handed the waiter both of their menus.

She'd come to the upscale French restaurant, Loiseau's, at his enthused suggestion after she'd decided to allow him to take her out to dinner.

She had been torn. She'd come to the office, not sure what to expect, and with the surprise outcome of both men wanting to take her out, the tension in Brandan's office had been palpable.

Her objective was to petition that they abandon their plans to buy the block of land and toward that end, she debated which man would be the one more likely to hear her side. Which one would really listen to what she had to say.

She was a painfully honest woman, even to herself, therefore she acknowledged there was the added tantalizing element that both men were interested in her. And she doubted it had much to do with urban renewal and development.

For reasons beyond her, or ones she chose not to examine closely, she'd decided to take Mateo up on his offer of dinner and conversation. She'd had communication with Brandan for over two months, and all the man had managed to do was infuriate her, and have her long to strangle his neck.

She'd then taken a look at him, his big body casually leaning against his desk, observing her with a look that sent crazy chills running down her spine, and revised her opinion.

Hmmm. As thick as his neck was, she doubted she could wrap her hands around them to make good on her threats. She'd caught him staring at her, one corner of his mouth hitched in a smile that made her teeth clench, as though he could read her thoughts.

After seeing the smirk on his infuriating, albeit handsome face, her mind was most definitely made up.

She accepted Mateo's offer, telling Brandan she didn't want to cause him to change his plans for her. At her decision, some of the smugness dropped and she saw his face tighten when Mateo had escorted her out of the office.

She'd not been able to resist looking back over her shoulder as they left. She'd caught the tic in the corner of his mouth, denoting his irritation, along with the hooded look in his eyes when his gaze had centered on Mateo's hand at the small of her back as he ushered her out the door.

"Yes, it is. I come as much as I can. Particularly with a beautiful woman. Makes it that much more . . . appealing."

Leila gave him a small smile in acknowledgement of the compliment. Even if it was a tad on the cheesy side, she thought.

After she'd agreed to accompany him, Mateo immediately insisted he drive and Leila had politely told him no. She didn't like the predatory gleam in his eyes, and no matter what he thought her reasons were for agreeing to go with him, hers were purely for business.

And well, *maybe* a bit of spite thrown in, against Brandan.

At any rate, she didn't give him an explanation, despite the fact that he seemed to be waiting for her to do so. After a small awkward pause, after she'd told him she'd drive herself and follow him, they'd caravanned to the restaurant.

Now, as she sat across from him, she glanced around at the romantic candle-lit restaurant.

It was decorated in subtle, varying shades of reds. The stone walls were color-washed in crimson, with a faux finish that complimented the large murals depicting various scenes of couples, some subtle, some more overtly sexual, forms blending into the next, bodies molding against others. It all added to the overall sensual vibe of the restaurant.

She had to look at one mural twice to make sure she was seeing it right.

"Sensual, isn't it?" Mateo asked, bringing her attention back to him.

Just then the waiter returned and brought a bottle of wine to the table. With a flourish, he presented the bottle to Mateo and after his nod of approval, poured a taste into his glass.

After accepting the fluted glass from the waiter, he brought the wine to his nose, gently swirled the contents, and took a sip. Once again, Mateo nodded his approval and the waiter filled his glass, then poured a second one and handed it to Leila.

"Yes, it is," she agreed, lightly stroking her fingers down the side of the crystal wine goblet.

"I know the artist," he said, referring to the murals. "He's a friend. I've commissioned him to do some private work for me. He does commissioned works at a few local businesses. If you ever want to add something different in the way of decorating to your restaurant, I could introduce you to him. He's a personal friend," he finished, placing the glass of wine down on the soft cloth-covered table.

She looked him over suspiciously from beneath lowered lashes as she took a careful sip of wine.

His overall beauty, again, struck her, totally fascinated her. It wasn't that she was attracted to him, sexually. Not at all.

There was no strange chemistry arcing between them as there had been with Brandan, yet there was something about Mateo that pulled at her.

He emitted an aura of blatant sexuality, as though it were second nature to him. His dark hair had a slight wave, his thin wide lips curled upward, even when he wasn't smiling, and the gleam in his chocolate eyes screamed of . . . sex.

It unnerved her that she couldn't pinpoint what about him was a bit unsettling.

Shaking it off, she smiled and answered, "That would be nice. We're planning to give Aunt Sadie's a new look. Something fresh, hip, with a twist, maybe bring in some old classic style to give homage to my great-aunt. She was a woman with style," she said with a smile.

"I'll make sure I get you his contact information," he said. "Avant-garde projects are his favorites. He agreed to create the murals for Loiseau's when he found out the restaurant was named after the famous chef, Bernard Loiseau. It appealed to the tortured artist soul in him, I guess," he replied, and shrugged an elegant shoulder.

Leila raised a brow and titled her head. "How so?"

Mateo leaned back in his chair and smiled. "Rumor has it that the prominent chef had a history of bipolar disorder, and committed suicide when rumors circulated in France that his restaurant was in jeopardy of losing one of its prized star ratings. But as I say, it is only a rumor. At any rate, Renaldo—my friend and the artist responsible for these beautiful murals—found the story and the chef fascinating. For that reason alone, he agreed to create the murals."

"Hmmm. Interesting," Leila agreed, and took a sip of the wine.

Just like everything else in the restaurant, it was perfect. She swallowed the bit of natural jealousy that arose and continued,

"About the restaurant . . ." Leila smoothly turned the conversation to the reason she'd accepted his offer of dinner.

"Yes, about Aunt Sadie's," he said, and again, she caught the subtle smile as though he held a secret humor. "That is why we're here. To discuss why you are the only one of the owners who refuses to sell."

Leila sat up straighter, tossed a few of her locs over her shoulder, and raised a brow, glad they were getting down to business.

As soon as Mateo and Leila left, Brandan swiftly gathered his briefcase and laptop and left, impatiently punching in the his date's number—what was her damn name?—telling her there was a change of plans for dinner, and to meet him at Loiseau's, instead of the earlier agreed upon club.

He wasn't fooling himself, thinking the change was because he suddenly had no desire to go to the popular nightclub for food and dancing.

He knew Mateo. He knew that he would take Leila to Loiseau's, and he damn well was going to be there as well.

Now, as he and Angela entered the restaurant, after sliding the maitre d' three crisp hundred dollar bills, they followed the tuxedoed man toward a table.

Scanning the restaurant, it wasn't long before he spotted Mateo and Leila, and he grinned. From his location, he'd be able to see the couple without them seeing him.

After pulling his date's seat back, Brandan sat down as well and ordered drinks from the hovering waiter. Brandan glanced back over at Leila and Mateo, making sure he had them in his sights.

He felt like a damn fool, or some amateur dick scoping out his target. But damned if he was going to let his partner get too close to the woman before he'd had the opportunity to find out what it was about her that got him hard whenever he was in her presence, though that had only been twice.

Plus, he was way past the age where being next to a pretty girl should have gotten his dick so hard he could hammer nails with the damn thing.

Squinting his eyes in the dimly lit restaurant, he was able to zero in on them, then clenched his teeth together when he noticed one of her hands clasped between Mateo's.

The sneaky bastard was reading her palm.

He'd seen him do that tired move more times than he could count.

He'd gotten the "gift" from his grandmother. Mateo had told him that despite his father's protest that it didn't look good for someone of his standing to have his mother setting up shop in the market reading palms and predicting futures, she'd ignored her son and continued doing what she had done in her homeland of Columbia before the family had moved.

As a boy, Mateo had always been fascinated with the practice, and after his grandmother told him he too had the "gift," he learned the art of palm reading.

Yeah, right.

Just another way to get close to a woman, Brandan thought cynically.

"Oooh, I like this! I've never been here before."

Brandan reluctantly turned away from the cuddled pair and smiled at his date.

"I'm glad you like it," he replied.

"I said to myself after you called, 'Angela, now why is he changing restaurants? What surprise does he have in store for Angela?' And you bring Angela here! I've been wanting to check out Loosow's since they opened last spring. What a surprise, Sweetie!" she laughed, butchering the name of the restaurant and letting out a high, shrill giggle that drew other diners' attention toward them.

Angela. That was it.

Although it irritated him how she referred to herself in the third person, Brandan was glad she had this time, as he kept drawing a blank when trying to bring her name to the forefront of his mind.

"Good," he said though he doubted she was really listening, as she kept on speaking.

He smiled and nodded at what he guessed were the appropriate times, but he didn't really know or care.

She had several irritating habits, and referring to herself in the third person was just one. She could go on for hours talking nonstop, not noticing if he edged a word in, in her shrill, strongly accented southern drawl.

He hadn't asked her out for her scintillating conversation anyway, more out of boredom if anything.

Lately, all his female companions had merged into one homogenous blurb in his mind. None were distinguishable from the other.

All tended to be the same. Petite, because for some reason those were the ones he attracted more than any other type. Blonde or brunette, didn't matter which, banging body, and into themselves and what they could get out of a man.

Completely self-absorbed. Angela was no different than the rest. And that had been the way he liked it, until recently

The last time he'd gone to dinner at his partner Damian's home, he'd brought one of them with him at Wanda's—Damian's wife's—request.

The next day at work, Damian made an offhand comment about her being like the rest. He said it in a joking manner, but it had struck Brandan.

Something was missing from his love life.

Not the sex.

He could get that easily. Flash a handful of money, flashy car, and nice trinkets, and it was his for the taking. His eyes slid to the woman across from him, chattering away like there was no tomorrow.

He knew women were drawn to him because of the money, the perceived power. It was a heady combination. From the time he started playing ball in college, and later pro, it had been a sweet exchange.

In exchange for great sex and ready availability when he needed it, he gave his women what they wanted. Generous when it came to gifting, as well inviting them into a nightlife that catered to the rich and famous.

But of late, it wasn't enough. He wanted more. Though he volunteered to coach football at a local youth center, along with Damian, he felt as though something was lacking in his life.

He glanced back over at Mateo and Leila in time to see him pulling her chair back for her. She smiled at him and quickly walked away from the table, weaving her way through the restaurant toward the back.

Quickly, he turned to Angela and excused himself. He briskly followed Leila's retreating back, wondering what had happened in the few seconds of his mental musings that had her racing away from his partner.

7

Leila washed her hands in the sink and peered down at them, noticing the fine tremor as the water ran down her fingers.

She laughingly allowed Mateo to "read" her palm, thinking it was a cheesy effort on his part so he could hold her hands. Really, what were they, in the eighth grade, she thought, but she went along with it.

She had no idea she'd be left unsettled and shaken to the degree she was now, after the "reading" was over.

Mateo cradled her hand in his, his lean fingers trailing a path along the dark lines in her palm. Leila waited patiently for him to explain what each line meant, and as she knew he would, he went into a spiel on what each line represented.

"You see this line?" he asked. "This line represents your life line." The pad of his thumb outlined one of the creases, and he continued without looking up at her. "Yours shows that barring unforeseen accidents, you'll have a fairly long life. Prosperous even."

He went on to explain several other lines. "This one is your love line," he said, then stopped, a frown settling across his wide forehead. "Hmmm," he murmured, running his thumb across the line in a back and forth seesaw movement.

"And?" Leila prompted, intrigued despite herself, knowing full well this was all a part of some game he was playing. Another player out to score. Albeit in an original way, with the whole my-grandmother-was-a-soothsayer thing, but still a game.

"You have a large capacity for love," he continued, and Leila hid her smirk. Now he'd get to it, that she was a woman made for love, that she'd never met the right man to—

"But, you've haven't met the man yet who does it for you," he finished the thought in her mind and she hid her surprise. But really, what else would a man say when trying to get a woman in bed, she thought, and bit her lip to stop from laughing.

"They're all the same to you, indistinguishable from the next. And easily interchangeable. And easily they irritate you, within a short time."

She began to grow uncomfortable and laughed nervously. It was just some game, she reminded herself.

He didn't know her, didn't know anything about her. It didn't matter that his words eerily echoed what her great-aunt had once said to her after she'd dumped her latest boyfriend. What Sadie had said was that she had a tendency to let them work her nerves too soon, that if she found fault with any and every little thing a man did, she'd be irritated for the rest of her life. And alone.

"You're strong willed. Independent for sure," he laughed as though to himself, totally immersed in what he was doing to the point that Leila felt as if he'd forgotten she was there. "At times *too* strong."

Okay . . .

Then he looked up at her, a strange look in his dark brown eyes, a serious look. Although she knew nothing about him, it was an expression she wouldn't have expected to see in his eyes. No slick flirtation, no sly sexual vibe was he throwing off.

"You'll love once. A real love, and that's all. You're the type of woman that draws men to you with effortless ease," he laughed softly, "with the type of ease other women are envious of, and you're not even aware of. But no one has made an impression on your heart. None of them have managed to touch you in any profound way. Haven't gotten past that shield you carry."

Her breath had caught at his words.

"You'll know the man when you meet him. When you do, it won't be calm, or sneak up on you gradually. It won't take many days or months of dating to know that he's your man. You'll know the minute you lay eyes on him."

Leila had laughed it off, and tried to withdraw her hand, but he'd kept his grip firm.

He peered at her intently across the candlelit table and told her, with regret in his dark eyes, "It's too late for that man to be me. Seems you've already met your man. He's your other half," he'd said, and Leila had grown even more uncomfortable with her "reading," unable to shake it off as some ridiculous nonsense.

With more force than before, she pulled her hand back, and unconscious of the meaning behind her actions, had wiped her palm down the side of her skirt, as though to erase the words he'd uttered.

His expression had lightened and he'd allowed her to remove her hand.

The hair at the nape of her neck had stood up, goose bumps had feathered down her arms and she glanced around the crowded restaurant feeling strange, eyes on her, as though someone was watching her.

When she'd hastily gotten to her feet, mumbling that she needed to get away, he'd said nothing. His dark eyes had instead followed her as she'd pushed back her chair and quickly gone to the restroom.

Leila shook her hands, shaking off the excess water, and turned off the gold-tipped faucet, stared at her reflection in the smoky mirror, and blew out a shaky breath. She refused to admit the effect Mateo's "reading" had on her.

She shook her head as though to erase the image of Brandan that had sprung to her mind, an image that had been hovering in her subconscious since she met him early that morning.

"Are you okay, miss?"

Leila turned away from her reflection in the mirror, smiled absentmindedly at the waiting attendant, and nodded her head before accepting the soft towel the woman held out for her.

Brandan ignored the curious glances cast his way as he leaned against the wall outside the women's restroom, arms crossed, and waited for Leila to come out.

He glanced down at his watch, impatient.

She'd been in the bathroom for nearly twenty minutes, and the longer he waited the more he wondered what Mateo had said that sent her flying from her chair.

He'd not been able to see her expression from his distance away, but the hurried way she stood, her chair almost toppling in her haste to get away, and the long strides that had taken her across the restaurant in less than a minute had been telling.

Just as he glanced up, the door opened, and although he'd been waiting for her, expecting her to come out, he was caught by surprise when she opened the door and took halting steps, her head down, a deep frown crossing her smooth forehead.

She would have walked past him had he not pushed away from the wall and stood in her path. With an "umph" she bumped into his chest, and he reached his hands out to steady her.

She looked up at him, an apology on her wide, sensual lips,

before her eyes widened and she realized who she'd walked into.

"Wha—what are you doing here?"

"Enjoying your dinner date?" he murmured, ignoring her question.

He slowly ran his hands down her arms, ending at the tips of her fingers. So close to her, Brandan saw her response to his touch, feeling the rush of small bumps flash across her smooth honey-colored skin.

Despite her height, coupled with the heels she wore, she still had to look up to meet his eyes. Just barely, but enough for Brandan to notice her small breasts rise with the sudden breath she took, and her nostrils flare at the tips.

Her wide-spaced light brown eyes stared at his mouth.

His cock jumped in response to *her* reaction to him.

Shit.

What was it about this woman that had his body acting like a randy-ass prepubescent boy, he wondered.

When she tugged her arm away from him, he reluctantly allowed her to go.

"Yes, it's a beautiful restaurant. But you didn't answer my question. What are you doing here? I thought you had a date with Tiffany," she said, a frown creasing her forehead, her brows puckering.

"Angela," he corrected easily.

She knew what the woman's name was, of that he had no doubt. She was a sharp woman—he'd found that out from their interchanges over the last few months.

She'd been irritated that he'd had a date. And although that shouldn't please him, shouldn't matter one way or another, it did.

"And you didn't answer my question. Are you enjoying your dinner date?" he murmured, his eyes trained on her lips. She wore no color on them, none that he could detect this close, nothing but a shimmering of gloss, but they were a soft light pink color. His gaze followed her tongue as it snaked out and made a quick swipe across the fuller bottom rim.

Just then a large woman walked past them, brushing against him before issuing an apology. Brandan used it as an excuse to push her gently against the wall while he boxed her in.

When she simply looked at him, not saying more, he pressed closer, both physically and mentally. "Why did you go out with him? Why not me? I was the one you came to see, the one you want . . . to talk to about your business."

"Like I said, you had other plans. And I don't want you, I just want you to leave my business alone. Nothing more, nothing less," she insisted, her tone cool. But her body was telling him something else.

Without touching her, he felt her body heat reach out and sear him as her chest sharply rose up and down as she took short shallow breaths.

Yeah, she wanted him as badly as he wanted her.

"Keep telling yourself that, maybe you'll start to believe it."

He raised a hand to touch her cheek, wondering if it was as soft as it appeared, before he could stop himself. He never pressed a woman like this. He wanted a reaction from her. And damn if he had any intention of stopping.

She placed her hand on top of his before he could make the connection and stared at him with an intensity that stole his breath. She shook her head as though to clear her thoughts and shoved his hand away.

"I don't need to remind myself of anything, Mr. Walters. Our only connection is Aunt Sadie's Café. Now, it's time for me to go back to my dinner date. If you'll excuse me . . ."

Leila brushed past him, making sure she put as much swagger into her stride as she could as she strolled away, plastering what she hoped was a confident half smile on her face as she approached Mateo.

She felt Brandan's eyes burning a hole in the back of her head, but wouldn't give him the satisfaction of turning around.

She finished the dinner with Mateo, but feigned a headache when he suggested they have a nightcap. She agreed instead to call him about setting up a meeting to further discuss their situation, and the current stalemate that she, he, and his partners were facing.

8

"God, what a night!" Leila said, and plopped down on one of the bar stools surrounding the counter.

It was nearly ten o'clock, and the café was nearly deserted. With only a smattering of diners left, she was finally able to sit down for the first time in hours.

"Business is booming. We keep this up, and we'll have to buy both of our neighbors' shops."

Leila glanced over at her best friend, lawyer, and accountant, and sometimes busboy when she needed him, with a tired smile.

"Always the optimist, that's what I love about you, Hawk," she said and eased off her heels. She accepted the cup of tea he placed in front of her with a murmur of thanks.

"It's a start," he said casually.

Leila looked at him, and although the remark was offhand, she bit her bottom lip, something she did whenever she was uncomfortable. Something she rarely did in Hawk's company.

She was uncertain if he meant it was a start regarding the business, or their relationship going to the next level. And of late, that was the cause of her discomfort around him. And it saddened her that she couldn't return his feelings.

She and Hawk had been friends for most of her life. In fact, she couldn't remember a time when he wasn't around.

Her great-aunt had taken him in when Leila was a child and he was a teenager. He'd moved to Texas from a Cherokee Indian reservation in Phoenix, having followed a woman there who was five years his senior. When the woman abandoned him, he'd been on his own.

She'd learned of the nature of his relationship with the woman when she'd once peeked into her great-aunt's office at the back of the diner, and seen her aunt's large arms wrapped around the boy as he cried and told her about his life.

She'd only been able to pick up bits and pieces, and she'd been far too young at the time to understand the significance of what he was telling her great-aunt, but she'd overheard enough and understood enough that tears of sadness had run down her cheeks.

Quietly, though they hadn't known she was there, she backed away, giving him his privacy as he poured out the rest of his story to Aunt Sadie.

He'd begun working at the restaurant, and Sadie had turned one of the storage rooms into a bedroom for him. She'd invited him to stay with her and Leila, but the young man had a sense of pride even then that wouldn't allow him to do that. With his first check from Sadie, he started giving her money for rent.

Leila remembered seeing her aunt trying to refuse accepting the money, but soon gave up as she realized it made the young man feel better to do so.

When her aunt had died, they all realized why the normally dominating woman had given in so easily. She'd taken the money he'd given her and put it into an account for him, and over the years it had earned quite a bit of interest. Both Leila and Hawk had been stunned, though they knew she was a generous woman.

"Leila, you're like a sister to me." His words brought her attention back to him.

"I know," she grinned at him. "And I don't know what I'd do without you, Hawk."

She leaned over and hugged him tight. They didn't say anything else, just hugged each other, but Leila felt content. His simple statement and the meaning behind it rid her of the discomfort she'd felt, thinking he had feelings for her.

Around the time her great-aunt had died, Leila had been devasted, and seeking to find comfort had gone to Hawk. He'd held her, but wouldn't allow things to progress further than mild kisses and caresses, telling her that when she was no longer in grief, if she still desired him . . . to come to him. The look in his dark, mysterious eyes had sent hot awareness coursing through her body, an awareness she was no longer a child with a mild crush on an older boy, but a grown woman.

However, when her grief had abated, she'd realized that her feelings for Hawk were not those of a lover's. She didn't want to chance changing the dynamics of their relationship by sleeping with him. She loved him too much. He meant far too much to her to do that.

When she pulled away, she felt a familiar sensation—the same one she'd had last night, as though someone was burning holes straight into her back.

She turned around, her arms still linked around Hawk's lean shoulders, to glance toward the door to see what—or who— was causing the tingling sensation.

Though she already knew good and well who was responsible.

The café doors opened, and Brandan Walters's overly tall, overly muscled, overly . . . dominating body stood in the doorway.

Her heart thumped against her chest so harshly, she feared it would leap out and fall on the floor. Even from a distance, she noticed his eyes were narrowed, and a frown settled across his craggy features. As though he was displeased with her hugging Hawk.

As if he had anything to do with *who* the heck she hugged.

The two locked gazes, and Leila forgot all about Hawk—though her arms were still loped around his neck—until he nudged her, forcing her attention away from Brandan.

In Hawk's dark, nearly black eyes, a look of concern shone brightly. "Someone you know?" he asked.

"No . . . I mean, yes . . . but he's not important." She dismissed Brandan, telling her best friend the bald-faced lie without batting an eyelash.

"Are you sure he's no one of importance?" Leila felt her face heat when she followed her friend's gaze down to her breasts.

She always wore an apron when she worked, many she'd inherited from her grandmother, and others she'd found on her own. Some were sexy half aprons, and others were full. The one she was wearing she'd pulled out of the back of her closet that morning, was new and one she hadn't worn before.

It was red and sheer, more sheer than she thought it would be. So sheer that the small lace demi-bra, and the silk long-sleeved blouse she wore as well weren't able to hide her body's reaction when Brandan entered the café.

She resisted the urge to cross her arms over her chest to hide the way her nipples stood erect, poking past the flimsy material.

She simply gave Hawk a *look* and turned away from him, unconsciously pulling the bottom rim of her lip into her mouth. Flutters tore through her stomach as she watched Brandan lazily stroll inside and take a seat at one of the booths.

When Tricia, one of the only waitresses still working, picked up a menu and headed his way, Leila waited until the woman handed him the plastic-backed menu, took his drink order, and returned to the front counter, her hand massaging the center of her back.

"Hey, Trish, it's almost closing time. I can handle the last customers. Why don't you head on home and get off your feet," she said, and the tired waitress smiled and moved her hand from her back to rub her large, rounded belly.

"Oh, girl, thanks. I am *bushed*," she said tiredly. "If you're sure . . . ?"

"I'm sure. Go on home. Hawk and I will lock up."

With a grateful smile, the waitress handed Leila her order pad and pencil. She walked toward the back to collect her things, in what Leila called the pregnancy waddle. Her legs were spread slightly apart, aiding her balance while housing something the size of a football—she adjusted her thinking in Trish's case—a watermelon—within her body.

It wouldn't be long, maybe a week at the most, before Tricia wouldn't be able to work, and Leila would be forced to find a replacement until she returned from maternity leave. She put that, along with the other nine million things she needed to do, to the back of her mind, and walked toward Brandan, whose head was buried deep in the menu.

"Find anything appealing, Mr. Walters?"

Brandan's eyes flew from the menu up to the woman who asked the question, her voice low, slightly husky, and so sexy it made his dick jump in his pants.

From her voice alone.

Fuck.

"There's plenty I see that's appealing. What do you suggest?"

Her light brown eyes widened at his words' obvious double meaning, her lips tightening and the ends of her nose flaring.

She placed one long-fingered delicate hand on her hip, tilted her head to the side, and looked at him, a bored expression on her face.

She must be one hell of a poker player, he thought. She had the disinterested perfected to a T.

But he'd been playing poker since he was a kid, beating grown men and making the money he needed for the various football camps his mother couldn't afford to send him to. He recognized a good game face when he saw one. And besides, she either needed to invest in a better bra to hide her body's response, or take the damn thing off all together for all the good it was doing.

He felt his humor restored for the first time today.

His glance slid over her. Her long dreads were in a topknot, and several locs had escaped the haphazard bun to frame her face, falling down the length of her back. The ones that were not in the bun were multicolored—some were a copper color, others a light brown, almost blond—while the rest were a dark brown. His fingers itched to dive into them, deeply, and loosen the long locs of hair.

She wore a plain white silk blouse with small silver buttons, the top buttons undone to the top of her small breasts to reveal the deep slit of her cleavage, where, between the small mounds, the end of a silver charm nestled.

She also wore a small red, sheer, ridiculously frilly apron that tied at the back in a big bow. But hell if he didn't want to unwrap the bow to get at the gift inside the pretty package.

On her feet she again wore high heels, but this pair was backless, the type women could slip their feet into. He didn't know what they were called, but they were sexy as hell, especially on her as she stood before him, semi-balanced on one foot, her other foot easing in and out, in and out, in a hot see-sawing glide that had him hypnotized.

He silently thanked whoever had created the style.

"I meant on the *menu*, Mr. Walters . . . is there anything on the *menu* that you find appealing," she said, snapping his attention back to food and away from sliding feet and sweet beaded nipples.

"Sugar, I know what you meant," he replied, and when she simply arched a brow in response, he smiled and handed her the menu. "I'll have whatever you suggest," he replied.

"How about a nice bowl of Aunt Sadie's signature Texas chili? It's the house specialty. That is, if you can take the heat."

"Hmmm, don't know how much . . . heat . . . I can take this time of night." He leaned back and grinned at her, enjoying the exchange.

"You're a big strappin' Texan. I'm sure you can handle a little spice, can't you, big boy?" she mocked and grinned an angelic smile.

He trusted that smile as much as he would a coiling rattlesnake.

For all her faults, his mama didn't raise a fool.

He opened his mouth, ready to order something else when he caught the look of triumph dancing in her eyes and decided what the hell. No way in hell was he going to let her think he couldn't handle anything she could dish out.

In or out of the kitchen.

"I think I'm man enough to handle it."

With a nod and a completely devilish grin on her face, she accepted the menu from him. In the exchange the tips of their fingers touched and a spark of electricity arced from his hand to hers.

You would have thought she'd been bitten by the same snake he compared her smile to, the way she snatched her hand away so abruptly.

If they continued on like this, pussyfooting around each other, sparking and igniting, they were liable to set the whole damn place on fire.

She turned away and walked back to the counter toward the

tall, lean man she'd been wrapped around when he'd walked into the café, and spoke something in his ear.

Brandan saw the man laugh and look toward him and from the distance he could have sworn he saw sympathy in the man's eyes. Brandan shrugged. Nothing she could dish out could he not handle.

However, the sympathy from the man leaning against the counter did nothing to alleviate the need to punch him into the kitchen wall after he'd witnessed the hug they'd shared.

Damn, what did the woman want, a harem, Brandan thought moodily, and sipped the sweet tea the pregnant waitress had supplied him with before scurrying out the door.

He'd drilled Mateo without mercy, to no avail, when he'd called him that morning.

Normally Mateo was more than happy to fill him in on his nighttime games, but as they'd spoken on the phone, he'd not told him one damn thing that had happened. Instead, he'd had the nerve to laugh at him, telling Brandan that if he was so curious, why didn't he go to the café and ask Leila herself. Then he hung up the phone.

He'd told himself it didn't matter. She didn't mean anything to him, and if his damn Casanova wannabe partner had more than a simple dinner with the woman, more power to him.

Afterwards, he had joined Damian to go to the youth center and coach, just as he normally did on Saturdays, but midway through their practice he admitted to himself that he did care what happened.

A hell of a lot.

Too much.

He'd finished practice and spent the remainder of the day acting like a schoolboy with a crush, trying to shove thoughts of her out of his mind. But in the end he admitted it was useless.

He glanced around the diner.

It was the first time he'd actually seen it. Neither he nor his partners had ever actually been inside the shops they were buying. It had never been necessary before, their only interest was in the land.

The décor of the café was offbeat, but had its own charm.

Most of the tables were intimate, holding no more than four chairs, and the spattering of booths with benches where the old wood gleamed, polished to a high glossy finish, added more charm to the old café.

There was a smattering of prints that were by no means high art which adorned the walls, yet the pictures blended perfectly with the café's eclectic décor.

In the center of each table was a small glass vase with fresh flowers. Surrounding the vase were small red see-through glass candleholders. His waitress had lit his as he sat down, and he thought it a small bit of charm, adding to the overall cozy feel of the café.

There weren't many customers left, the last remaining few were either drinking coffee or paying their bill. He watched as Leila smiled at her customers, her charm reaching out to them though she appeared to not even note the effect she had on them, men and women, as she smilingly accepted the money, her charm effortless.

She moved from one table to the next, casually talking, her low husky laugh reaching over to him to envelop him, pulling at him.

He followed her with his eyes, her slim, shapely backside gently swaying back and forth in the close-fitting knee-length skirt that was not in the least bit provocative, or at least it shouldn't have been. Yet the split in the back gave him an enticing glimpse of the back of soft, smooth looking . . . lickable knees.

His shaft stirred in his pants when she dropped her pen and bent over to retrieve it, and the skirt hitched up to reveal more of her honey-colored thighs. Damn. Unable to look away, he watched her stand up and gently tug at the hem of her skirt.

She turned slightly, her glance finding his centered directly on her rounded bottom. She quickly turned away and with a brisk step, headed back toward the kitchen.

9

Brandan continued to watch Leila interact with her customers, taking an occasional drink of the sweet tea, wondering when she'd make her way back over to him.

He also idly wondered if she always wore such slitted skirts and high heels when working. Not that he was complaining.

He felt a male grin of pure appreciation cross his face while watching her rump as she bent over, and her long legs take her from table to table as she mingled with her customers.

He'd always been attracted to a certain type of woman— usually the small dainty type were his cup of tea. Not too small that she made him feel like a pedophile, but small enough that she fit perfectly beneath him.

But this woman, with her curvaceous yet athletic looking body, had him longing to feel what it would be like to have her underneath him, giving back as much as she took as their bodies twined together, wrapped around each other as he stroked into her.

Brandan subtly adjusted himself in his pants, and widened his legs, automatically giving himself more room as his dick began to swell, just thinking about what it would be like to be inside her.

When his food arrived, the flavorful aroma instantly assaulted his nostrils and made his mouth water.

Instead of a traditional bowl, the steaming hot chili was held within a toasted brown-bread bowl, with a piece of cornbread on a small plate beside it. Brandan eagerly picked up the fat round spoon and stirred the aromatic concoction of black and red beans, tomatoes, onions, peppers, and fat hunks of sausage.

His culinary talents weren't anything to brag about, despite the fact that his mother had cooked for a living most of her life, so he wasn't able to name what other ingredients were in the chili. All he knew was that it all looked delicious.

He took a careful mouthful, unsure what to expect, despite the wonderful smells. He had been certain she'd make sure it was blazing hot and spicy even by Texas standards after her parting quip.

He was surprised, pleasantly so, when it had just the right amount of heat and spice, but not too much to singe the fine hairs in his nose.

"Can I get you anything else?"

Brandan looked up, surprised that she'd approached him and he hadn't noticed.

As he swallowed, his eyes glanced over her tall, voluptuous body, and his instinct was to give a resounding "Hell, yes," there was something else he wanted.

He swallowed the response though, along with the mouthful of chili.

She raised a brow when he shook his head no, instead of responding the way his body dictated. He decided his initial response probably wouldn't have been the brightest move on his part.

"Can you have a seat and sit with me for a while?" he asked instead. "There aren't too many customers left and I'm sure your waitstaff can handle them. Why don't you sit down and talk to me?"

She looked around the café, indecision stamped on her expressive face.

"Isn't that what you've been wanting, the opportunity to talk about your business, to persuade me . . . my partners and I, to look elsewhere for the project?" he pushed. "Unless you and Mateo have already come to an agreement about the situation?"

At that, she whipped her head around, and several of her upswept dreads tossed across her face.

She tucked her hair behind her ear and her red tongue darted out to swipe across the upper swell of her full lips.

"No, we didn't exactly get around to that," she said, and Brandan felt unreasonable jealousy—yes, he knew it was unreasonable, he had no claim on her—sweep over him, wondering what in the hell they *had* "gone over."

"I guess I can sit and talk . . . for a minute. I've got to get ready to close, and I only have one waitress and a busboy left."

"Is that your 'busboy,'" he asked, nodding his head toward the tall guy in the corner who hadn't taken his eyes off them the entire time they'd been talking.

She turned toward the counter to see who he was talking about, and he leaned back in his seat, taking a drink of his tea.

A corner of her wide mouth hitched in a smile and she turned back to him.

"No."

When she said nothing more, not clarifying who the hell he was, Brandan grit his teeth, but let it go.

Again, he had no claims on her. If she wanted a harem of men to screw, who was he to say anything, he thought in dismissal, ignoring the taunting laugh of his subconscious mocking him.

* * *

Leila sat down across from Brandan and was immediately aware of their close proximity. Although he sat across from her and the table comfortably sat four, his overall ... *largeness* seemed to dwarf his surroundings, leading to her feeling extremely irritated and out of sorts.

After she'd taken his order, she'd busied herself with her regulars, doing her damnedest to try and forget his presence.

As if.

He was hell-bent on making it an impossible thing to do.

She'd felt his eyes burning holes straight through the soft fabric of her blouse. Several times she had flushed in embarrassment when her body had reacted, chagrined that he could make her nipples throb simply from him being in the same vicinity.

She crossed her arms over her chest and ignored the sexy grin he threw her way at her telling response.

"This is amazing. Please give my compliments to the chef," he said, indicating the chili which, from the looks of it, he was close to demolishing.

"Thank you. It was Aunt Sadie's trademark recipe, one she made sure I knew how to prepare. It's always been the most popular thing on the menu, no matter what time or season."

"It's amazing."

"Thank you," she smiled. "Mine is nowhere near as good as Sadie's. But the customers don't complain. They seem to enjoy it."

"I'm sure she'd be proud. I bet it's just as good as your aunt's. Don't knock yourself."

His words eerily echoed her great-aunt's praise, and she felt herself soften toward him.

"I wasn't sure I'd catch you still open. I thought you closed shop at nine," he commented, glancing around at the last remaining customers.

"Oh, we do, but the customers don't always know that," she laughed, some of the tension easing from her. "Especially the regulars. They usually hang around until a little after closing. We don't kick them out,"

"Makes for longer nights, I would imagine," he said, and Leila shrugged her shoulders.

"Yeah, but they've been our bread and butter for years. Some of them have been coming here since it opened, forty years ago," she replied fondly, glancing over at Mr. Clemmons, the elderly man who sat drinking the last of his coffee. With a satisfied smile, he raised a hand for the waitress to give him his bill.

"You see that older gentlemen over there?" she asked, pointing to Mr. Clemmons. "And that dollar bill framed on the wall near the register?" She then pointed to the small framed dollar bill.

He dutifully looked at both before turning back to her. "Yes."

"Both were Aunt Sadie's first." She laughed when he raised his eyebrows. "Get your mind out of the gutter," she threw the quip at him and refrained from returning his deep laugh.

"Sorry. Can't help it. Go on," he encouraged.

"*Anyway* . . . Mr. Clemmons and his wife were Sadie's first customers. They bought two cups of coffee and split an apple fritter with that dollar," she smiled in nostalgia.

"That's sweet," he murmured, and Leila looked at his face, a mingled expression of compassion and understanding that made her breath catch.

She cleared her throat. "When his wife died a year ago, around the same time that my aunt did, I didn't think I'd see him around here. Last month he started coming back again. Sits in the same spot and orders a cup of coffee and an apple fritter. Sadie would be happy to know he's back."

She fought against the tears burning the back of her eyes and turned away from his scrutiny. Her eyes flew to his when she felt his big hand cover hers for a fraction of a moment and run the rough pad of his thumb over the back of her hand.

When she'd gotten her emotions checked, she put on a bright smile and eased her hand away from his. The moment was short, yet intense. The type of moment she was beginning to understand were not so abnormal between the two of them.

Uncomfortable with her thoughts, as well as his simple comforting touch, she placed both of her hands in her lap.

"I had no idea Aunt Sadie's had been around so long. How long have you worked here?" he asked, and the slight change in subject was a relief.

"Hmmm, let's see . . . twenty-six years?" she said, and laughed when he coughed into the cup of tea.

"I was four years old when I came to live with my great-aunt, and I've been around the café my entire life. So it feels as though I've 'worked' here most of my life," she said. "In fact, Aunt Sadie used to have a jazz pianist set up right over there," she said, pointing to a small area in the corner of the café. "And for some reason I had it in my mind that I had real talent, my toy tambourine and I, and I was hell-bent on being in the 'band'."

"And your aunt indulged you," he stated, a half grin on his face.

"Yeah, she was like that. Never believed in crushing anyone's dream, no matter how far-fetched!"

"I bet you were good."

"Not!" She choked back a laugh. "Nowhere close. But the customers didn't mind when I'd get up and sing the only song I knew."

"Which was probably something along the lines of 'Twinkle, Twinkle, Little Star'?" he guessed, and she grinned and gave him two thumbs up for his knowledge.

"Yep, while beating the *hell* out of that little tambourine! Lord, have mercy." They both laughed, and Leila felt closer to anyone than she had in a long time, besides Hawk, sharing the small anecdote.

"So when did you leave the cutthroat industry of musical entertainment and decide that your gift was in the culinary arts?" he asked once their laughter subsided.

"I've always loved being in the kitchen, was always underfoot when Aunt Sadie or any of the others were cooking. They took pity on me, taught me the fundamentals, and I experimented. Some of my concoctions were something only a mother would love, or an indulgent aunt," she quipped. "But a lot were good. I found out that my true love was baking. I graduated from high school and got a scholarship to attend a great culinary school, and the rest is history," she finished lightly, naming one of the top culinary schools in the world, modest, yet proud.

"The rest is history?"

Leila looked away and noticed that the café was nearly empty, that the last customer was paying their tab and heading out the door.

She turned back to Brandan and saw a light of curiosity in his eyes.

No. The rest wasn't history.

But she didn't want to think about how excited she'd been when they'd gotten the loan approved to expand Aunt Sadie's, after they'd gotten their new catering business, how excited both she and her aunt had been with the opportunity to expand the business into that area.

Months before her aunt suffered the first of three back-to-back strokes that had ultimately caused her death.

The thought of her aunt no longer with her still hurt so badly, at times she woke up and thought it was all a nightmare. Hoping it was nothing more than a horrid dream.

Unfortunately, it was all too real.

She shook her head no. "Like I said, the rest was history."

Brandan didn't remember the last time he'd enjoyed simple conversation with a woman.

Yes, the sexual energy was there between them, so vibrant, so *charged*, it felt as though it had its own life force. Yet beyond the obvious sexual attraction, he felt as though he *knew* her. He didn't know the small things about her, what her favorite color was, her favorite music, or anything so mundane. Yet the connection was real and went beyond that.

Their email exchanges had given him a clue as to the type of woman she was. Strong, take-charge, confident.

What they hadn't provided was something no written communication could, that she had an aura of sensuality and vitality around her that was unique, different. Something that reached out and grabbed him by the short hairs and, he shook his head, wouldn't let go.

Damn, he was sounding like Mateo when he'd start talking about all that metaphysical stuff, but hell, it was what it was. There was something uniquely different about her, something that seemed to "fit" for him.

He couldn't explain it, but had every intention of exploring whatever it was between them.

He reached out a hand toward her, and again lightly caressed her smooth skin. He felt his heart thud against his chest when she didn't withdraw. Instead she turned her palm over, allowing him to twine his fingers with hers.

"Leila, I tallied the sales for you, babe, and put the money in the vault for deposit on Monday."

Brandan straightened in his chair and bit back a cuss. He'd been so wrapped up in Leila, the two of them seemingly in a world of their own, that his surroundings had faded away to nothing.

He let the curse fly when she hastily withdrew her hand from his and looked guilty up at the man leaning against a chair at a nearby table, a sardonic look on his lean face.

"Oh, thanks, Hawk! I'm sorry, I didn't realize—"

"Hey, no problem. You know you never need to apologize

to me," the man—Hawk—responded, and gave her a look that suggested a casual, intimate familiarity, one Brandan had no intention of allowing to continue, even if it was platonic.

Brandan stood.

He reached out a hand and saw the surprise flash across Hawk's deep olive-toned skin before he put his hand out to shake Brandan's.

"Hi, I'm Brandan Walters."

"Yes. I know who you are. I'm Jarred, Jarred Wikvaya," he said, and the two shook hands. Brandan noticed that despite his tall, lean frame, he wasn't weak. His frame was densely packed, his grip strong, as he glanced down at his long, lean fingers wrapped around his own hand. "Hawk to my friends."

"Nice to meet you, Jarrad," Brandan replied before turning back to Leila.

"I'd better get out of here—"

"No, you don't have to. I mean, you can stick around."

She'd also stood, and Brandan felt a sense of personal triumph when she obviously wanted him to stay, despite her friend's obvious wish for him to go.

He took both of her hands in his, and pulled her closer.

"No, it's late, and I know it's been a long day for you. I'll come by tomorrow . . . is that okay?" he asked, and when she nodded, a small smile on her full lips, it took everything in him not to reach down and kiss her. Everything not to pull her close in his arms and feel every delightful curve against his body.

He looked up and caught eyes with Hawk, saw his narrow as though he'd read Brandan's thoughts. The two men exchanged looks, Hawk's warning, Brandan's challenging, staking a claim.

"Yes, sure . . . that would be okay," she replied and Brandan looked away from Hawk and down at Leila. She'd taken off her shoes as they'd sat talking, and now she had to look up further into his eyes.

He reached a hand out and thumbed a caress down the soft line of her cheek. "Tomorrow," he promised, and with that he turned around and left.

"Nobody of importance, Lee?" Hawk asked, and Leila turned to face him.

She opened her mouth to speak but promptly shut it when words escaped her. Taking a deep breath, she crossed her arms over her chest and stared after Brandan as the door swung close on his departure, wondering how he'd come to be important to her in such a short amount of time.

10

"Have you and Roberto talked any more about you buying his space?"

Leila looked away from the screen of her laptop and sighed. She removed her glasses and folded them, placing them on the small table near the pull-out sofa she was currently sitting on.

Unfolding her legs from beneath her, she winced. She'd been going over inventory as Hawk had been reconciling her books for her, and had sat in the same folded-up position for—she glanced at her clock—over an hour.

"God, I didn't realize it was so late."

She stood and stretched, and padded over barefoot to the desk where Hawk was crunching numbers for her.

"Well?" he asked, concern etched deeply in his brown eyes.

"No," she sighed. "In fact, the last time I brought it up to him, it didn't feel like he really wanted to talk about it. He kinda gave me the brush off," she admitted.

"Probably because of the plans to buy out the block," he stated the obvious, and grimaced when she punched him on the shoulder.

"Ya think? Yeah, but what really pisses me off is that he was ready to sell. All we needed was the financing, and then this happens."

This time Hawk wisely refrained from stating what "this" was. Instead saying, "Yeah, well, Lee, you have to understand where he's coming from. They're offering five times what the property is worth now. He's ready to retire, and with the amount of money they're offering, he can do it in style."

She turned away and began to massage the bridge of her nose. "I know, I know. But sometimes it's not about the money, Hawk. Roberto and Aunt Sadie were friends for years, they were both the first tenants here. They always looked out for each other. You'd think that would mean *something*."

"I know, Lee, I know."

There was really nothing more to be said.

They both understood the reasons for the elderly man's recent reticence in discussing Leila buying the business, why most of the other shop owners had recently stopped returning her calls: she had asked for their support in signing a petition to declare the area a historical landmark, therefore preventing Sanchez, Walters and Reed from buying the land and turning it over to the highest bidder.

It still didn't ease the sense of betrayal Leila felt from those around her, many of whom she'd known most of her life and thought of as family.

"All done here, anything else you need from me, sweetie?"

Strong, lean fingers began to massage the back of her neck and she leaned her head to the side to give him better access.

"Ummm, no. Not unless you have a million dollars so I can buy out the block myself," she laughed.

He leaned down and gently kissed her on the cheek. "If I had it, it would be yours," he returned lightly.

Leila smiled and turned around, watching him pick up a colorful canvas bag, sling it over one shoulder, and smile back at her, his expression tinged with concern.

"Don't worry, it'll all work out."

"I know it will, Hawk."

Once again tears burned the back of her throat. She'd been so emotional lately that the least thing tended to do that to her.

"Have I told you lately how awesome you are and that I wouldn't know what to do without you?" she asked.

"Who, me?"

"Yeah, you."

"Couldn't be."

"Then who?" he finished the silly childish rhyme and they both laughed.

"Yeah, but I never get tired of hearing it, brat," he said and walked out of the office after giving her a wink.

Leila followed him moments later, and after making sure everything was locked up, lights out, she was on her way out the door when she noticed a slip of paper tossed in the trash can.

"I thought I emptied that," she groused and reached down to retrieve the lone sheet of paper. Her eyes scanned over the contents and within moments she balled up the sheet and tossed it back in the trash.

Quickly, she locked up, and with a determination in her step, hurried to her car and drove the short distance to one of the shops along the block.

After parking her truck, she quietly made her way to the back of the shop, opened the door, and eased inside.

"I hear what you all are saying, I do." Brandan held up a stalling hand when Ms. Mayflower opened her mouth to speak. "Please, let me finish," he said as gently as he could, not wanting to offend the elderly woman.

But if he allowed her to, she would again, in painstaking detail, illuminate all the reasons why she was ready to retire and how if it wasn't for *"that girl,"* referring to Leila, they'd all be much richer and happier . . . and satisfied.

"She's just like that old aunt of hers, God rest her soul," she said, and quickly made the sign of the cross before continuing her diatribe, lips pinched, face twisted up. "Always telling us what was good for *us*. We are all grown here, we know what's good for us, and what's good for us—me, y'all," she said, pointing a bony finger around the crowded room, "is to finally get what is due to us, so we can move on!"

A smattering of murmurs accompanied her comment, and although Brandan knew the majority of the occupants of the room loved Leila, they were clearly frustrated with her refusal to sell.

Unbeknownst to Leila, over the course of the last few weeks, he'd received emails and phone calls that clearly showed their growing ire.

And although he wanted—needed—to bring the sell to a close, a small part of him was angry with the way she was being treated.

Over the last couple of weeks, he had been frequenting the diner. Most of the times he made it in just before closing, and she would sit and talk to him for long stretches of time. A few times he'd gotten up earlier than usual and after his daily run, had made it through his daily routine in record time in order to come by the diner for breakfast.

After the first few times, he knew he was growing on her. When he would enter the café, within moments their eyes would meet, and although she tried to hide her pleasure at seeing him, he'd caught the flash of that sexy dimple in the corner of her lips before she could erase it.

They'd avoided talking about the sale of the café. He knew he should be trying to persuade her to sell, but whenever he saw her, the furthest thing on his mind had been trying to convince her to sign away her café.

One part of him didn't want her to. She belonged right where she was; her passion for the café went beyond simply owning the business and catering to her loyal customers. Aunt Sadie's was her link to her deceased great-aunt, one that he didn't want to destroy.

The others in the room began to talk among themselves, their discontent with the situation clear.

He sighed.

The last time he'd come by Sadie's had been several days ago, before he'd had to take a trip to Austin on business. Just walking into the inviting café, with it's down-home good smells, familiar looking customers, ones he'd come to know were her regulars, had filled him with warm feelings he'd never experienced before, either growing up or as an adult.

Her regulars were like family to her. She smiled and told jokes and laughed with them. And not those fake tinkling laughs the women he knew gave, the ones that were either purposefully seductive, or polite little giggles.

No, she gave full-out laughs, the kind where the corners of her almond-shaped eyes would nearly close and her face would split wide in a smile. She had a full-out, honest laugh. One that was as appealing as she.

He had come in at breakfast, sneaking in early before the downtown traffic had become hell, and she'd been sitting with one of her customers, one he hadn't seen before, but one he could tell was yet another devotee of Leila.

He'd laughed. Hell, at least this one was a woman, and he didn't have to worry that it was another hapless male to add to her stable.

Not that she couldn't have a woman after her.

There was only the two of them in the café, as it was five in the morning and she'd just opened the doors. But the pair weren't giving off any sexual vibes that he could sense. Particularly as Leila looked so casual sitting there with the woman, her typical high heel shoes on the floor next to her, the two drinking coffee and laughing like two friends, not like lovers.

As soon as she'd seen him enter, she whispered something to the other woman, who looked at him and seemed to be fighting back a smile. She pulled Leila down and whispered something back in her ear that had both women giggling like schoolgirls, and Leila had pulled away and sauntered over to him.

He'd rewarded her saucy behavior by pulling her into his arms and kissing her fully on the mouth.

"Hmmm. What—what was that for?" she murmured, looking up at him, her eyes crinkling in the corner.

"Just because."

"Just because . . . ?"

"Just because I think it's time we settled a few things between us." He pulled her back into his arms and kissed her again, lightly pressing his tongue deep into her mouth and capturing her tongue with his.

He'd expected her to resist, pull back, but she didn't. Instead she settled deeper into his embrace. Wrapping both arms around him, she ran her hands through the back of his hair, pulling him closer.

Brandan tightened his hold, placed one hand on the curve of her waist and the other into her head, wrapping several of her long dreads around his hands, and deepened the kiss.

When his shaft stirred to hot and immediate life, he almost forgot they weren't alone, and pressed her closer. A cough . . . several coughs . . . from the lone customer brought them both out of their private little retreat.

Wild color filled her golden brown cheeks when she pulled away, just as several customers were entering the café.

"You are bad," she admonished him, in a slightly breathless tone.

Brandan only smiled, and watched her sweet hips and long legs carry her away with that sexy walk of hers as she greeted her new customers.

He turned around and laughed out loud, shrugging when the woman she'd been talking with was staring at him, shaking her head with a deep smile on her pretty face.

"Look, I know you all want to sell, and I'm doing my best to make that happen."

"Humph! If your best is hangin' out at that café every day flirtin' with that girl, then I think it's 'bout time we come up with a different game plan," Ms. Mayflower interjected, and Brandan penned the woman with a glance.

"I'm not sure what you mean by that, ma'am. Anything going on between *that* girl and myself is purely business. No need for you to worry. I'll get her to agree, make no mistake," he said out of anger.

The old woman was really starting to get on his nerves. This wasn't the first of her sly innuendoes about his motivation in going to Aunt Sadie's. In fact, he'd not told any of them about his regular visits because it really wasn't anyone's business. That was, until the old woman had made a comment earlier in the meeting about it, making sure everyone within earshot heard her.

Nosy bitch, he thought, and immediately felt bad for thinking of her like that, but out of all the tenants in this deal, this woman was the only one who disliked Leila, and he didn't have a damn clue why.

"Can you promise us you'll convince her to sign soon? We're not getting any younger, you know."

Brandan had had enough. It was time to go, and he wanted to go by Aunt Sadie's before Leila left. He hadn't been able to get to the café in several days, and like a kid with a crush, he was desperate to see her.

He glanced impatiently at the clock mounted in the far corner of the room, and just as he was opening his mouth to bring the meeting to a close, he spotted Leila.

The look on her stricken face tore into his gut like a tsunami, devastating and complete.

She turned and rushed out of the room before he could take two steps toward her.

11

Angry tears ran down Leila's face, unchecked. She swiped them away with an angry balled-up fist as she put the keys into the ignition, revved the motor of her jeep, and peeled out of the small parking lot.

How dare he!

"Damn it, how fucking dare he!" she cried out and swerved, narrowly missing the curb as she angrily downshifted on the gear stick and swung out into the darkened street.

Listening to him as he told that old Ms. Mayflower how he was "handling" the situation, how he would make sure they all got theirs, filled her with so much anger she could barely see straight.

She should have known better.

"Stupid me! I thought he cared about me. All he cared about was trying to work me into agreeing to sell Aunt Sadie's. And hey, maybe get a little pussy in the process. Damn his ass!" she cried and sniffed, before moving one hand from the death-grip hold she had on the steering wheel to feel around in the dark interior of her Jeep for a tissue.

She glanced behind her and narrowed her eyes after she noticed the bright lights of another vehicle following close behind her.

"That had better not be his ass following me," she mumbled, and after several miles she knew without a doubt that it was.

"He can follow me 'til hell freezes over, for all the good it's going to do him," she murmured, continuing her one-sided diatribe with herself.

When she pulled into the driveway of her loft, she calmly turned off the ignition and jumped out of her Jeep, grabbing her purse, and walked toward her door.

He turned in behind her within moments of her arrival, and unfurled his long frame from behind the wheel of his low-slung sportscar.

"Leila . . . wait!"

Leila turned to face him after she'd unlocked the door.

"Baby, please—"

"*Baby*? I think not. What. Do. You. *Want*?"

After asking, she turned away from him, and looked out over the dark street. As hurt as she was, as angry as she was, she couldn't stand to look at his face, and had to give herself a moment.

She turned back to face him and in the porch-lit night, she saw the fine tinge of red running along his cheeks. The fact that he called her baby seemed to register on him and he looked as surprised as she at the endearment.

"I can explain. It wasn't what it looked like," he said, and she laughed harshly.

"I *know* what I saw and heard, Brandan. I'm not stupid. Come on, now, give me a little more cred than that! But you know, in all actuality, you don't owe me any explanations. You don't owe me a damn thing. Now, I'm tired. It's been a long day."

She turned to leave.

He reached out and pulled her back around to face him.
"Please . . ."

"Please what? What can you possibly say?" she cried and pulled away from him.

"Can I come in? Do we have to discuss this outside?"

Leila bit her bottom lip and stared up at him, undecided.

"Please, just let me in," he begged, his voice low.

She turned and opened the door. Once inside she made a motion with her hand for him to follow her. She ignored the flip in her stomach when she saw the look of relief flash across his handsome face, but backed away when he reached out to touch her.

His hand dropped away as she turned around and entered the loft, throwing her purse on the small sofa in the middle of the room, and she turned to him.

"So, you'll take care of it? You'll take care of me, huh?" she said, and crossed her arms over her chest.

When his cheeks flushed red, she quirked a brow and waited for his response.

12

"It wasn't like that, I—"

"Oh, no? Then what *was* it like, Brandan? From where I stood, it appeared as though that was *just* what it was," she countered.

With that, she slid her shoes off her feet, although sliding wasn't exactly what she did. She kicked them off so hard they skidded across the ceramic tile flooring and landed with a soft whoosh against a corner of the room.

Damn. She was pissed off.

"Look, I don't know how much you heard." He began to walk toward her as she busied herself in her kitchen, opened a cabinet and furiously slammed a old-fashioned looking red tea kettle in the sink, and filled it with water.

He crossed his arms over his chest and waited for her to calm down. There wasn't any use trying to talk to her until then.

But he wasn't about to leave and allow her to stew and think all kinds of shit about what had happened, things that weren't true, without defending himself.

He glanced around the loft, and although his mind was on her and her alone, he admired the eclectic design of her home, one that mimicked the café, a curious blend of antiques, modern, and straight-out funky looking furnishings dominated the large, open loft.

The living area, in fact the entire loft, was open, and the only area that was sectioned off was the kitchen and, his eyes spanned over the area, the bedroom. Or the bed to be exact. It was raised and positioned on a high dais. There was also a sectioned-off area which he assumed was the bathroom.

His eyes went back to the bed dominating one corner of the large loft.

It was a four-poster canopy, complete with sheer red netting that wrapped around the circumference of the bed, enveloping it, giving it the appearance of a warm, inviting cocoon.

He turned back to her and caught her staring at him.

"You know what? I really thought, stupid me, that there was more to—" she waved her hands around and then blew out a harsh breath, "us, whatever . . . hell, I don't even know what to *call* this strange relationship of ours," she admitted, running a shaking hand over her hair.

"What's so strange about it?" he asked, walking closer to her. "We're two people who are getting to know each other. Two people who are attracted to one another. All the rest, is it really important?"

"This was a bad idea," she said, slamming the teapot down on the counter, facing him.

"What was a bad idea? You inviting me in, or you throwing a tantrum over nothing?" he asked.

"I know what I heard!" she said, coming from behind the small kitchen island.

When she went to walk past him, he grabbed her wrist.

"You need to let go of me. Now," she said, her mouth tightening, eyes narrowed as she stared down at his hand, loosely wrapped around her wrist.

When he ignored her, kept his hand firmly circling her wrist, she jerked her arm, snatching it out of his grip. When she moved to walk away from him, he grabbed her, hauling her close to his chest.

"Let me go. You're going too damn far," she bit out furiously.

"No, not until you listen to me, Leila! I wasn't trying to manipulate you, trick you, sabotage you, or whatever the hell else you're thinking!"

"Let me go," she said again, as though he hadn't heard her the first time.

"Damn, you're stubborn! What do I have to do, to say, to show you that you mean more to me than what I can get out of your property?"

A furious expression crossed her face, and when she hauled back a hand as though to hit him, he caught her wrist, holding it tight, yet not tight enough to hurt her.

"I wouldn't suggest you do that," he murmured, his breath coming out in harsh gasps as though he'd just run a marathon.

"No?" she asked, her breath coming out equally harsh. "And what do you suggest I do? And what are you going to do about it?" she threw the challenge at him, the ends of her nostrils flaring as her amber eyes roamed over his face.

"This," he bit out, and covered her mouth with his.

She grabbed onto the back of his head and pulled him tighter, closer. With a harsh groan he lifted her in his arms, and with long strides carried her to her bed.

He didn't bother to release her lips as he swiftly divested her of her clothing. He simply snatched her skirt down her long legs, buttons and zippers ripping, and nearly tore her panties in half as he ripped them from her body.

Seconds later he'd taken off her blouse, and after fumbling with her bra, removed it as well.

"God!" he murmured as he pulled his lips from hers and gazed down at her laying beneath him, her golden-colored small breasts tumbling free. He firmly cupped one in his hand, thumbing the tight wine-colored nipple until it spiked hard and long.

Dizziness swarmed in Leila's head when he took her nipple deep into his mouth, pulling the rest of her breast within the warm, wet cavern, and suckled her hard.

As he nursed her breast, she shoved her hands between them, unfastened the buttons on his jeans and eased a hand inside his shorts.

When she grasped his penis, she slid her hand over his thick shaft, and felt her own cream ease from her vagina at the thought of how hard and thick he was, and how good he would feel imbedded deep inside her.

Her anger vanished, going up in smoke while her passion, a lustful passion she'd had for months for him, even before they'd met, burned bright and hot. Temporarily, anger and hurt feelings were set aside.

Her body hummed with pleasure as his mouth, so wet, so warm, pulled and tugged at her breasts.

He pulled his mouth from her breasts and she cried out.

"Ssh, it's okay, baby," he murmured, and helped her shed his pants before tossing them over the side of the bed. He lifted his body from hers, pulled his shirt over his head, and turned back to face her.

Her breath caught at the sight of him in the dim light, kneeling on her bed. His thick shaft was long and so full, curved against his lightly furred stomach, and the bulbous knob thumped past his navel.

With a glint in his eyes he rolled on top of her and snaked his big, hard body down hers to settle between her thighs.

He leaned into the V of her legs and inhaled.

"Damn, your pussy smells good," he groaned before pushing her legs up so that her feet lay flat on the bed, her knees wide apart.

Expecting to feel the strong sweep of his tongue against her folds, her body arced off the bed when she felt the tip of his tongue tap against the sensitive seam between her pussy and ass, his fingers digging into the cheeks of her buttocks, spreading it wide, so he could continue his freaky assault.

"No, God, what are you—"

She gasped, her words cut off when he plunged a thick finger deep into her core, while rimming her with his hot, wicked tongue.

He held her down when she would have bucked him off, trailing his tongue along the seam between her buttocks and pussy and down her inner thigh.

"Ummm," she moaned and reared her body up, reaching down to grasp his head. With a guttural laugh he shoved her hands away and pinned them to side of her hips.

"No direction. I know how to steer, Lee," he said, lifting his head to gaze at her.

The look in his eyes was so hot, so . . . hungry, it stole her breath. She bit the edge of her bottom lip and at his nudging, lay back down.

With a satisfied murmur he went back in, licking, stroking, and devouring her pussy. Her body hummed, her pussy flooded cream, and blood rushed to her head as sensation upon sensation hit her.

She mewled when he separated the lips of her vagina, and inserted one thick finger inside while steadily lapping at her cunt. Leila squirmed, rotating her hips around the invasive finger.

"You like this, baby?" he asked, and she felt his smile against her mound when she moaned an affirmative.

When he pulled his finger from out of her well, she cried out, pressing closer to him, wanting to feel his hot, talented fingers deep inside her body.

In the dark she saw him lift his finger to his mouth and lick off her cum from his finger.

"Nice and wet. And so damn sweet," he murmured.

She tried to choke out a response, but he chose that moment to push her legs further apart and press his tongue deep inside her pussy.

"Oh God, Brandan, what are you doing?" she cried when he hollowed his tongue and speared deep inside her.

Her mewling cries became harsh, guttural, when he plunged two fingers, then a third, and finally the others deep inside her.

Her head tossed back and forth on her pillow as the pressure built, unbearably sweet painful pleasure swept through her while he slowly rotated his hand inside her body, dragging his balled fist in and out of her creaming core.

When he eased a finger of his other hand deep into her ass, the orgasm hit it hit hard.

Her torso jerked upward, she grabbed onto his head, ignoring his silent edict that she not, and ground herself against his head, her thighs death-gripping the sides of his face, her hips pumping to meet his piercing dual thrusts until her body exploded.

She released his head and her body fell to the bed. She grabbed the pillow and slammed it over her mouth in an effort to quiet her cries of release, nearly blacking out, her orgasm was so intense.

When she came back to awareness, he was crouched on top of her, his hard shaft stabbing against her stomach, and a look of intense lust shone in his light blue eyes.

The combination was lethal, deadly, to her already overwrought body. Her pussy throbbed and her gut clenched, and when the fine hairs on his chest rasped against her breasts, her nipples stood out in aching, stiff little points.

He grabbed his cock in his hand and began to feather it back and forth across her mound, toying with her clit and the lips of her vagina.

She closed her eyes, ready to feel all of that incredible dick deep inside her.

"Please tell me you have a condom," he pleaded, his breath coming out in harsh gasps.

Leila's eyes flew open as realization dawned.

God, she'd gotten so wrapped up in the pleasure he was giving that protection had been the last thing on her mind.

Although she was on the pill, she never, *ever* had sex without protection, something her Aunt Sadie had drilled into her from the time of adolescence.

That she'd been ready to do so with Brandan, with him not wearing a rubber, the thought not even crossing her mind, was something she'd analyze later.

Much later.

"Yes. Side drawer. Hurry."

He bounced off the bed. Her eyes stayed glued to the rock-hard muscles in his tight, naked ass as they flexed when he bent down to retrieve the box of prophylactics. He ripped open the box and grabbed several small foil packages.

At her raised brow, he laughed. "No way in hell is one going to be enough."

Leila gulped.

Her heart skipped several beats.

13

Brandan shut his eyes as he slowly invaded her slick heat, savoring the feel of her pussy walls clamping hard on his cock.

He'd licked and devoured her pussy, eating her sweet cum like it was nectar from heaven, finding her hot spots with his tongue.

And for the first time, as he slowly rocked into her, he resented the use of a condom.

She was so hot, so goddamn . . . wet, he could feel her heat sear his shaft, her pussy warm and wet, tightly gloving him.

"Shit!" he grunted as he fed her more of himself. He stopped when she gasped, her pussy clamping down on him like a vice.

"Wait . . . God . . . you're so big. Damn!" she cried out. He stopped, although everything in him screamed for him to spread her legs further and shove into her tight creaming cunt.

"Okay . . . okay, baby, we'll go slow . . ." He ground out the words and felt his entire body shake as he fought back the inclination to fuck her hard. To shove his cock into her as far as it would go until he reached the back of her womb.

She wrapped her arms around him, her short nails scoring

his back. He welcomed the slight pain, his body trembling with the effort to hold back, to wait until she was ready for him before he went any further.

"God, baby, I don't think I can wait much longer," he said, his body now dripping with sweat, trickling down in hot splashes on her small, ripe breasts.

"Okay, okay, I think I'm ready. Ummm, you feel so good. So hard . . . so thick."

"Keep saying shit like that and I'm fucking you now, hard and deep, whether you're ready or not," he said, releasing a pain-filled laugh when he felt his cock grow even harder with her moaning reply.

She laughed a breathless laugh, and he heard her swallow.

When the walls of her pussy relaxed around his penis, he ran his hands down the sides of her body until he reached her hips. Grasping them, he then began, in short experimental shallow thrusts, to flex into her.

He pressed a hand between them, withdrew her own moisture and circled her blood-filled rigid clit in tight circles until he felt her cream ease down his hands.

When her hips rose to meet his, his thrusts became stronger as he slid in and out of her slick honeyed depths.

Within moments, they'd each caught the other's rhythm, and Brandan increased his depth of stroke, taking clues from her. With each movement of her hip and every contraction of her pussy on his shaft, he adapted his strokes to maximize her pleasure.

Leaning down, he captured one of her erect nipples and suckled on it, lapping and tonguing her as he rode her.

The pressure mounted with each jab and stroke until she screamed, "Yes . . . like that . . . please, God . . . yes . . . Brandannnn . . ." He cut her cries of pleasure off, slanting his mouth over hers, grasped her hands within his, and held them high above her head.

With each corkscrew thrust, as he jammed her body, his balls tightened painfully with the need to release his seed.

The orgasm almost broke free when he released her hands and cupped her tight muscled ass, and he stroked into her once, twice, and then a final time.

He pressed her into the bed, covering her completely, and ground into her sweet snatch.

Within moments, she broke.

She screamed, bucked against him strongly, almost unseating him, but he held on, stroking into her willing, warm core, determined to give her pleasure, his body taut, on fire, with his need to come.

When he felt her pussy clench, her inner walls tightly clamping down on his shaft, he threw his head back, every muscle in his body strained, and came.

His cum was so intense, it was startling in its intensity. A loud roar filled his ears, stars flashed before his eyes, yet he battled against the blinding release to catch one final look at her before his orgasm engulfed him.

Her expressive face in the dim moonlit room, as she held on to him, was the most beautiful thing he'd ever seen.

Her eyes were tightly shut, her lips, red and swollen, were partially opened, and tears of release ran down her pretty honey-colored cheeks.

As he continued to stroke her, before bliss completely took over, he was stunned to feel matching dew moisten his own eyes, their cries melding in harmony, ending on a wailing note of passionate accord.

14

Leila lay on the bed, looking drained, spent. Satisfied.

With her eyes closed, she drew in deep breaths of air as her body calmed after her wild release. His hungry gaze raked her body. Her big, beautiful thighs were spread wide, one drooped over the edge of the bed.

Even in the dark Brandan could see her pouty clit peaking out from the dark triangle, that thatch of hair at the apex of her thighs.

So goddamn sexy.

He had to fuck her again. Now.

He rolled the condom over his shaft and mounted her. She opened surprised eyes and groaned along with him when he eased back inside her hot, sweet, willing pussy.

"Baby, I don't think I can take you again so soon," she groaned, and he gently kissed her closed lids before trailing kisses down her soft caramel-colored cheek that tasted as good as it looked, over to her lips. Her ripe, red, luscious lips.

"It'll be okay, I'll be gentle," he promised.

He shifted his hands beneath her head and brought her face close to his as he deepened his kiss in time to his deeper strokes, and thrust his tongue inside her warm mouth.

"Ummm," she sighed when he swiped inside her mouth, running his tongue around the walls of her mouth, the roof, before slowly lapping his against hers.

"Feel good?" he asked, releasing her mouth.

"Yeah," she smiled, a small, purely feminine smile that made his breath hitch in his throat.

Laying her head back down he maneuvered their bodies so that she lay in front of him before he eased his dick back inside her, carefully separating the swollen lips, and he pushed into her until he was imbedded all the way back in.

Leisurely he made love to her, alternating his depth and strength of his strokes, from shallow to deep and slow, he rocked into her.

He held onto her breasts and she arched into his palms, her sweet round bottom nestled tightly against him as she accepted him.

He took his time with her, easing a hand in front to brush his fingers over her mound, separating her so that he could toy with her swollen clit.

They made love that way, him rocking into her from the back, her head lying against his chest, accepting his loving until the storm, gentler this time, broke, sending them both into ecstasy.

"So, you've been setting up meetings with the others?" Leila murmured lightly, her voice hoarse and strained.

It was the early hours of the morning, and her body, sore and aching from their all-night lovemaking, was firmly nestled against Brandan's.

She felt the thick muscles in his arms, tense with her question, before they relaxed, and he continued to stroke feather like caresses down the length of one arm.

He moved one of her long locs behind her ear, and kissed her lobe, pulling it into his mouth before slowly releasing it.

She moved her head away.

He sighed, turning her around to face him. .

"Lee, it wasn't like that. I promise you. They invited me to their meeting. I didn't set anything up."

With the early morning light filtering into the room, past the wide wood blinds of the windows, she was able to see the sincerity in his eyes. But it didn't erase the burning sense of betrayal she'd felt.

"I wish you would have told me, Brandan. I mean, I know you're still after the property and all, but I thought . . ."

He leaned down, captured her lips in a soft kiss. "Thought what, Leila?"

The question seemed to be asking more than what was obvious. What had she thought?

She ducked her head, unsure . . .

He lifted her to meet his eyes, one finger beneath her chin. "Thought that what is happening between us goes beyond interest in your property?"

She looked him in the eye, answering, "Yes. I thought so."

He pulled her into his arms. "It is. Much more than that." He held her, his head resting lightly on hers.

"So, what do we do?"

"I won't lie and say I don't want your property, Leila. I do. But what's happening between us matters more to me." He sighed. "Neither will I lie and say I have the answer, a compromise that will work. One that will make you happy, one that will make my partners happy. Or even one that will make your neighbors happy. They all want to sell, Leila."

Leila felt tears burn the back of her throat. "God, I know.

Don't you think I know that? But what am I supposed to do? I can't let Aunt Sadie's go. It's my last link with my aunt, a woman who raised me like her own daughter. I can't let her down like that. I can't sell out," she cried, burrowing her head deep in his chest, worry, anger, and helplessness suddenly crashing down on her in waves.

Brandan tightened his hold on her. He was at as much of a loss on what to do as she. The only thing he could offer was comfort. He ran his hands over her long locs, noticing the fine tremble in them.

He'd never been affected by a woman, never felt such an emotional attachment to anyone, such that to see her cry, distressed, made him feel helpless.

"You know, I wish I'd had someone like your Aunt Sadie in my life growing up."

Her soft cries began to wane and she raised her head to seek his eyes.

He smiled down at her. Although her face was puffy and flushed, her eyes reddened from her tears, she was still the most beautiful woman he'd ever seen.

Damn. He had it bad.

He thumbed a caress down her soft cheek, wiping away the last of her tears.

"My father skipped out on us when I was a kid. We never did have much, and my parents and I were basically homeless," he laughed without humor.

"I'm so sorry," she said softly.

He saw the sympathy in her eyes and smiled. "Well, we weren't ever actually out on the streets. Just went where my father could find work, usually in ranching and cattle. My mom usually got hired on in the kitchens."

He leaned down to kiss her before continuing. "Dad had a hard time keeping it together. Got drunk one time too many and didn't show up for work, and the next day we had to pack up. Time to move on."

"That must have been hard."

"Wasn't great. But it could have been a lot worse. A lot of the ranchers hired illegals to work. They'd bring their families sometimes, and share the same cramped quarters that we had. It wasn't an easy life. But none of us knew better—it was the only life we had," he finished, remembering the days of his childhood. As a boy, he hadn't been aware of just how poor he and his family had been. It had taken adolescence and bussing to urban area high schools to realize that.

He remembered the shame of showing up to school in mended jeans and too-tight hand-me-down clothing, and the teasing that ensued before he became aware of just how poor he and his family was.

He shook off the shame of a painful past and pulled her on top of his body.

"Where are your parents now? Your mom? What happened when your father left?"

"Mom kept on doing what she knew, working in the kitchens whenever she could get hired on. Things actually got better once dad left," he said lightly.

He didn't feel like going down memory lane, memories of his father's raging and subsequent abuse whenever he got drunk, how he'd take his anger out on his mother until Brandan had finally stepped in.

The result of his interference was that he still bore the scars, both physical and mental.

"That's all in the past. Why don't we focus on the future?" he asked, ignoring the painful memories, and the light of sympathy and curiosity that burned bright in her amber-colored eyes.

He leaned around her body, sought and found a condom,

and with her warm body on his, he sheathed his burgeoning erection.

"I can think of much better things to concentrate on," he said, lifting her by the waist and slowly lowering her onto his shaft until his balls tapped against her mound, and her warm, welcoming sheath gripped him.

15

"An offer came through from the Rodriguez brothers," Mateo told Brandan as he strolled into his office.

"Asking price?"

Brandan glanced away from his monitor, removed his glasses, and massaged the bridge of his nose before setting the glasses on his desk.

"Hell, above asking," Mateo laughed, tossing the fax on Brandan's desk before sprawling down in one of the chairs facing him.

Brandan glanced over the copy and raised a brow.

"I'll say," he murmured and placed it to the side. "It's a good investment. They'll sit on it for a while and turn around and make a huge profit when they resell it," he said offhandedly, knowing the nature of the real estate commercial business well.

The Rodriguez brothers' business was similar to theirs—they bought large land plots and then resold them to investors, mostly for commercial deals. And made a hell of a lot of money in the process. The longer they waited, the higher the tag when they sold.

"No doubt."

They discussed the deal for several minutes, among new deals they had on their plate, before Mateo mentioned a fundraiser he was going to attend.

As he was speaking, a ding alerted Brandan that he had an email message. He smiled when the small envelope appeared on his computer and saw it was from Leila.

He hadn't seen her since they'd made love a week ago, having had to go out of town on business. He'd just gotten back to the office, and had every intention of leaving early to rectify his absence.

She didn't know he was back in town—his intent was to surprise her and pick her up and take her out. In all the time they'd known each other, they hadn't yet gone out on a real date.

He shook his head, thinking how their relationship had gone from zero to one hundred miles per hour in three seconds flat.

"I'm going to invite Leila to accompany me," Mateo stated, and Brandan turned his eyes away from the computer and back to Mateo.

"What the hell are you talking about?" he asked, narrowing his eyes.

"To the fundraiser. I want to take her to the fundraiser. Senator Montoya will be there."

"And?"

"And he's a sucker for a good hard-luck story and a pretty face. He may be able to exert some influence and help her out," he finished, goading Brandan.

"I don't give a shit what he's a sucker for. She's not going anywhere with you," Brandan stated baldly.

"Well, why don't we let Leila be the judge of that?"

"And when in hell did you decide you wanted to 'help' her out? I thought you wanted to buy the land," he demanded.

"I like her. What can I say?" he responded, shrugging a shoulder.

"I don't give a damn how much you like her. Leave her alone," Brandan said, his voice calm and devoid of emotion as the two men stared at each other.

"And if I don't?'

"Mateo, don't fuck with me on this. Leave it alone," Brandan repeated in a deadpan voice as the two men measured one another—one with a deadly gleam in his eye, the other's mocking.

Brandan glanced around the brightly lit ballroom, his gaze running over the glitz and glamour and fashionably turned out crowd, seeking Leila.

He'd gotten caught up in business and hadn't been able to call her until several hours after his conversation with Mateo.

Surprised and pleased that he was back in town, he could hear the smile in her voice when she greeted him.

They'd gotten caught up with each other's news, engaging in the type of conversation new lovers often conducted, her deep husky voice soft, sweet, almost girlish in tone, when he told her what he planned to do to her when he saw her next, before he'd steered the conversation around to the fundraiser.

"Yes, actually, Mateo called me a few hours ago and invited me. I didn't know you were back in town," she'd said and he'd heard the hesitancy in her voice.

"So, when the cat's away, the mouse will play?" he'd asked, anger flooding him.

"What are you talking about?"

He heard the hurt in her voice, but ignored it. "You're not going."

"Wha—what do you mean, I'm not going? Since when do I

need your permission as to what I can and cannot do, Brandan?" The hurt turned to anger, yet Brandan ploughed on.

"I'm serious. Call him up and tell him you have a change of
plans," he demanded, knowing he sounded like a dominating ass,
but not really giving a damn. She wasn't going anywhere with
Mateo.

"And if I don't?"

Brandan cursed, her words mocking him, echoing Mateo's.

When he said nothing, trying to check his anger, she continued. "Senator Montoya will be there. And unlike you, Mateo
seems to actually want to help me save Aunt Sadie's." She
threw the words at him and Brandan reacted.

"Mateo doesn't give a goddamn about you or Aunt Sadie's.
His only concern is trying to fuck you. Don't fool yourself," he
laughed harshly, and knew he'd gone too far when she gasped.
"Damn, I didn't mean that . . ."

"Yes, you did," she paused. "But really, is he any different
than you?" she laughed harshly.

"Damn it, Lee—"

"Look, I gotta go. I need to close up early so I can get ready.
And Brandan, please don't make the mistake of thinking you
own me just because I let you fuck me," she said, and before he
could refute her claim that all he'd done was "fuck" her, he
heard her quietly disconnect the phone, leaving a soft buzzing
in his ear.

He savagely pressed end, and slammed the phone down on
his desk.

"Damn!"

Now, as his eyes scanned the crowd searching for her, his
gaze zeroed in on her. Like a lighthouse beacon, she stood out
from the crowd.

She, tall and so gorgeous she made his breath catch, was talking to an older man. He walked closer, watching her animated

beautiful face as she laughed and spoke to the man he recognized as Senator Montoya.

She had her long dreads—locs, he corrected himself, remembering what she'd told him the correct name was—long and loose, hanging down her back in a thick curtain, pulled away from her face.

She was wearing a short black dress that draped her long, fit body, molding her soft curves and ending above her knees.

His hungry gaze traveled down her gentle curves, down her long shapely legs, legs that had been wrapped around him as she called out his name while he stroked into her.

"Shit," he mumbled, forcing his thoughts away from the two of them making love before he embarrassed himself in the crowded room of sophisticated partygoers.

He shook his head when a tuxedoed waiter offered him a fluted glass of champagne, and purposefully strode toward Leila.

16

"I've been looking all over for you, darlin'," a familiar baritone whispered loudly enough for Senator Montoya to hear. Leila felt her cheeks warm in anger.

He nuzzled the side of her neck briefly, and smooth as butter on a hot skillet, deftly removed from the man's outstretched hand the card the Senator was in the process of handing her.

"Ted, would you mind if I took the beautiful young lady away from you? She's promised me the next dance."

The shorter man winked broadly, a huge grin on his face as though the two men shared some joke beyond her weak feminine grasp, and left.

The sympathy she'd seen on his face as she'd spoken to him about Aunt Sadie's had been replaced by a look of what appeared to be relief, as though he'd been rescued.

Leila opened her mouth to speak, to bring the retreating Senator back to her side. Immediately, Brandan pressed her tighter against his hard body. She felt his warm breath against her temple as he spoke for her ears alone. "Let it go, Lee. I warned you not to come here."

"Let *me* go," Leila gritted between clenched teeth.

She felt the muscles in the corner of her mouth twitch with the effort to keep the smile on her face, so others wouldn't know what was going on between them.

The band struck up again, music filling the ballroom, and Brandan turned her around to face him. "Let's dance."

Her angry yet hungry eyes raked over his handsome form, decked out in a black tuxedo, complete with bolero tie, his big body looking resplendent in his formal clothes.

She wanted to maintain her anger with him, the last words they'd exchanged still heavy in her mind, and knew that if she was in his company for more than five hot seconds and danced with him, she'd fall victim yet again to their crazy, electric chemistry, something she didn't feel like doing until she got a grip on her emotions.

She turned away from him, intending to put as much distance between them as she could, but he pulled her back.

Without waiting for her reply, he held her hand firmly within his and led her around the fast-filling dance floor. Once he'd gotten them a space, he turned her around and pulled her close.

He wrapped his arms around her waist, bringing her body flush with his as he moved his body and hers in time to the slow, sensual beat of the band.

"What are you doing here? What did you hope to accomplish by coming here with Mateo, Lee?" he asked, giving her no time to compose herself as his hard body brushed against her. Hypersensitive to his touch, she sought to pull back.

He immediately pulled her in again, tightening his hold around her waist.

"What do you care? It's not your neighbors losing their businesses, their livelihoods, not your children losing their park! And you most certainly don't care about me!" She refrained from sticking out her tongue at him. Just barely, as she tacked on that last bit out of spite and anger, remembering their last conversation and they way he'd *told* her not to show up at the fundraiser with his partner.

"Does this feel like I don't care?" he asked, bringing their lower bodies into closer alignment.

Leila's heart slammed against her chest, and her mouth went dry when she felt his hard length pressed intimately against hers.

Leila closed her eyes and shut down her body's immediate reaction, refusing to get caught up with him again. "That doesn't impress me," she lied blithely.

"Not if you don't want it to, it can't," he said, and subtly ground his cock against her body, disguising the bold sexual move as a dance move, as he pulled her hips closer to his and swayed back and forth, side to side, his heat searing through the thin black fabric of her dress.

Despite her best intentions, she leaned into his body, welcoming his touch, and opened her thighs to better accommodate him.

They swayed together to the music, their bodies pressed close, blending, merging, instinctively in tune with the other.

When the song began to end, she shoved away from him and broke out of the sensual spell they'd weaved.

She quickly left the floor, seeking out the ladies' restroom. Blinded by tears at how easily he got around her, and weaving her way through the crowd, she was desperate to escape the tantalizing promise in his eyes.

Once in the restroom, Leila was thankful it was empty. She'd purposely chosen one that was far from the ballroom, figuring no one would come to it, and with the lateness of the hour, the likelihood was slim that a hotel guest would meander inside as well.

She needed to be alone.

What was wrong with her that just one touch from Brandan

sent both her emotions and her sexuality into overdrive? When she was willing to, if not forgive, temporarily shove to the back of her mind the things he said that really pissed her off . . . and act like a cat in heat rubbing and grinding against him on a crowded dance floor.

Damn . . .

"Aunt Sadie, what in the world am I going to do?" she murmured out loud, staring at her reflection in the mirror.

She could almost hear her great-aunt respond: *Well, baby girl, you have to make a decision that you and only you can make. You need to decide what it is you want from this man, what he wants from you. You need to stop trying to analyze the whys of your feelings, and just feel, baby. Life is so short . . .*

Leila squeezed her eyes shut tightly to erase the threat of tears that threatened to fall.

She knew it was all in her head, her conversations with Aunt Sadie. But sometimes, it felt so real . . .

She took a deep breath, opened her eyes, and washed her hands before she walked toward the door.

In the process of opening the door, her heart slammed against her chest when Brandan walked through the opening, determination settling across his face and in his stride.

17

"You can't be in here! What's wrong with you?" Leila demanded, but when he continued to advance toward her she quickly spun around and ran into one of the bathroom stalls and slammed it shut.

But not quickly enough.

He tore open the door, and with a screech, Leila backed up until the back of her knees hit the toilet.

She would have fallen had he not grasped her by the crook of the arm. With a thud and an "oomph" of breath escaping her lips, she was hauled against his chest.

With her mouth wide open she stared at him, fearing he'd plain lost his mind following her into the bathroom, and not sure what to say, completely speechless as his big body crowded her in the small stall.

He grasped her chin with his thumb and two fingers and lifted her face, forcing her to look directly into his eyes. As their gazes connected, she noted that within his light blue eyes was a strange gleam, one that scared her as much as it excited her.

He drew her closer. Yet didn't say a word.

Leila was thrown off balance with his quiet, watchful stare.

Staring into his face, his eyes, she saw her own reflection stare back at her. His penetrating gaze seemed to look directly into her soul, as though he were seeking to discern her every thought, her every emotion.

At the thought, a new tingling awareness coursed through her body, sending chill bumps to curl around her spine. Cupping his palms around her cheeks, he dropped his mouth and covered her lips with his, giving soft, whispering caresses with his lips that soon turned to long, drugging, and devouring kisses.

"I told you not to come here, Leila," he whispered hotly against her lips once he released her.

"And I told you, you don't dictate—" her words were cut short when he lifted her easily, and hiked up her skirt to her waist before he wrapped her legs around his waist.

"No . . . what are you doing? I don't want thi—" Her breathless protest was cut short when he slanted his lips over hers and turned, fumbling behind them to lock the door to the stall.

She heard the rasp of his zipper, and with his other hand he ripped her panties from her body and watched with dazed eyes as the flimsy scraps floated to the floor.

"Brandan . . . are you insane?" she whispered, her chest heaving as she turned her eyes back to his.

He nuzzled her neck, sending electric pulses of heat racing over her body. He licked her, grabbed the lobe of her ear between his teeth and pulled. One hand found and caressed her clit before he slid between her now-slick folds to slip inside her, and withdraw her own moisture to lubricate her.

Her body arched sharply, her back slammed against the door as he pressed his fingers deeper.

"Do you want it? Do you want me, Leila?" he asked.

She should have been angry.

She should have been afraid of the hot, intense look of determination brightening his light blue eyes, and struggled to get away from him.

She should have done and been all of those things.

But, she didn't. She wasn't.

Instead, she reached out for him, as desire and anticipation swirled around and over her, covering and submerging her until she felt weak and drowning in a sea of need.

A need only he could fulfill.

She wanted . . . needed him with a desire that was limitless, one that knew no boundaries, and one she wasn't going to analyze . . .

With her breath coming out in a shallow rhythm, she nodded her head yes.

18

Leila's heart was slamming against her chest like a jackhammer.

Not waiting for her garage door to open, she slammed on the breaks, grabbed her purse, and after fumbling with the door, yanked the key out of the ignition and raced out of the car.

The very thought of the feral look in Brandan's eyes sent fear mingled with insane lust through her veins.

She couldn't believe what they had done.

Taking her in the women's restroom, of all the places in the world, like a damn animal. And she'd let him do it. In the end, she'd all but begged him to.

On legs that were still wobbly, she raced toward her front door. After a few fumbles, she managed to find the right key to the door. Just as she was inserting the key, a low rumble alerted her that Brandan was hot on her heels.

After their torrid activity in the restroom, she'd gathered her things and fled, leaving him to run behind her to try and catch up.

She'd thrown her useless panties in her purse, and raced down the hall. At the door to the ballroom, she'd left a message telling Mateo she'd gotten a headache and was going home.

As she'd impatiently waited for the keys to her car, she'd sent a prayer heavenward in thanks when she saw someone reach out and pull Brandan's arm, forcing him to stop and speak, giving her enough time to get into her vehicle and speed away, as though the hounds of hell were after her.

"Damn it!" she cursed, looking over her shoulder to see his low black Lamborghini slide next to her beat-up Jeep in her driveway. The powerful engine had barely been cut before he was out of the driver's side.

Fumbling in earnest, she got the key in one lock and glanced over her shoulder to gauge if she had enough time to get the other two unlocked, when his tall, dark, menacing-looking form quickly advanced on her.

"Shit, shit, shit, shit, *shit!*" she mumbled.

Her heart thudded, hiccupped, and stuttered.

She spun around and nearly wept in relief when she unlocked the last one all of three seconds before he made it to the door.

Once inside, she turned to slam the door shut.

But not fast enough.

One large black, ostrich-skin cowboy boot lodged between the door jam.

Leila chose not to wait around for him to catch her. She kicked off her heels and took off running.

Where the hell she was running to, she had no idea.

But the chase was on.

19
_____

Brandan's lips stretched into a predatory smile.

So she wanted to run, did she?

He took his time, gave her a head start.

Just to make it that much more—tasty—when he caught her.

As he walked through her home, he heard the echo of her racing steps in the dark, quiet loft.

He hoped that if she ever decided to leave the restaurant business, she wouldn't turn to a life of crime. Her stealth abilities sucked.

As he walked around the loft, he headed straight to the back where he knew she'd be, and found her in the kitchen, paying no attention to his surroundings in his single-minded intent.

He turned in the darkened room and saw her staring at him, her nostrils flaring, chest heaving, her purse clutched against her chest as though it were some magical shield that could protect her from him.

"Come here."

"Come here," he said again.

Although he spoke in a low tone, the demand in his voice

was subtle, and the look in his bright blue eyes promised a delicious retribution if she were to disobey his request.

But still . . .

"Make me."

She had all of two seconds before he was on her.

"Look, what we did in that bathroom was crazy, and I don't want a repeat performance, thank you!" She shoved against his chest with all the strength she had, but to no avail.

He picked her up as though she weighed no more than the purse she held clutched in her hands, a crazy glint in his light blue eyes, and carried her through the dark loft toward her bed, tossing her in the middle.

She'd only bounced twice on the bed before he was beside her, grasping both of her hands within one of his big ones and stretching them above her head.

Deftly he removed his belt and with the expertise of a master scout, secured her hands, murmuring against her ear. "Wouldn't want you to try and escape before we can even begin."

"What are you doing, you big brute? Let me go!" she panted, her breath coming out in harsh gasps when he tightened his impromptu restraints. "No damn *way* are you doing this, Brandan! I'm serious, let me up!"

He inserted one big hand inside the bodice of her dress, thumbing her extended nipple, before pulling the fabric to the side and capturing her turgid peak in his mouth and slowly releasing it.

Leila clamped her legs tight to prevent the cream from easing out of her vagina, valiantly ignoring her body's reaction, and renewed her struggles in earnest.

He stood and swiftly shed his clothing, and in the dark, his long cock stood stiff and proudly erect, curving against his ripped abdomen, pulsing.

Her pussy, the traitorous hussy, clenched at the sight. She shut her eyes, her heart pounding.

She heard a telltale rip and reluctantly opened her eyes to see him sheathing his rod, his big hands almost obscene looking as they roughly smoothed the prophylactic over his straining dick in one quick movement.

He slanted his mouth over hers just as she was about to let him know what she really thought of his caveman, over-the-top antics, muffling the curses she was ready to let fly.

She fought him, kicking at any available body part she could reach, not really giving a damn if it was one he *might* need in the future, that is, if he ever wanted a family.

He rolled with her on her California king bed, their limbs tangled together until she was trapped beneath him, one of his hands grasped her bound wrists.

"If I let you go, do you promise to be a good girl?" he licked the shell of her ear, and brought the lobe into his mouth with his teeth before slowly releasing it.

"Answer my question. Will you be a good girl if I let you go?"

"I got your good girl, buddy," she said and renewed her struggles in earnest. She just barely kept her laughter in check with their WWW moves on the bed.

"Be still and let me in this pussy," he growled, and shoved his tongue deep inside her mouth. He loosened the belt, allowing her hands to be free. He moved down her body, shoved her skirt up her legs, and nosed aside her slick folds. When he thrust his tongue deep inside her, her body completely lifted away from the bed.

She grabbed his head and instead of shoving it away—as she should have—she pulled him deeper, tighter, closer. She threw back her head, her eyes rolling backwards as a tingling, almost burning sensation swept over her.

The pressure continued to build, until her limbs shook and her breath came out in harsh hiccups, as his long tongue rolled and frolicked inside her body.

"Stop, please, stop!" she begged, incoherent in her desires, instinctually seeking to back away from his hot strokes.

He anchored her to him, and tongued her in long, wicked glides. When he shoved two fingers inside her weeping core, she broke.

He wasted no time. As she was riding the wave of her orgasm, she felt his shaft glide on home, pushing past her swollen, passion-thickened vaginal lips, and press deep inside her core.

Leila arched her back sharply and dug the heels of her feet into the bed as he fed her his dick in tortuously slow increments, until he was all the way in.

"Please . . . wait," she panted and growled low in her throat. But he ignored her plea, pushed her legs further apart, and pressed all the way home.

He didn't stop until he was completely housed with her, didn't pause until he had every inch inside, until her core was filled to the brim with his massive cock.

Brandan stared down at the sexually abandoned expression on Leila's beautiful honey-colored face, saw the red tinge underscoring her skin, and grit his teeth, trying to give her enough time to accustom herself to him.

"You okay?" he asked, his voice rough, raw.

He remained still as he could inside her, but couldn't prevent his hips from flexing, slowly grinding against her. He felt the minute her slick walls relaxed their death-grip on his cock, and with a sigh he felt her move against him.

She kept her eyes closed and gave a short nod of her head, her lips partially opened, small puffs of air escaping from between their full rims.

With a groan he grabbed onto her hips and began to thrust in shallow strokes into her.

She clenched around his shaft, milking and clenching him as he plunged into her sweet honeyed depths.

The walls of her pussy grabbed onto his cock desperately, causing flames to shoot electric fire directly from his balls and cock straight to his gut like a bolt of lightning.

She felt so damn good wrapped around him.

He hadn't meant to fuck her in a damn bathroom stall, of all places.

Shit.

They'd been dancing around each other for so long. He couldn't get a handle on their relationship—one minute they were burning hot, and the next they were at each other like two pit bulls . . . and when she'd defied him, coming to the fundraiser with Mateo, despite his threat of what would happen if she did, he'd seen red.

All rational thought had flown out the window, and his vision had become tunnel. He had to get at her, had to claim her as his. Nothing else had mattered.

She belonged with him for as long as it took for them both to get the other out of their system.

She was his, despite the anger and tension surrounding them, despite the fact that she denied this . . . this . . . connection between them.

He'd known they'd be amazing together. No way in hell it would be anything else, not the way she was built . . . the way she moved. But he hadn't expected the emotional entanglement that had come along with it. He burned hot for her, constantly. She was on his mind every damn waking moment of the day. He thought about her constantly . . . he ran a hand down the swell of her hips, trailing down her smooth thighs.

Their chemistry was explosive, unlike anything he'd ever experienced with a woman, ever thought was even possible.

Brandan clenched his teeth together, and grunted deep in his throat when her inner walls pulsed on his dick with delicate yet robust ferocity.

And then she moved.

Slowly she ground against him in a sensual beat only she heard, and his strokes became stronger, his dick pressed deep into her body before stroking back out until the knob of his shaft sat at her slick entry, only to plunge back inside.

"Ummm." The mewling sigh of pleasure only served to make him harder, and brought an answering growl from his own mouth as she met him stroke for stroke.

He thought his body would incinerate when she angled her hips so that he hit the walls of her pussy in such a way his dick felt as though a thousand tiny feathers were running along the length of it.

He'd never felt anything like it in his life. It was as though her pussy was alive.

Vibrant and unpredictable. Just like her.

"Damn!" he bit out the expletive.

He grabbed her hands in his and forced them high above her head.

Her eyes were like slits, nearly closed. Her pleasure, a tangible, breathing entity, made his cock thicken to painful proportions inside her. His heart beat heavily against his chest, and his balls tightened as he watched her panting breaths escape from between her pouty, juicy lips.

He picked up the tempo of his thrusts, driving inside her relentlessly, his body on fire, sweat dripping from him to her, mingling and running down the midline of her breasts, pressed together with her arms in position.

With every powerful jab inside her wet heat, her head bounced against the wall, against one of her thick pillows. He couldn't—wouldn't—stop the hard, pounding thrusts.

Being inside her was more exhilarating than anything he'd ever experienced.

As he dragged in and out of her heat, with each plunge her

small, beautiful breasts jostled and swayed, gently slapping against each other. With a growl, he held her hands within one of his own, and moved the other down to nudge away her locs from the top of her breasts and grasp as much of one perfectly rounded mound that he could.

He molded and massaged the firm orb with strong fingers before he pinched and tugged on the long, dark wine-colored nipple. She gave a mewling, kittenish sound of pleasure, arching her back and pressing more of her breasts into his hand.

His breathing came out in harsh groans as he stared down at the picture she presented. Caught up in her pleasure, her beauty was mesmerizing.

Her head lay to the side of the pillow, her eyes were closed, and she had captured the bottom rim of her lush lower lip with her small top teeth. Her long locs were wildly spread, partially obscuring her breasts and stomach, providing her with an intimate blanket.

His nostrils flared. Her natural scent, mixed with the smell of sex, enveloped him, ensnaring him in her unique web.

Brandan bent down to inhale her, nuzzling aside several long locs to breathe in her intoxicating scent.

She mewled, rooting closer to him, and he leaned down to lick the side of her neck with the flat of his tongue.

"Delicious," he murmured against her neck.

Her taste was sweet and salty. A hedonistic combination of milk chocolate and peppermint.

Brandan took his time playing with her breasts, swirling his tongue around the large chocolate disk of fat areole with the flat of his tongue, up and over her plump sweet nipple, before he pulled it deep inside his mouth while he rocked into her pussy.

"Brandan . . ." she cried in a strangled voice, her body surging up to meet his thrusts.

"Is it good to you, baby? Do you like what I'm doing to you? What we're doing to each other?"

"Yes . . . yes," she cried out.

"I need to come now," the words were torn from his throat. "Are you ready?"

She closed her eyes and widened her legs, which allowed him to dig into her that much more. She rolled and twisted her hips, skewering his cock with abandon.

Brandan knew he couldn't last much longer.

"*Now*," he roared.

He reared his body up, away from hers. He firmly gripped her lush hips with his hands, digging his fingers into her flesh and furiously pumping inside of her, trying to hold on to the pleasure of her pussy as long as he could.

In hard strokes he rocked into her. Every thrust, every jab of his cock, he took them both that much closer to release, that much closer to rapture.

"Ooh, *God!*" she screamed. "Yes!"

He released his grip on her hips, grabbed both of her wrists again with one of his hands, and held them pinned above her head. He pumped into her furiously, delivering short staccato thrusts, jamming into her body, rocking them both into ecstasy, so harshly, her head easing toward the headboard so that he had to adjust her body, moving her back down toward the middle of the bed.

The only sounds in the room were her moaning wails, his heavy breathing, and the bed banging against the wall.

Brandan slammed his mouth over hers, swallowing her cries, and screwed into her with tight, controlled, circular motions, savage pleasure crawling through his gut with every clench of her pussy clamping his dick.

When he felt his balls swell, throb, as they tapped against her ass with each stroke, he knew it was time. He couldn't hold back any longer. He was seconds from detonating.

He relented, gave up the battle.

Throwing his head back, he shut his eyes tight and growled deep from within his throat as all the blood rushed from his head with the power of his orgasm. He felt his cum spurt in painful streams from his body with the power of his release.

20

When he flipped their bodies so that she lay draped on top of his big, hard sweaty body, Leila lifted a limp hand and laid it on top of his chest, her body relaxed, at ease. Sated.

She felt boneless.

"That's what will happen whenever you challenge me, Lee," he murmured, the hairs on his chest tickling her cheek as he rumbled the response.

Leila's heart seemed to skip a beat at his response, and she felt the hairs on the back of her neck stand up on end.

Despite the laxity of her limbs and the all-around good feeling she had—the kind of feeling a woman got when she'd been good and pleased by a man—damn if she'd let him think he was the boss of her.

No man was the boss of her.

She ignored the taunting laugh in her head telling her she sounded like a taciturn toddler.

She forced her relaxed limbs to cooperate and before he knew what hit him, she'd flipped his body away, silently thanked her instructor, Master Yong, for the skills he'd taught, and had jumped off the bed. After landing on the balls of her feet, Leila swiftly spun around.

Brandan, now sprawled on the bed, his legs splayed apart, and his gorgeous cock . . . damn it, Leila forced her eyes away . . . He continued to lie where she dumped him. Before he could hide it, a look of surprise on his face forced a pleased grin on hers. "Get out," she demanded.

He laid back, propped his leg to the side, his penis, no longer erect yet still thick, lay enticingly to the side of his inner thigh.

Leila looked away.

"You heard me, Brandan . . . I want you to go," she insisted.

She turned to face him, ready to see a mocking look on his face.

There was none. Instead, he leaned up and gently held his hand out to her, silently begging her to take it, to take him.

She took a deep breath. She didn't want him thinking he could get away with manhandling her.

"I'm sorry," she said. The apology seemed to shock him more than her, and despite her ambivalent feelings, she felt a smile tug at the corner of her lips.

What in the world was she going to do with him, with her confusing feelings for him, and their odd relationship?

Leila sighed, and placed her jumbled thoughts and confusing feelings to the side.

She placed her hand in his and allowed him to draw her back to the bed.

He pulled her body in front of his, her back to his chest, and wrapped his arms around her, before resting his head lightly against the top of her head.

Leila expelled a breath of air, and curled her body inside his, and fell asleep, her thoughts a chaotic swirl of tangled emotions.

21

"Wow, you look . . . different, but cute! I don't think I've ever seen you wearing anything so casual before. What's the special occasion? Supporting the Spurs?"

Leila laughed, and spun around in her pink and white Nikes, showing off her outfit of faded jeans and a San Antonio Spurs' jersey, before she quickly glanced around to make sure all her customers were taken care.

Once she was assured they were, she asked, "May I?" indicating the seat opposite one of her favorite customers, Danita Adams.

"Girl, of course!"

Leila pulled back the chair and sat down, unable to keep the grin from her face. "I have a date to go see the Spurs pull out a can of whoop-ass on the Nuggets," she replied, laughing.

"Oooh, who with? No, let me guess . . . that big, fine, Stetson-wearing tycoon who's been sniffin' around you for the last few weeks?" Danita laughed when Leila's grin widened.

"Ummm, girl, spill the beans! What's been going on with you two? The last thing I heard from you was that he was hell-bent on trying to steal your land, and you were just as hell-bent on stopping him. A regular Hatfield—McCoy type of relationship," she laughed, and Leila laughed along with her at the analogy.

"Yeah, well, we're at an impasse with that one."

"Called a temporary cease-fire, did you? Ummm, must be some good loving going on for that to happen." Danita replied, raising a brow as she drank her tea.

"I am not saying a *word* about that. My lips are sealed!" She replied, moving two closed fingers across her mouth as though she were zipping them shut.

"Your lips may be sealed, but I'd lay ten-to-one odds that's about all that's sealed!"

"Oooh, no you didn't!" Leila burst out laughing. "You are too much!"

"You may as well spill. You know you want to, anyway . . . what's been going on since the last time we spoke?" Danita asked, propping her elbows on the table, a mischievous grin flirting around her small, pursed lips.

Leila sighed, and immediately began to spill. Just like Danita knew she would.

She hadn't talked about her relationship with Brandan with anyone. The only one who was aware of what was going on was Hawk, and she didn't feel comfortable talking about it with him, although he was the closest person to her. It felt somehow . . . strange when she'd tried to. Instead, she'd kept all her doubts, fears . . . and excitement to herself. She had no real close girlfriends, just casual acquaintances. Danita was the closest she had to a real "girlfriend." It was a strange relief to have someone to share her burgeoning feelings about Brandan with, at last.

Danita had moved to San Antonio a few years ago at the urging of her assistant and good friend, Larissa, after completing her dissertation to earn her clinical license in psychotherapy.

After striking out on her own, she'd gradually earned a solid reputation as an outstanding therapist, and within two years of opening, now had a nice office in private practice in an exclusive area of town.

But she'd worked hard for every bit of success she'd acquired.

Before she had been able to afford to move into her own office space, in the very beginning, she'd come to Aunt Sadie's early in the mornings, before the diner grew crowded, tugging her portal office of cell phone and laptop.

When it wasn't busy, Leila would sit down with the woman and talk, and although not exactly friends, they'd formed a bond, the type of bond two women who were in business for themselves, struggling to be successful, created. From there it had grown into a friendship, one that Leila valued.

She'd lightly spoken about Brandan with Danita, telling her how they'd met, and how confusing she found their relationship. And how she had never felt so alive as she did when they were together. Now she brought her friend up to speed on where they were in the relationship.

"In all this time, you two haven't actually had a date, huh?" Danita asked, and when Leila shook her head no, continued. "Well, from the sounds of things, you've been doing a lot more than the typical dinner and movie . . . girl, I ain't mad at ya," she quipped, a wide grin crossing her pretty dark brown face.

"No, which is why Brandan decided we were long overdue *for* a date," Leila laughed.

"So, it's official? You two are an item?"

Leila cocked her head to the side, considering her friend's words. "Well—" she began, but before she could finish, Danita interrupted her.

"Hmmm, looks like your man is here."

Leila turned around and felt a ridiculous blush warm her face when she saw him in the doorway.

He was dressed as casually as she, a baseball cap replaced his typical Stetson, his long legs were encased in faded button-fly jeans, and his big feet were sporting running shoes.

He was wearing a Spurs' jersey—matching the one she was wearing—and she grinned, remembering how he'd brought it by the restaurant the day before and told her she had to wear it. To support the team. It was all about the team, he'd assured her.

She rose as he approached her, and as she had with Danita, Leila spun around for his inspection.

"Yeah . . . papa likes," he said in a deep, sexy drawl.

"Oh, so you're my daddy now, huh?"

He brought her close and kissed her gingerly on the lips. "Hell, no, there's nothing fatherly about the way I feel about you, the things I plan to do later tonight," he said, stroking a hand over her bottom and pulling her tight so she could feel the thick ridge of his cock at the V of her legs.

"Hmmm, hmmm."

Leila turned when she heard her friend's subtle cough.

"Sorry, she just can't seem to keep her hands off me!" Leila slugged Brandan good naturedly on the arm and laughed, waving to her friend as he turned her around to leave.

She called out a farewell to Hawk, who was helping her out so she could go out with Brandan, and the pair left the café.

As Danita watched them leave, a wistful smile crossed her face. Feeling as though someone was watching her, she turned and caught eyes with the waiter who was intently staring at her. After several moments, moments where she felt as though she were caught in a crazy time warp, unable to look away, he finally was the one to break contact.

Danita shivered, despite the warmth of the diner and the sweater she wore, and she rubbed her hands over her arms, warming herself.

22

"What a game! Boy, there's nothing like live action. It beats the heck out of watching the game on TV!" Leila enthused, the adrenalin obviously still pumping.

Brandan sat in one of high-backed stools, and with pure male appreciation, watched her bustle around her kitchen, taking out pots and pans, and chattering nonstop, reliving the game, as she began to prepare him food.

She had changed clothes, and now wore nothing more than a pair of short lounging shorts—where he could see her tight, round cheeks peek out when she stood on tiptoe to grab a box of pasta from the back of one of her cabinets—a sports bra, and one of her sexy aprons. And no panties.

The no panties had been his idea, one she'd laughingly agreed to.

He grinned in complete masculine appreciation as he watched her fill the pot with water and place it on the stove.

He'd paid more attention to her than the actual game. Her cheeks had flushed with excitement while she leapt out of her seat throughout the game, cheering on the Spurs or booing the ref for a bad call.

It had been slow inching along in the back-to-back build up of traffic as they exited the AT & T Center. They would have made it out a lot sooner, with his VIP seating and parking, but when he'd told her he could introduce her to a few of the players, her eyes had widened, and for the first time he heard her actually squeal in excitement.

"I had no idea when I suggested a Spurs game, that you were such a fan," he said.

"Yep. True blue! Aunt Sadie and I never missed a game. Once, when I was younger, she took me to a game, a live one, and I was hooked. We couldn't afford to make it a regular habit, but whenever they were playing a playoff game, she made room in the budget," she smiled in memory.

"She sounds like one of a kind, your Aunt Sadie."

"She was." Leila tossed the comment over her shoulder as she opened the refrigerator and leaned inside to hunt down what she needed. As she bent over, exposing more of her softly rounded cheeks, Brandan groaned.

"I never wanted for anything, but at the same time, luxuries like ball games and movies were rare. I appreciated it, particularly as I grew older, how much she sacrificed to raise me."

He felt rather than saw some of the happiness leave her, as her back was turned to him. He rose from his chair and walked over to where she stood in front of the stove, staring down at the water as it began to bubble, coming to a boil.

He placed his arms around her and pulled her tight against his chest.

She picked up the noodles, eased them into the bubbling water, and began to stir them in the pot. "It's the main reason why I can't let Aunt Sadie's go. I feel like if I do, if I give up and just sell, I'll be letting go of something I can't ever get back."

Brandan sighed. After hugging her, he moved away and leaned against the butcher block island, crossing his arms over his chest.

They had been avoiding all talk of the sale lately. Anytime

she tried to bring it up, he would steer the conversation away. Anytime his partners asked him how things were going, how close he was to convincing her to sell, he gave the standard answer that it wouldn't be long.

"Leila, you know you're going to have to sell. You're going to have to face that," he said, breaking the silence.

She whipped her head around to stare at him, an incredulous expression on her face. "What?" Several of her long locs whipped across her face as she did. With an impatient hand, she pulled them back into the ponytail at her nape.

He pushed away from the counter. When he tried to take her into his arms, she pushed him away and stared up at him.

"What do you mean I *have* to sell? I don't have to do anything I don't want to."

"When are you going to face the fact that you're causing more harm than good to yourself and your neighbors by refusing to sell?"

"I don't know what you're talking about!"

He brought her back into contact, forcing her to look at him when she would have turned away.

"Yes, you do. Come on, Lee."

"No, why don't you tell me, Brandan?"

He grabbed her by the arm. "Look, you need to face facts—"

"What facts?" she yelled, her breathing now harsh as she stared at him.

"Facts that you can't bring back your great-aunt by holding on to that damn café. You can't keep it together, no matter how strong you think you are, all by yourself. By taking our offer, you'll be doing yourself and your neighbors a hell of a lot more good than by being stubborn and holding on to some unreasonable hope that you'll make that café more than what it is."

"And just what is that, Brandan?" she asked, her voice quiet.

"A run-down, forgotten diner, one which anyone with half a brain would have sold a damn long time ago." As soon as the words left his mouth, he wished to God he could have retracted them.

Her face lost all color; she closed her eyes and seemed to deflate right in front of him.

"Baby, I'm sorry, I didn't mean that . . . can we just forget about it for now, talk about it later," he begged, his voice hoarse as emotion swamped him as he looked at her, shoulders slumped, face averted from his.

He tried to pull her back into his arms. She pushed against him, saying, "Not this time, Brandan. You won't get around me with sex. Not this time. I want you to go. Now," she said, her face set, her eyes boring into his, unflinching.

"Leila . . . I'm sorry. I didn't mean it."

"If you ever had anyone who you cared about taken from you, if you ever cared more about anyone than yourself, than you would understand *exactly* why that "run-down forgotten diner" means more to me than anything you'll ever have. No amount of money in the world can replace that "run-down forgotten diner." Obviously, this is something you'll never understand, and I'm tired of trying to explain it to you."

She said nothing more, just turned away from him and turned off the overflowing pot of noodles, setting it to the back burner of stove.

She removed her apron, hung it on one of the hooks, and turned off the light in the kitchen, as though he wasn't even there.

Before she left the room, she turned, and faced him. "You know the way out."

Brandan stared at her retreating back and bit back a curse as she walked toward a door that led to her bathroom, opened the door, and walked inside without a backwards glance. Seconds later, he heard the sound of pipes churning with water as she turned on her shower.

23

"Ummm, what smells so . . . uh, different?" Leila asked after walking into the dark diner. Expecting to smell a delightful aroma after Hawk had promised her a meal she wouldn't forget, presumably to cheer her up, she wrinkled her noise at the un-mistakable smell of something . . . the Lord only knew what . . . seriously burned. "Oooh, that is funky," she murmured low, not wanting Hawk to hear her and hurt his feelings.

As she walked inside, a frown marred her forehead as her gazed raked over the diner.

The overhead lights were cut, the only illumination being from the lights over the counter, and at one table, which was beautifully set, a bright light burned from the flickering flame of a candle set in the middle.

"Uh, Hawk, what's going on?" she asked. After their last conversation, she was confused. Although he'd admitted that he'd had feelings for her, feelings he'd kept to himself because he knew she didn't feel the same way, a small knot of tension swelled in her belly. Maybe he'd only been telling her what he thought she wanted to hear.

"Hawk? Where are you?" she called, walking toward the kitchen.

"It's not Hawk, Lee. I don't think Hawk would like to claim what I've created. He tried his best to teach me a simple recipe. I don't think I got it right, though."

Brandan walked from behind the swinging doors and Leila swore, angry that she'd been set up and mentally vowing to tell Hawk just what she thought of his meddling.

Her eyes swept over him. The memory of their last exchange, the words he'd said, harsh, ugly . . . hurtful, sprang in her mind. Without a word, she turned to go, walking as quickly as her feet would carry her back toward the door.

"You challenge me."

His words stopped her in her tracks.

"No one has ever done that on a personal level. The closest I've ever come to someone caring enough to challenge me was in football."

Her fingers relaxed, releasing their death-grip on the brass-knobbed door. She slowly turned around to face him, and was struck by the open vulnerability on his face, in his expression.

He held out his hands, palms out in a gesture of entreaty.

"Please. Don't go. Don't leave me."

Her eyes ran over him, from the top of his tussled hair, down the food-splattered shirt—which probably had been crisp and white when he had first donned it, before his venture into cooking for her—down to his dark slacks that also bore witness to his cooking abilities. Food and other unknown particles were splattered over them as well.

"Why? Why cook for me? Why do all this when you obviously have so little regard for Aunt Sadie's? So little regard for how much this café means to me? How do you have the nerve to pretend to really care, go through all of this . . . this . . . *mess* . . . just to take it all away from me?" She choked out the words, forced them from her throat, a throat that was clogged with unshed tears as she thought of how, since she'd signed the papers to sell, Aunt Sadie's would soon be reduced to a pile of rubble.

"Because I wanted to show you that you matter to me. That your wants, your desires, mean more to me than what I can make by buying your land. That it's not worth it if it means losing you, having you doubt my feelings for you. I—" he stopped, and turned away from her.

Leila slowly walked toward him and stood behind him, hesitant, not sure what to do, what to say.

He ran a hand through his hair, mussing it, spiking it over his head. Leila's eyes widened when she noticed the fine tremor in his hands.

More than anything else, this affected her deeply. To see him obviously shaken, unsure, was more telling than anything he could possibly say. He turned back around and faced her, his face tight, holding back the emotion she could see threatening to shatter him.

"I love you, Leila. I didn't expect it to happen. I don't exactly know when it happened. Hell, I didn't even want it to happen."

She inhaled sharply at his words. His confession caught her off guard. Completely off guard.

"I can't take you playing with my feelings, Brandan. I don't play games. I'm not wired that way." She heard the tremble in her voice, knew that he heard it, too, and that he felt her vulnerability as plainly as she saw his.

"Lee, I've never been more serious in my life. I want you to be a part of my life. Permanently. No one has ever made me feel the way you do. I know most of our relationship has been drama-filled, as you would say. But what I feel for you is real. And I'll be damned if I let it slip away, allow you to slip away, over a piece of land. Please. Believe me. Nothing else matters but you," he begged huskily, holding out his arms, silently asking her to forgive him, to accept him.

In the weeks since she'd last seen him, she'd been miserable.

Alternating between anger and abject misery, she'd been impossible to be around. She knew it, could tell from the way her small staff had studiously avoided her.

Yesterday, when she'd sat in her office, she'd picked up the document waiting for her signature.

As usual, whenever she needed her most, even if only in her mind, Aunt Sadie had spoken to her.

Baby, it's okay, everything is going to be okay. Ain't no piece of land going to sever our connections, child! What we had, what we still have, goes a lot deeper than Aunt Sadie's Café. Aunt Sadie's was my legacy to you, but it isn't the only thing I've left you. I've left you my determination. Whenever you set your mind to do something, you do it! I like to think you got that from your auntie. I've left you my spirit of adventure. Think of the wonderful adventures you'll have starting out new, fresh! A brand new Aunt Sadie's, one that will be everything we knew it could be! And I would like to think I left you with boundless love. Love all that you do, baby, but don't be too stubborn and not recognize love when it's staring you in the face . . .

And with tears running down her face, she'd signed the document and handed it to Hawk. He'd hugged her tight as she'd released the last of her tears.

Now she looked at Brandan, and what she saw in his eyes made her catch her breath . . .

When Brandan saw the look of acceptance in her eyes, telling him she believed him, he crushed her in his arms. Leila gasped in surprise when he slid his palms beneath her skirt and firmly gripped her buttocks.

She wrapped her legs around him and locked her feet around him, her heels resting on his firm, beautifully sculpted buttocks. Her breasts pressed firmly against his shirt when he pulled her tighter against his body.

He slanted his mouth over hers and they exchanged hungry,

desperate kisses until, with quick stumbling strides, he carried her to the small storage room. He toed the door open with a boot, and shoved the door aside.

He kicked it shut, mumbling against her mouth, "In case Hawk decides to come by and check out how our dinner is going."

They didn't even make it to the small bed in the storage room before they were at each other.

Buttons easily slipped from their holes as they hastily undressed, exchanging small laughs and sighs as they tore the other's clothes from their bodies.

When they were finally undressed, nothing between them, just naked skin gliding against skin, he lifted her back into his arms, wrapped her legs around his torso, and pressed her back into the wall, him covering her like a warm blanket.

The contrast of male skin pressed hotly against her front, and the cool hard surface of the stone wall on her back, was a tantalizing icy hot contrast. Leila moaned and relaxed her legs, allowing her outer thighs to lay flush with the wall.

Brandan ran his tongue down the seam between her breasts, licking beneath one small globe before engulfing it into his mouth, flicking his tongue in rapid strokes against her blood-engorged erect nipple.

She grasped his head, wrapped her arms around him, and shoved her hands deep into his hair, pushing her breasts further into his hot, willing mouth.

She groaned as made greedy wet sounds with his mouth feasted on her breasts. He drew her hard, stiff nipple into his mouth, and bit into the thick nub until she cried out from the pleasure/pain.

Releasing it, he blew on the slight injury before swabbing it with his tongue and moving to the other breast.

As he nursed that one, his hand trailed down her body, seeking the heart of her. Separating her moist folds, he tested her readiness for him, inserting one big finger inside her pussy before withdrawing her juices.

"Brandan," she whispered the words, her gut clenching when she saw him lick his finger, his hot gaze on her, making her dizzy.

He leaned down, kissing her, transferring her own essence from his mouth to hers.

"Are you ready for me, baby? I don't think I can hold out any longer," he bit the words out harshly against her temple, his breath fanning the soft hairs around her temple.

"Umm, yes, please, give it to me," she demanded. Without waiting for him, she eased her hand away from his head where she'd been holding him hostage as he sucked her breasts, and cupped his heavy sac.

His balls were tight, like two juicy plums. They were filled with his cum, ready to explode.

"God, yes!" she cried, her cream racing down her legs as she rolled her hips against him. So desperate for him to feel her with all ten-plus inches of his magnificent cock, she was ready to explode along with him.

"Damn, keep saying that, and this won't last long," he laughed, a painful sounding laugh.

Moving her hand to the side, he grasped his shaft in his hand and teased at her pussy lips, rubbing the big, round knob of his cock back and forth against her straining clit, between her slick folds.

If he didn't give her what she needed, didn't ram that big, beautiful hard cock deep inside her soon, Leila *knew* she'd expire, right on the spot.

"I warned you not to play with me, Brandan," she cried out, torn between crazy wantonness and humor when he laughed at her.

"Sorry, baby, won't happen again," he promised, and began to ease into her. As usual, when he began his steady, relentless thrusts, he completely stole her breath as her body stretched, trying to accept his width and girth.

"Oh, God . . . you feel amazing. Hot, thick . . . so amazing," she whimpered the words.

The feel of his naked penis sliding into her was pure heaven . . . Damn.

She grabbed onto his forearms and halted him when he was only halfway in. The feel of his naked cock sliding into her brought her up short, her eyes flying open.

"What? *What is it?*" he asked, his facial features distorted, as though it pained him to stop.

"A condom . . . we don't have a condom," she panted.

He grabbed both sides of her face and forced her to look into his eyes. "Do we need one?"

The question startled her, while at the same time filled her with fearful excitement.

24

Brandan waited, forcing himself not to press on home, not to embed himself as deep into her warm shelter as he could, and waited.

As painful as it would be to stop, as hard as it was not to press into her, he waited.

This had to be her decision.

His mind was made up. Hell, it had been before he ever met her, and he hadn't even known it.

She was his. Now. Always.

But he wouldn't take the decision away from her. He studied her intently, watched the play of emotions flash across her expressive face as his heart thud heavily in his chest.

Until she smiled.

That shy, slight, hesitant smile of hers where the small dimple in the corner of her mouth always seemed to be winking at him, and he closed his eyes and sent a prayer heavenward in gratitude.

He leaned forward and nuzzled the crook of her neck, running his face back and forth, lightly kissing her, so full of emotion he knew if he tried to speak he'd embarrass himself.

"What are you waiting for?" she asked huskily, and Brandan groaned when he felt her long, graceful fingers press into each of his buttocks and push his cock all the way in.

The feel of her sweet pussy clenching down on his naked erection, no condom to interfere with the pleasure, and the knowledge that he wouldn't have to pull out, that he could come deep inside her, sent an electric arc of pleasure straight to his balls.

He gripped her big sexy thighs and nipped at her shoulder, growling when she laughed and bit him on the opposite shoulder.

"*Damn*, Lee." He moved his neck to the side, giving her better access. She sucked and bit at his neck before thrusting her tongue into his ear, in time with him sliding deeply, in and out of her welcoming sheath, fucking her in easy glides.

He quickened his depth and pace, began deep-stroking her, the way he knew she liked to be done, pushing her legs to the side so he could hit it at the best angle, an angle guaranteed to send them both over the edge.

With each plunge of his hips, she gave back as good as he, meeting his thrusts, her hands roaming over his back, clutching him, bringing their bodies together as he continued to flex into her.

She felt so damn good wrapped around him he clenched his teeth together and grunted deep in his throat, trying to hold back his cum. With every sweet clamp of her pussy, he felt his balls tingle and sting with the need to release as he dragged in and out of her honeyed depths.

He shoved away from her, grabbed her thighs, spread her as wide as he could, and pummeled into her, his thrusts focused. Staring deep into her eyes, he refused to allow her to look away as he felt the cum swell in his balls.

He wanted her to *see* him as he fucked her ... as he *loved* her.

She grabbed both sides of his face and gently brought his face to hers and kissed him gently. She bit down on his bottom lip, mimicking what he so often did to her, and drew him deeper inside her mouth, just as she drew him deeper into her body.

And then she did her *move.* That move where the walls of her pussy clamped down on his dick in short pulsing, staccato throbs.

Damn.

The feelings, both physical and mental, were his undoing and he lost it. Completely.

Instead of slamming into her, as he wanted, his body and mind demanded he do something else. Gentling his moves, he allowed the pleasure of her body, their bodies together, to merge, to swamp him, as he reveled in the feel of her, without condom, skin to skin.

He rolled his hips, screwing into her perfect body in slow rotations until he could no longer hold back his orgasm.

"I've got to come, baby," he bit out.

"Yes, yes . . . yes!" she cried.

She rolled her head back and forth against the wall, her hands clutching at his shoulders, as he braced his hands behind her and made love to her.

When he came, he shoved his head back and roared his release as his seed erupted in near painful jets. He grimaced as he continued his thrusts, pressing her body deep into the wall, his cock shoved deep inside her tightening snatch, trying to reach her womb in an instinctual need to plant his seed deep inside her.

When both of their breaths had calmed, Brandan felt her slip her trembling legs away from his hips.

When she stumbled, he caught her, afraid she'd fall down to the floor. He picked her up and felt his own legs wobble, and they exchanged mutual light, low laughs.

He was as shaken as she, and if he wasn't damn careful, they'd both end up in the middle of the floor in a useless puddle of exhausted limbs.

He carried her the short distance to the bed, and carefully lay her down before laying behind her. Running a shaky, caressing hand over her hair, he pulled her locs up and away, and rolled her body so she lay on top of him, the top of her head fitting just beneath his chin.

Within minutes after he'd positioned their bodies, they were asleep. The only sounds in the room were of their mutual soft snores . . .

When Leila woke, she was curled tight against Brandan's big body with one of his brawny arms slung low over her hip. She turned her head to the side and watched his chest move up and down in easy breaths, letting her know that he still slept.

Very carefully, she lifted her body, moved slightly away from him and pulled at her locs, as several were trapped between their intertwined bodies.

She ran her eyes over him. A slight shadow stamped his cheeks and lower jaw, and his lips were partially opened as he slept. Even in repose with his big body relaxed, there was an aura of smoldering sexuality and heat surrounding him that drew her like no other ever had.

He stirred, moving so his legs were spread, opening him to her perusal. Damn. Even in sleep, he was the picture of male perfection.

She pulled her bottom lip into her mouth with her top teeth, and reached down to cup his scrotum. She lightly stroked the tips of her fingers over twin juicy plums, the hair covering his balls soft to the touch.

Moving her body so she lay parallel to his hips, Leila circled his penis, ringing her fingers over it, before carefully grasping it with her hand. Softened, she was now able to ring her fingers around the circumference of it. She swiped her thumb over the tiny eye at the top, still stick and dewy with his cum.

She brought her thumb to her mouth to taste him, an unknowing smile crossing her lips.

"Hmmm," she murmured, the taste of him tangy yet sweet. She leaned in and inhaled his musky, warm scent. Her breath blew the fine dark hairs surrounding his groin, and his penis, once soft, began to thicken.

Fascinated, she watched it twitch, as though it had a mind of its own, welcoming her touch. She leaned closer and ran her tongue up the back of it, along the central vein that ran from his sac to the round bulbous head of his cock, before slowly easing him fully into her mouth.

A warm, wet mouth on his shaft brought him to shocking wakefulness.

Brandan pried his eyes opened around the stickiness of sleep. He groaned when he shifted his head to the side, and peered down to see Leila working his cock with gentle expertise as he slept.

Damn, what a way to wake up. A lazy smile stretched his mouth wide.

Sleepily, he pulled her body on top of his, positioning her so that her hips straddled his face. She released his shaft and peered at him over her shoulder in surprise.

She smiled, a dimple appearing in the corner of her lips. "I couldn't resist." Her voice was low, scratchy, her big eyes gleaming mischievously.

"Don't let me interrupt," he replied, and brought her mound down closer to his face. He spread her legs farther apart and he heard her swift intake of breath when he separated her plump lips and stroked her tight little clit with the flat of his tongue.

With a sigh, she turned her head away and drew him back into her warm, wet mouth and with leisurely laps of his tongue, he in turn feasted on her pussy.

She rode his face, slow and easy, her vagina spread open and her juices running down his face, and Brandan greedily ate her as though he was a starving man and she was his first morsel of food.

Their mutual orgasm swept over them, gentle and complete, and when they'd both caught their breaths, their hearts returning to normal, he pulled her up to lay on top of him.

"You know, if we keep doing this, we're going to have to buy a bigger bed for our little getaway," he said, twining one of his big fingers around one of her locs with absentminded attention. "Although I don't think a bigger bed will fit in here, do you?" he asked casting a doubtful eye around the small quarters.

Leila lifted her head and laughed at the look of studied concentration on his face as he looked around the room. She lay her head back down.

"Maybe when we buy out Mr. Gomez's store and expand, we could get a decent sized bed that will fit the both of us, in case we want to, you know . . ." his voice trailed off and he wiggled his eyes comically. "What do you think?" he finished, and suddenly it hit her, exactly what he was saying.

Leila's breath caught and she lifted her body abruptly up from his chest until she was straddling him.

"*We?—Mr. Gomez's—what*??!" she stuttered, her heart racing, the back of her eyes burning with the threat of tears as she tried to grasp what he was telling her.

He grabbed her and sat up on the small bed, placing her in front of him.

"Listen. I know how much Aunt Sadie's means to you. I know that it is more than a café, more than a job, a way to make a living," he began, and when she opened her mouth to speak, he placed his forefinger against her lips.

"Ssh, baby. Let me say this." She closed her eyes and lightly kissed his finger before he slid it away from her mouth.

He wrapped his arms around her and scooted back against the wall with her tight against his chest. "I grew up moving from ranch to ranch, place to place, home to home, with none that I could ever claim as my own. My mom . . ." he stopped, and Leila held her breath, waiting for him to continue, waiting for him to open up and share his life, his history with her.

"My mom did the best she could, I suppose. It couldn't have been easy on her, trying to raise me without my dad around. She did the best she could," he repeated, and if it sounded as though he were trying to convince himself more than he was her, Leila decided it was best to let is slide for now. She knew this wasn't easy for him.

"We moved around a lot. My mom and I. The only life we knew was ranching. Even when dad was around, we never stayed in one place long. Depending on what rancher or farmer was hiring, that was where we called home for most of my life. When dad left, nothing much changed, except the beatings. At least we didn't have to put up with that anymore.

He laughed a humorless laugh.

Leila pressed deeper into his embrace.

"I didn't know," she murmured, feathering her fingertips over the backs of his hand in an unconscious effort to soothe away past hurts.

"No one did. I learned early not to tell 'family business' after one of my teachers asked me how I'd gotten the first of many black eyes."

"God, I'm sorry, Brandan." The words were so inadequate she knew, but she meant them. The thought of what he went through sent sharp arrows of pain to her heart.

She'd grown up in a loving home with her great-aunt and had never known what it was like to be abused, and had never known anyone who had been, with the exception of Hawk. And even with him, she'd had to piece together what his life had been like before she and Aunt Sadie had "adopted" him.

As close as they were, Hawk had never shared what made his eyes get that faraway look, or the rare glimpses of pain she'd seen in them ever so often when he was unaware that she was looking at him.

"It started when I was too young to remember. Rough handling grew to hits, grew to punches when he was drunk. The bad ones came when he would be fired after being caught drunk on the job. He'd come home, tell us to pack, go out and get drunk, come home, and take it out on mom. I tried to stop him once and that's when he started in on me . . ."

"It had to be painful to have a loved one hurt you, baby. I'm sorry," she said and felt closer to him than she had to anyone since her great-aunt had died, that he'd share something so painful with her.

"Finally, when I was about ten or so, mom got tired of it. Kicked him out and told him never to come back unless he could be a real man, a real father. That was the last time I saw him."

Growing up without a father had to have been hard, but Leila was glad his mother had finally gotten the strength to kick his father's sorry tail out of their home, their lives.

"What did you and your mom do? Where did you go?"

"Well, like I said, ranch life was all we knew. Whenever Dad got a job, mom got hired on in the kitchen, cooking, cleaning, whatever was needed. She continued doing what she knew. It was a living, kept a roof over our heads. Well, one of the ranchers my mom worked for was quite wealthy, had ownership in one of the pro football teams. One day a bunch of us kids were playing ball, after we'd finished our chores. He noticed me and I guess he thought I had a *little* talent."

Leila felt him shrug against her back and turned around. She laughed when she caught the cocky look in his bright blue eyes, and gently tagged him on the shoulder with a balled fist.

"Hey, that hurt," he grimaced and she laughed.

"A *little* talent?"

He leaned down and kissed her gently. "Yeah,"

They were quiet, each one in their own thoughts.

"So, what about us . . . this . . ." she waved her hands, words escaping her.

He turned her around in his arms.

"You mean, you and me?" he asked,

"Yes. I mean, is it only the hot crazy sex . . . or is there more to this chemistry, this whatever . . . than that?" She worried her bottom lip with her teeth until he replaced her teeth with his lips, giving her a short but sweet kiss.

"It is for me," he replied simply. "I can get hot sex anytime. Anyplace. What we have is more than that,"

She raised a brow and he laughed huskily. "I didn't mean it like that. The sex with us is amazing, you already know that. I've never had sex like this, but I think it's because I've never met a woman like you. Never felt like this with anyone else. Never been in love before."

Leila felt tears sting the back of her eyes. She ducked her head as emotions crowded in on her. She'd never felt as she did with anyone else either.

"How do you feel?" he asked, and when she saw the look of uncertainty and love burning in his bright gaze, her heart swelled.

"I've never had a man irritate me, piss me off—" she stopped and smiled when she saw his brows draw together, taking her statement as a rejection. "Or complete me like you do." His grin split across his face as she finished. "I have no idea how this is going to end, Brandan—" She stopped when he placed a finger against her lips.

"This is going to end with my ring on your finger, and the two of us living our lives together. When I said I loved you, I meant it. There isn't now, or never will be anyone else for me, Leila. I love you," he stated simply. "How do you feel?"

Baby . . . he loves you. Love is worth more than a building, more than a business, more than anything. Don't let it slip away from you. Grab on tight and don't let it slip away . . .

She'd always "heard" her great-aunt from the time she'd died. Yet she'd always simply thought of it as her mind's rumination and imagination. But, something about hearing her this time was different . . .

And remember when you sat in that old attic reading my Bible, you promised me you'd give me some grandbabies, Lee Lee . . .

This time she allowed the tears to fall as emotion crashed down on her, her heart beating erratically in her chest, the smell of flowers suddenly filling her nostrils, the distinct smell of freshly cut roses, her great-aunt's favorite.

"Baby, are you okay?"

She stared up at Brandan through a veil of tears and hugged him. "I love you! And yes, yes, yes, I'll marry you!"

As he held her tight, tears fell freely as she distinctly heard the husky, much-loved laughter of Aunt Sadie echo softly before fading away.

Danita

25

"All I'm saying is I wouldn't mind having a little adventure or two. Just to break up the monotony every once in a while would be nice. Nothing too dramatic, just a little somethin' somethin'," Larissa Jones told her employer and friend, rolling her eyes in disgust. "It'd be a nice break from my boring-ass routine, that's for sure. What's wrong with that?" she grumbled.

"I'm not saying anything is wrong with it, 'Ri. In fact, I know just what you mean." Danita Adams looked at her best friend, and took a thoughtful sip of her Diet Coke.

"You? Girl, you've got it all. Hell, I wish I did half as much! Fine man, great career, moved on up to the east side in that new condo." Larissa laughed and took a healthy bite of her double-decker Reuben sandwich. Her tongue snaked out to lick the French dressing that had oozed from the sandwich away from the corner of her mouth.

"How in the world do you know what I'm talking about?" Larissa continued above the noise of the busy diner as the two women sat in their favorite table at Aunt Sadie's Café, their favorite haunt, having dinner together after putting in over twelve hours at the office.

Although it was late, nearly ten o'clock at night, the restaurant was packed. In spite of its cheap decorations and crowded space, where you were practically sitting elbow-to-elbow with other diners, it was worth it. The food was mouth-watering and Aunt Sadie's was always packed until Leila, the owner, finally shooed the customers out, closing the restaurant for the night.

Danita had been coming to the diner since she'd first moved to San Antonio. After completing her dissertation and earning her doctoral degree in psychology, she moved to the city and started her practice, with her friend Larissa as her assistant.

In the early days before she'd found an affordable place to set up practice, Danita would come to the diner in the late afternoon, and although it wasn't open for business, the owner, Leila, would invite her inside and serve her a hot cup of tea and a muffin as she worked.

It was then that she'd come to know the owner, and despite the fact that she often had worry lines bracketing her mouth, Leila would chat with her for a few minutes, with a word of encouragement or two before leaving Danita alone to do her work. She in turn would retire to her office in the back to "crunch numbers that aren't there" as she would say, with a small, tired smile on her face.

When the two mile block of small shops and restaurants had been bought by a large conglomeration, Danita had worried for the owner. She knew the diner meant everything to her, and she had been fighting selling her small property, especially when she began to get pressure from the neighboring owners, begging her to sell so they could accept the lucrative offer from the large conglomerate. Many of the shop owners were older, and ready to retire. With the amount of money they were being offered, they had dreams of finally be able to retire in style and enjoy their twilight years.

But Leila had resisted, confiding in Danita that the diner was all she had left of her great-aunt, and she'd do everything in her might to keep it.

With relief, Danita had been happy for her when she'd learned that although Leila had sold the building, the restaurant would soon be moving to bigger and better digs across town in the next six months, thanks in large part to Leila's new husband, Brandan.

Danita's glance fell over the man in question.

After he and Leila had met, the man had fallen hard and had pursued Leila relentlessly.

Leila had resisted, claiming there was no way in hell she'd consort with the man trying to take her business away, but had fallen like the proverbial ton of bricks, despite her valiant struggles to the contrary.

Since their marriage, the tall ex-football player turned real estate magnate could be found at the diner helping out his wife and her small staff as she began the transition to her new place.

Feeling the slightest bit of envy, Danita watched him sitting at the counter in one of the high-backed stools, suit jacket thrown over the back of the stool, white sleeves drawn up his thick forearm, and small square-framed glasses perched on the end of his nose as his eyes scanned over the screen of his compact laptop, large fingers flying over the small keyboard.

When Leila swished past him, his arm snaked out and wrapped around her waist to bring her tall, lithe body close to his, and he gave her a leisurely kiss. When he finally released her, with a dreamy smile on her face, she floated back to the kitchen.

"You're not having second thoughts about Warren, are you?" Larissa snapped Danita's attention back to their conversation, one of her finely arched brows raised in question. "I thought you two were doing well," she finished, taking a sip of her drink, her eyes trained on her friend.

Danita sighed and placed the chipped, near empty glass down on the cheap vinyl red and white checked tablecloth.

Warren should have been the man of her dreams. In every department he had it "going on," as Larissa liked to remind her. Not only was he attractive, he also worked for one of the most prestigious law firms in the city, would probably make full partner before the year was out, and came from one of the most prominent families in the area as well.

Her father had been beside himself when she'd brought him home to meet them at Warren's insistence. Danita hadn't been ready to do that, fearing her close-knit family, as well as Warren, would read more into it than what it was.

She enjoyed being with him—it was a heady experience being on the arm of one of the most eligible bachelors in the country.

Their lovemaking was at times . . . predictable, and sometimes less than satisfactory. Despite the fact that there were times she hadn't gotten hers, after he came, he'd kiss her, roll over with his mouth wide open, and be snoring within minutes.

And if occasionally he'd been so caught up in his latest acquisition for one of his high-powered clients as an investment attorney so that he talked about nothing else for hours, that, too, Danita tried to brush to the side.

When she'd first met him at a fundraiser, she hadn't known who he was. Leila had been with her at the affair, and had gleefully informed her who'd she'd just "dissed and dismissed." Shrugging nonconcern but secretly pleased that a man like Warren obviously wanted her, Danita continued to ignore him. Even when he'd found out her work phone number and had called, she'd had Larissa tell him she was unavailable.

He had pursued her with a vengeance after she'd not returned his calls, and after several weeks of courting her, she'd finally given in and gone out with him.

But, try as she might, feelings of frustration and irritation at his egotistical ways had been sneaking up on her of late, making her really start to question the relationship.

"I don't know. I'm just feeling restless lately. Can't quite explain it. No big deal, really. I'm sure it's nothing I can't work through. Haven't you ever felt like that?"

Before Larissa could respond, the waiter, one who looked strangely familiar, came hustling over to the table, a smile on his lean, handsome face. Both women remained silent.

"I'll just get these out of your ladies' way," he said smiling, a deep dimple slashing on both sides of his high cheekbones.

As he leaned across the table and retrieved the glasses in front of them, his hair, secured with a wide tan leather clip, flipped over his shoulder, and Danita's eyes ran from the thick, dark, silky black ponytail to his face.

A face that looked as though it was sculpted by a master artisan, she thought in appreciation of his masculine beauty. Long and lean, it fit the rest of him. His dark eyes held the slightest bit of a tilt in the corners, and his eyelashes were thick and as dark as his silky black hair, giving him an exotic look.

Her gaze ran over the rest of his face, cataloging his long, somewhat hawkish nose, and his wide thin lips, hitched up on one side in an easy smile.

"Are you finished with this, ma'am?" he asked. Danita's eyes left his face and glanced down at his hand, so lean yet strong looking as he grasped the edge of her plate. She raised her face back to his and felt her face heat as he picked up her plate and deposited it in the pan he held holstered to his hip by one arm.

Just then, Larissa's cell phone rang and she fumbled in her oversize bag to retrieve it, and flipped it open to speak.

"Can I get you anything else? Maybe a refill of your drink?"

the waiter asked Danita, and again she mutely nodded her head, holding out her glass.

When their fingers touched, she quickly withdrew after he'd taken the glass, feeling a small spark arc from his warm fingers to hers, placing her hands in her lap and feeling all of ten years old when his smile deepened at her reaction.

Out of nowhere, images of the two of them, naked, sweaty limbs twined around each other, tumbling on a bed of black silk sheets as he stroked into her body, flooded Danita's mind.

The kaleidoscope of images slammed into her mind—his hard, gleaming, naked back covering hers as he rocked into her body from the back, his thick cock pumping in and out of her in strong easy glides, her face pressed against the bed, moaning in delight as he paid homage to her body.

The images were vivid, startling and graphic. So much so that Danita gasped, horrified when her panties were slick she'd gotten so wet.

While the images flashed through her mind, her gaze locked with his, and the smile on his face slipped.

He stared at her, his dark eyes deep and mesmerizing as they traced a visual path over her face, her eyes, down her nose, over her lips where they stopped. Danita's hand went to her lips, and softly she feathered her fingers over them, feeling as though it were his lean fingers tracing the hot path over her lips and not her own.

When his gaze moved down her body, her hand, seemingly of it's own volition, followed his actions, running feather light caresses down her own throat, watching him watch her as her hand trailed over one breast, softly, so softly she barely felt it, she allowed her fingers to stroke over her tightening nipples that strained against her bra as though begging her . . . begging him . . . for a kiss, a caress . . .

Her mouth was desperately dry.

She ran her tongue over her bottom lip to ease the dryness,

and his dark eyes followed the path before he looked back into her eyes, his chest rising up and down heavily.

Realizing with a start just what she'd been doing, with her heartbeat so loud she was afraid that Larissa, and the unsuspecting star in her private porn flick, could both hear its pounding, she broke visual contact with the waiter, and with relief saw Larissa was still on the phone, her body partially turned away as she murmured into it.

Danita sat back in her chair, a fine sheen of sweat breaking out across her forehead. She raised a shaky hand to tuck a strand of hair behind her ear.

She could feel his eyes on hers, but studiously ignored it, resisting the temptation to look at him again. After what felt like hours, but could have been no more than mere seconds, she chanced looking up.

When she did, she saw that Larissa had ended her call and he'd taken her plate as well. As he removed Larissa's plate, he upped the wattage on his smile, his even white teeth a brilliant contrast to his copper-colored skin.

He turned around and their gazes met again, but she quickly averted her eyes.

In her peripheral vision she saw him turn away with the large dishpan cupped under one muscular arm, and weave his way through the crowded café.

"Danita? Danita? Helloo, anybody home?"

Two manicured fingers snapped in quick succession in front of Danita's eyes, startling her, forcing her to turn her gaze away from the departing man.

"Do you know that guy?"

"Uh, no. I'm sorry. I was just—"

"Daydreaming. Yeah, I know. You seem to be doing that on the regular here lately," Larissa responded. She tilted her head to the side, and her dark brown eyes were full of concern. "What's going on?" her friend asked, lifting a finely arched brow in question.

"No one—I mean, nothing is on my mind." Danita hoped she didn't catch her slip.

"Something *is* on your mind. You may as well tell me. You know I won't stop asking until you do." Larissa laughed and Danita smiled slightly in return.

She knew her friend wouldn't stop, not until she'd gotten a satisfactory answer from her. Just like a dog after a bone, Larissa would be unrelenting in her search until she ferreted out the answer.

But as close as the two women were, Danita didn't have a clue how she would even *begin* to tell her friend what was going on.

Especially since she herself didn't know.

Everything in her life was going well. Her practice was growing, she had a condo filled with beautiful furnishings, a wonderful family, even if they were constantly watching her, and a man any woman would love to call her own. What else did she want, she wondered, suddenly feeling morose.

When the waiter came back over and set their drinks in front of them, Danita thanked him, trying not to allow her gaze to travel over his long legs that were encased in faded jeans or over the front of his jeans at the button-fly that was considerably more worn than the rest of the jeans. She crossed and recrossed her legs under the table.

When their gazes locked again, for a moment Danita feared he could read the crazy, instant lust she felt, the wild way her body was reacting from him being so near her. It was as strange and heady as it was puzzling.

It was a relief to Danita when he broke the connection and turned to Larissa, placing her drink in front of her. After he left the table, her heartbeat returned to normal and she answered Larissa's question.

"Girl, it's nothing. Just something I need to work through, that's all . . ." she replied with a weak smile.

Danita picked up her glass and gazed down at the amber-colored liquid and slowly twirled the thin straw around and around inside the glass, her mind a million miles away.

26

"Hey, thanks for pitching in, Hawk, I really appreciate it," Leila said, tucking a loc behind her ear. She dragged her attention away from the printout inventory in her hand and smiled as Jarred "Hawk" Wikvaya walked into the bustling kitchen, a pan of dishes cupped under his arm.

"No problem, Lee," the tall Native American man said, smiling in return.

After sliding the large plastic tub onto the gray metal counter, he walked over to where Leila stood perusing the document held in her hand.

"Have you had a go over the final drafts of the financial statements yet?" he asked.

"Yep, I have, and it all looks great! Every 'I' dotted, all 'T's crossed. Everything looks in order. I'll go over everything one final time and we should be good to go—should be able to hand it off to Brandan tomorrow," she said, opening the door and motioning for him to follow her into her office. "Thanks again for handling the legal end of the sale for me."

Hawk followed her in, his eyes raking over the familiar small, cramped office, boxes stacked on top of each other, the walls nearly bare of the many pictures that once hung, now wrapped up and ready to be moved away.

He walked over to one of the boxes and lifted the lone framed picture, smiling down at it.

Leila glanced up and noticed the picture he held, one of his thumbs lightly caressing the glassed frame. Hawk looked over at her, a nostalgic smile on his face. "Not packing this one away yet?"

"No," Leila replied softly.

He glanced back down at the photo. "I sure do miss her. She was the closest thing to a mother I had. If it hadn't been for Aunt Sadie, I don't know what my life would have been like. They broke the mold when they made her," he replied and cleared his throat, looking up at Leila.

"Yeah, she was definitely one of a kind," Leila replied softly.

"She was the reason I didn't end up in juvie hall or somewhere worse."

"Aunt Sadie had that effect on people. She never gave up on anyone. Always saw the best in everyone. Not a day goes by that I don't think about her, Hawk."

When he glanced up at her, he noticed her amber-colored eyes glistening with unshed tears, and placed the picture carefully back down on top of the stack of boxes, clapping his hands together. "Okay, what else do you need for me to do? I'm ready to work, boss. Those documents aren't going to sell themselves," he said in an attempt to lighten the mood.

Although the sadness still lingered in her eyes, with a determined smile Leila agreed, and the two went to work on the pile of documents neatly placed in folders on top of her desk.

"Well, like I said, if I had a man like Warren, and a stable, *monogamous* relationship, Danita, girl, I think I'd be one happy woman. What's more—"she stopped speaking when her cell phone rang for the second time in less than thirty minutes.

She picked up the phone and after seeing who it was from, rolled her eyes. "I'm not answering that . . . as I was saying—"

Danita lifted a brow, "Answer the phone. If you don't, he'll just keep calling anyway," she laughed and with an exaggerated sigh, Larissa snatched up the phone and pressed a long, manicured finger on the talk button. "Yes, Stephen?" she asked. She tried to playing it cool, as though she was irritated, but within moments the man obviously said something she liked, and no matter how she tried to put up a front for Danita's benefit, Danita knew she was enjoying whatever he was saying to her.

When she turned her body to the side and began to speak low into the phone, and started giggling—which she only did when Stephen started talking sex to her—Danita shook her head and ignored her friend.

Restless, she began to drum her nails on the table, her eyes searching the thinning crowd, looking for who she didn't know.

Hearing her own mocking laughter in her head, she knew just who she was looking for. No use trying to kid herself. She was hoping to catch sight of the busboy/waiter among the remaining diners and staff. Disappointment flooded her when she didn't see him, and she glanced at the clock when she noticed a few of the waitresses waving good-bye as they left the diner.

Damn, he'd probably clocked off and hadn't come by to tell her.

As soon as she thought of it, she realized how ridiculous that sounded, even in her own mind. Just because he'd gotten her all hot and bothered, to the point that X-rated images of the two of them paraded through her mind, didn't mean the feeling was mutual.

And even if it was, just what in hell would she have done about it? she thought. She wasn't likely to take up with a busboy and engage in a hot and heavy sex marathon, despite her crazy wayward thoughts.

"Hey, uh, would you mind if I took a rain check on the movie?" Larissa asked, ending her conversation on the phone, her face flushed.

Danita started to make a comment about how easily she caved in, but the look on Larissa's face stopped her. She already felt awkward enough, no sense teasing her about it. "No problem, I think I'm going home anyway, go over some of my case notes, and turn in early."

"Thanks, Danita! I'll call you later, okay?" she asked, but from the excited flush in her light brown cheeks and glitter in her eyes, her mood greatly improved, Danita didn't really expect to answer, doubting Larissa was paying any attention.

She began to dig in her oversize bag, and pulled out her wallet.

"Larissa . . . just go . . . I'll get the check," Danita said, knowing that it was more than likely Larissa would be picking up the tab for whatever she and Stephen would be doing, as the last she'd heard, her friend's current lover was sans job, or "between opportunities" as he put it. That is, if they even made it out of Larissa's bedroom.

She said good-bye when a no-longer-morose Larissa fluttered her fingers at her in farewell.

With a mental shrug, thinking to each his own, Danita resigned herself to spending the rest of her evening alone.

Nothing really new on that front, she thought, and moodily bit into her Reuben sandwich.

"It's just about closing time. I can't believe the diner's nearly empty!" Leila said, shutting the register drawer and inserting a small key on the side. The register hummed as it began to print out the day's tally of sales.

"Brandan and I *just* might be able to catch the last showing of *All About Eve!*" Danita said, gleefully clapping her hands together in anticipation of seeing the classic old movie.

Hearing his name, her husband lifted his head and removed his glasses. "Hmm . . . I was thinking more along the lines of something more . . . intimate, Lee. Maybe a little wine, a little cheese . . . a little lovin'," he asked with a hopeful gleam in his eyes.

"We can do that anytime. We'll get the super nachos at the movies and get you all the cheese you want on it, sweetheart," Leila replied with an impish grin. "How many chances will we get to see this special colorized edition?"

"Hell, hopefully never," he mumbled and Leila ignored him. With a resigned sigh he shut the cover on his laptop and stood. "Okay, okay, Bette Davis it is."

"Good! Hopefully it shouldn't be too long before the last customer leaves," Leila said, glancing around the room at the nearly empty café.

"Hey, why don't you two go? I can stick around and lock up for you," Hawk volunteered, his eyes still on the woman sipping the tea, a thoughtful expression on her pretty deep brown face.

"Lord, no, Hawk. I couldn't ask you to do that. You've done so much as it is!" she protested, but Hawk saw the hopeful look in her eyes. "It's Friday night . . . don't you have other plans?"

"No, just me, myself, and I tonight. Gregory is gone for the weekend, went to see his girl in Chicago, and another pal bailed on me, so I canceled the poker game," he said with a laugh, mentioning his ex-roommate and their weekly Friday night poker game. "The only plans I had were to finally get into the latest Tom Clancy, which I bought six months ago and still haven't gotten around to reading. Nothing major," he assured her.

"Well, if you're sure?" Before he could answer, she ran to

the end of the counter to grab her coat and purse tucked beneath the counter.

Brandan interrupted: "Man, you need to get laid. When was the last time you had a woman?" His question forced Hawk's intent stare away from the woman.

"I don't recall asking for advice on my sex life," he said, his face neutral.

Although he'd gotten to know Brandan, and grudgingly liked the man, he was still a far cry from being bosom buddies with him.

He knew Brandan loved Leila, would do anything for her, and had proven it beyond reason. Hawk was still coming to terms with their relationship.

He no longer had any romantic feelings toward Leila. Any lingering feelings he may have had were cast aside when he realized Brandan had captured her heart.

In his heart he knew he didn't care for her in the same way Brandan did, realized it with startling clarity when she'd told him that she loved the man, her face so brightly lit with love, it left no doubt in his heart that she truly did.

And in that moment, after he'd gently kissed her, he realized his feelings for her were nothing like those she and Brandan shared. He didn't even think he was capable of loving another with that same intensity.

Leila needed a man who loved her with all the passion and fire she deserved. A man that could give his whole heart to her, not one who could give her a pale imitation.

As Brandan helped Leila with her coat, again, Hawk's eyes were drawn to the woman sitting alone at the table. He heard Leila murmur a thank you followed by the sound of a kiss, yet his full attention was on the woman.

When Brandan moved in front of his line of vision to retrieve his things, he turned back to Leila.

"Hey, Leila, the woman at table five sitting alone—is she a

regular?" Hawk said casually, motioning with his head to the table where she sat.

She scanned the restaurant, squinting, her brows drawn together until her gaze lit on Danita, the only diner left among the handful that was sitting alone.

"Oh, you mean Danita. And no, you probably haven't seen her too often. The few times you're here I don't think Danita has been. But, yes, she's been coming to the diner for the last few years," she said, the corner of her mouth hitched in a small smile. "She's pretty, isn't she? Single, too. At least there are no rings on her finger stating the contrary," she added, the corner of her mouth lifting in a small smile.

When Hawk made no response, his face neutral, she touched his thick forearm with her fingertips. "Hawk, when's the last time you went out on a date with a woman? Just kicked back and had fun, no worrying about the plight of mankind?" When he felt his face tighten, he knew she picked up on his discomfort when she sighed.

"I'm not making light of your work, what you do is not only admirable, but needed. I'm just saying that once in a while you should think of yourself, and just have fun," she said.

Hawk glanced down at Leila, concern reflected within the light brown depths of her eyes, and he felt his face and body relax.

He could trust Leila. She cared for him, just as he did for her. She would never intentionally hurt him.

"I know you're concerned about me," he said and gave her a brief hug. "I'm fine. Don't worry about me." The two of them exchanged a shared moment of memories, memories of growing up, taking care of each other, of her great-aunt—a woman he considered family as well—telling them it was their duty to not only take care of each other, but to help anyone who needed them.

It was something Hawk had taken to heart, sometimes to

the exclusion of all else, sacrificing a real personal life in his desire to help those that society had cast away.

He took her face between his palms, smoothing away the lines of worry. "I'm fine. Now go have fun with that big brute of a husband who is now bearing down on us, looking like he wants to rip out my arms from their sockets for touching his woman," he said, and just to piss Brandan off, he laid a gentle kiss on Leila's soft lips.

"You butt!" she laughed softly, knowing he was kissing her to piss off Brandan, and handed him the key to the diner.

When Brandan reached her side, and pulled her tight against him, a deep frown on his face, Hawk's mouth stretched into a wide grin.

"Let's go, Leila, we don't want to be late." Turning his wife away, shooting a look of warning on his face aimed at Hawk, they left. Leila allowed him to lead her away, waving good-bye to Hawk over her shoulder.

Soon after they left, the remaining diners finished and paid their bill, leaving only he and Danita, alone, in the diner.

He finished closing down, quickly locking up Leila's office, and finalizing the accounting for the day.

The only one left was the woman—Danita. He wiped his hands on the white dishcloth and walked over to where she sat, lost in her own thoughts.

27

"Let me refill that for you."

Danita glanced up, startled, when the deep, low voice spoke and a hand reached over and removed her mug.

He refilled her mug and set it in front of her, surprising her when he set a second mug across from her on the table.

"Do you mind if I sit with you?" he asked, and she mutely shook her head. "There's no one else to serve, so you have me all to yourself," he said, and the smile he gave her was innocent enough, but the glint in his nearly black eyes and the flash of teeth that accompanied the smile set her heart thudding against her chest.

She glanced around and with a start, realized he was right; there was no one in the diner besides the two of them, not even Leila or her husband.

She glanced at the antique clock in the corner of the diner, the large hands and face displaying the lateness of the hour.

"I didn't know it was this late—I didn't even notice everyone leaving!" she exclaimed and began to remove her leather coat from the back of her chair.

He leaned over and placed a staying hand on top of hers, stalling her action.

"You don't have to go. There's no rush for you to leave," he assured her.

"No, I'd better go. I imagine Leila and Brandan want to get out of here. Quite sure they have better things to do with their time than wait for one lonely woman to get out of their hair so they can go on with their night," she said, though she could have cut out her tongue when she realized how pathetic she must have sounded.

"They already cut out thirty minutes ago or so. I told Leila I'd lock up for her."

Her somber mood changed to one of apprehension, realizing she didn't know anything about the man who sat across from her, his deep, dark, hooded eyes intensely focused on hers as he drank from his mug.

"Once in a while I help Leila out around the diner. We've known each other for years," he said, and Danita realized he was seeking to put her at ease, no doubt reading the apprehension from her.

Still, the man could be an ax murderer for all she knew. She sure in hell wasn't taking any chances just because he told her he and Leila were friends.

As she moved back in her chair, preparing to leave, her glance rolled over his tall, lean body as he sat across from her.

She had known Leila for well over a year and she couldn't remembering seeing the man before. Yet something about him was familiar.

"My name is Jarred—my friends call me Hawk—and yours?" he asked, speaking casually, as though she weren't about to get the hell out of the diner as fast as her two feet could take her.

She paused, her coat clutched in her hands when he said his name. Hawk.

She bit the corner of her lips, hesitating.

She remembered Leila mentioning on several occasions her friend Hawk, a man she'd grown up with. And on more than one occasion, Danita had wanted to meet the man who could put a smile on the face of Leila so easily.

She'd thought the two were lovers, as Leila would occasionally mention going someplace or other with Hawk. In fact, when Leila had met Brandan, Hawk's name had come up several times and she'd wondered if there was more to their relationship than brotherly/sisterly love.

However, once she'd seen Brandan and Leila together she'd known that, at least for Leila, there was no one else who held claim to her heart.

"Danita," she said giving him a small, tight smile in return, and slowly she eased back down in her chair and returned her coat to the back of her seat.

She picked up her mug and took a careful sip, warily watching Hawk over the rim, a nervous feel in the pit of her stomach at the thought that she was all alone with him.

The kaleidoscope of images she'd had of their bodies straining, limbs twining and tangled together, flashed through her mind.

Hawk raised the small mug of steaming tea to his mouth and drank, his eyes never leaving hers. He felt her nervousness, and knew that she would easily bolt from the restaurant at any moment. He wanted to keep her at ease, let her know that she had nothing to fear from him, wanted her to believe she was safe with him.

"So, Danita, what do you do?" he asked, hoping the easy question would make her feel more comfortable.

"I'm a psychotherapist. I work mostly with young women. Most of my client's ages range between eighteen and twenty-four."

"That's a challenging age," he replied easily.

"It is. It's the age where you're supposed to be grown up, not quite a child anymore, but not exactly an adult either."

"But it's rewarding working with that age group."

She tilted her head in a questioning look. "You sound like you're speaking from experience."

He smiled. "I have some." When he didn't continue, simply took another sip of his tea, she didn't press him for details.

"Yes, it is rewarding. Wish everyone felt the same." She didn't know what came over her, but she felt comfortable talking to him.

"What you do is rewarding. Sometimes reward isn't measured in dollars and cents. To help another in need is often its own reward. A single moment of understanding can flood a whole life with meaning."

"Very true." Danita was struck by the simplicity, the sincerity, of his statement.

"Thanks."

"Wise old family saying?" she asked, and felt like kicking her own butt if she could have reached it, as soon as the words flew from her mouth, especially when he coughed around the sip of tea he'd just swallowed.

"Not quite," he replied.

"I'm sorry—I assumed you were Native American, please—"

"I am. But the saying isn't from any Native American history. Read it once in a fortune cookie," he said, and when his wide mouth stretched into a grin, Danita laughed with him, relieved she hadn't offended him.

"But yes, you're right. It is rewarding," she finished.

"What made you want go into therapy as a profession?" he asked her, and Danita felt flutters in her stomach at the intensity of his regard.

"Hmmm, do you want the standard answer?"

He laughed. "We can start with that."

She took a sip of her tea and mulled it over. "I suppose I've always wanted to know what made us tick as human beings. I was always interested in knowing the inner workings of the human mind. I can't tell you how many times my mother came into my room as a child, and I'd have one of my Barbie dolls wearing a lab coat, sitting in one of the little chairs that came with my pink and diamond decked-out Barbie playhouse," she started, and he laughed.

Grinning, she continued, "And Barbie would have old Ken laying on the couch . . . in deep therapeutic session, discussing his latest emotional crisis. My mom would stand there with this strange look on her face and turn away. Didn't matter though. Barbie and I were determined to unearth the reasons behind Ken's reticence about asking Malibu Barbie to marry him after years of living together. I mean, come *on*, how long was she supposed to wait? They'd been dating since the sixties!" she finished, her face completely serious.

When she could no longer hold her laughter in check, it erupted, and Hawk threw back his head and laughed along with her.

After their laughter had subsided, a small, lopsided grin fell on Hawk's face, and his gaze was so intent, she suddenly felt very self-conscious.

"What?" she asked under his dark-eyed scrutiny. She touched her hair, fingering the errant strands that had escaped.

"No, don't" he said, reaching a hand up and covering her hand. She raised questioning eyes to his.

"It's been a long day, I must look a mess," she said, desperately wishing for a mirror to freshen her long-ago applied make-up and tidy her hair.

"You're beautiful just the way you are."

"I'm a bit disheveled. It's been a long day," she said, flutters dancing in her lower belly in reaction to his long, lean fingers stroking her fingers. He gently tugged her hand away from her chignon and placed it on the table.

She glanced down at their interlaced fingers on top of the old checkered table.

"If disheveled means sexy, than yes . . . you are disheveled." His smile, so hot, so . . . intent, made Danita's heart thump heavily in her chest.

"Do you work for an agency, or are you in private practice?" he asked, and Danita was relieved with the change of subject.

"Both, in a way."

"How's that?" he asked, and her eyes followed his as he took a bite of the muffin and swallowed, the strong muscles in his throat working the food down his body.

Their gazes locked, holding for what seemed like an eternity, but in actuality could only have been seconds.

"You said you did both? In what way?" With his question she mentally shook her head, and concentrated on what he was asking her.

"I started out working in child welfare," she said, and the sigh from her lips escaped without her awareness.

"That bad, huh?"

"Yeah, that bad," she agreed, remembering her short stint working in the state welfare department after completing her bachelor's degree.

"Lots of long hours, low pay, and sacrifice," he murmured. Startled, she glanced at him.

"Sounds like you know a bit about it," she replied, hoping he'd share something more of himself with her.

"You could say that." His smile, like hers, was bittersweet, yet he offered up no more information.

Danita opened her mouth to ask more, but instantly clamped it closed. If he wanted to tell her more, he would. No amount of prodding would help. She knew that from her years counseling.

Instead, she munched on her muffin and took the last drink

of tea, before continuing. "So, after grad school, I moved here at a friend's insistence. She'd met a guy and moved here after graduating from high school," she said with a laugh, thinking of Larissa. "Things didn't work out with the guy, but she loved the city. Went to college, got a degree in psychology, and offered to be my assistant."

"Was that the woman sitting with you earlier?"

"Yes, Larissa. We were supposed to go to a movie, but, well . . ."

"Change of plans?" he asked, and laughed at her expression.

"Yeah. Something like that," she agreed, and laughed with him.

"What about you?"

"What about me?"

"Any boyfriend in the picture?"

His bold question threw Danita. Unwanted thoughts of Warren came to mind.

"No. Yes. I mean . . . yes, there is." She knew her answer was about as clear as mud, but she hadn't figured out her relationship with Warren herself.

Of late, she wondered if she was going along with what everyone else wanted—expected—of her, rather than what she wanted.

She changed the subject, and for the next hour they exchanged light banter. But beneath the banter was a sexual tension, from the way he smiled when she would laugh, to his careful attention to her, refilling her tea without her asking it. When the grandfather clock in the corner of the diner chimed, signaling it was midnight, Danita was surprised how the time had gone by so swiftly.

She laughed self-consciously. "Lord, I've been talking your ear off. I must be boring you to tears," She laughed again. "You seem to bring out the jabber jaws in me. Are you sure you're not a therapist?" she asked.

Danita also realized that over the course of the last hour,

she'd talked more to a stranger, a man she didn't know, than she had with anyone else in a long time. So used to being the one people naturally seemed to tell all their problems to, she was unused to telling so much about herself, much less to a stranger.

He laughed. "No, I'm not a therapist, not by a long stretch. It's just easy for people to talk to me, I've been told. Not that I'm complaining. Not in the least!" he inserted when she bit her lip, knowing she'd just talked the poor man's ears off, nonstop, for over an hour.

"No, just the opposite. I'm enjoying getting to know you," he said, reaching out to lightly stroke her hand that was laying on the table.

"Is that what we're doing? Getting to know each other?"

"We are if that's what you want us to do," he replied in his low voice, sending tingling awareness coursing through her body, reminding her that they were all alone, no one around.

The normally bustling café was quiet, the overhead lights were turned off, and the main lights coming from behind the counter offered them a very intimate setting.

She smiled at him. "Yeah, I guess I do," she replied to his question. "I've talked so much about myself," she said, curious about the man who sat so intently in front of her, making her feel like she was the only woman in the world at the moment.

"Hmmm. Just a working man. Not much to tell," he replied.

"Come on! I've sat here for the last hour telling you my whole life story! I think you could throw me a crumb and tell me about you," she smiled, and the small, appealing dimple appeared in the corner of her pretty, bow-shaped mouth.

"Hmmm. A crumb, huh? I like to take long bubble baths with lighted candles. Scented ones. I'm particularly partial to the blackberry scented ones. But if you tell Leila's husband that, I'll deny it to the end. Gotta keep up the macho image," he replied, teasing her, hoping to see the cute dimple appear again.

When the pink tip of her tongue snuck out to ream her bottom lip, and her eyes widened, her chest rising sharply, the teasing left and Hawk was once again aware of the growing tightness, the sexual tension that lay silent between them, yet very much a part of their surrounding.

His penis thumped against the buttons of his jeans in reaction. He stared at her, and saw that she too was affected.

Her large, drowsy-looking brown eyes dominated her small face, and his gaze had constantly been drawn to her bow-shaped lips as she spoke to him. Now, as she sat across from him, her petite body nestled deep in her chair comfortably with her feet curled beneath her chair, he wanted to pick her up and sit her in his lap and get to know her on a completely different level.

He shifted in the vinyl-covered seat, his cock thickening, the semierection he'd had since he'd first laid eyes on her, thickening as images of the two of them together played in vivid movielike sequence in his mind.

Images like him stretching her small body out on the table in front of them and feasting on her delicate curves.

He reached across the space covering them, and touched her hand, one thumb caressing her soft mocha-colored fingers.

She looked up at him, startled. Her eyes widened and she inhaled a deep swift breath. Hawk knew she read his thoughts in his eyes.

Licking her lips nervously, she sat up in the chair, allowing her feet to drop, and hastily withdrew her hands from his as she glanced over at the clock for the third time in less than five minutes.

"I'd better go! It's getting really late. I'm sure you have a lot to do—" she began, quickly rising from her chair. She gathered her briefcase and purse, slinging them both over her shoulder, and grabbed her jacket. Before she could move more than a few steps, Hawk had risen from his chair, and moved to where she stood.

"You don't have to leave. Stay," he encouraged.

"No, really, I'd better." Danita laughed nervously, staring up into Hawk's somber face as his intense, dark eyes stared down at her, a small smile lifting the corners of his wide mouth.

"No. Stay." He kept his dark gaze on hers, the small smile on his face in place, and gently removed the strap of her brief case and purse, and placed them back on the floor.

Danita's heart thud loudly against her chest when he nudged her legs apart and stepped closer into the V of her legs, wrapped one of his hands around the back of her head, his nimble fingers tunneling in her hair, and pulled her closer.

Her eyes drifted closed and a soft breath of need escaped her lips when his mouth bushed back and forth against hers.

In feather strokes, he ran his mouth over hers, back and forth, and his tongue sneaked out from behind his mouth to lick across the seam of her lips. The light touch of his tongue was electric and Danita gasped, her mouth opening to admit him.

His tongue invaded her mouth, swirling around the moist walls, running the length behind her teeth, end to end, before plunging back deep to leisurely lap and tangle their tongues in a heated love play.

He withdrew from her mouth to place nibbling kisses over her lips, on her chin, before pulling the lower rim of her lip into his mouth by his teeth and suckling gently on it until she mewled. She pressed her body closer to his.

He pulled her tighter to his body until her breasts pressed hotly against the hard wall of his chest. The fingers of one hand tightened in her hair, while the other hand curved around the swell of her hip, palming her buttocks. Her nipples spiked, painfully erect, and she rubbed against him like a kitten as the kiss deepened.

When she felt the hard ridge of his arousal pressed against her, the velvet smoothness of his tongue bathing her mouth, her body completely yielded to his. On fire for him, she rubbed her body against his, yearning and creaming for his touch.

She heard a low groaning come from him as he made love to her mouth as though it was a drug, one he couldn't get enough of, stroking into her with an urgency her body longed for.

Of their own volition, her arms crept up and wrapped around his shoulders, pulling him down even closer to her. Long drugging kisses later, he tore his lips from hers, his nostrils flaring, his chest expanding with each harsh breath he took.

With his eyes staring down deep into hers, Danita felt hypnotized, unable to look away, as he pulled her silk blouse from the waistband of her skirt. He deftly unbuttoned her blouse, his eyes still on hers, until he undid the last one.

Hawk moved his gaze away, trailing his eyes down the smooth line of her creamy, chocolate-colored neck to the tops of her breasts that crested over the top of her lacy bra. His heart thud against his chest and his dick kicked against the rough zipper of his jeans, at the erotic picture she presented.

His hand trailed over the smooth creaminess of her chocolate-colored large breasts, over the satin covering of her bra, thumbing the bud of her nipple, that even behind the bra, was erect and pressing against the fabric.

He brought both of his hands up to trail down her curves, before spanning her small waist within his hands. Although her breasts were large, her waist was small, so small that he was almost able to span it with his hands.

But he wanted to see them. Wanted to feel, taste and caress them. The thought alone made the erection he had swell to the point of pain.

He quickly unfastened the closure to her bra, and the large globes bounced free, her nipples, fully erect, long and tight, hard as cherry pits and just as delicious looking, were surrounded by the large, flat disk of her areolas.

With a groan he moved his head down to capture one of the bright, cherry-colored nubs within his mouth.

He lifted her breasts, each hand cupping one of the large mounds, deciding which one he wanted to taste first. He flicked at her nipples and then licked and mouthed first one long bud, then the other, alternating his attention between them, playing with them, deeply engulfing one before allowing it to pop out, then going to the other.

Danita barely resisted grinding against his thick shaft and dry humping the hell out of that thick, delicious manhood she felt against the ridge of his jeans. Wet, God she was so wet, the cream from her vagina now saturating her panties.

When she moaned and placed her arms around his head to pull his head closer, arching her breasts fully into his mouth, Hawk glanced up, watching her eyes flutter closed while he suckled on her breasts.

Her obvious arousal at what he was doing flamed his even more.

He moved a hand to shove up her skirt, lifted her, pivoted, and sat down on the nearest chair with her sitting on his lap.

She faced him and he widened his legs, forcing her to straddle him with her mound pressed directly over his erection. He fumbled with the buttons on his jeans and swallowed a sound of both pain and relief when he freed his erection from the constricting denim.

His hand moved to pull at the side of her panties and he eased one of his fingers inside, feeling her liquid heat saturate his fingers.

Her hot little bud pulsed beneath his fingers as he rolled it between his thumb and forefinger. Taking her own moisture, after separating her vaginal lips, he spread it between her moist folds before easing his middle finger inside.

He clenched his teeth, in an attempt to prevent himself from taking his dick out of his boxers and feel her tight sheath wrapped around him, gloving him.

When she cried out, he pulled her head back down and covered her lips with his, continuing to drag his finger in and out of her drenching heat, devouring her lips with his own.

Moaning and crying around his lips, Danita pressed closer, grinding against his hand, seeking to get as much of his finger inside her body as she could.

When he removed it, Danita's eyes flew open, and she released a distressed cry of denial.

He placed his hands against either side of her face, the look in his dark, lust-filled eyes hot as his gaze roamed over her kiss-swollen lips.

"We've got to stop. If I don't stop now, I won't be able to, Danita. I'll take you right here and now," he spoke harshly, and closed his eyes, taking deep breaths.

Danita lowered her head, overcome with the kiss and his nearness, taking deep calming breaths of her own.

When he laid his cheek on top of her head, unbidden, tears sprang to Danita's eyes. His kisses, his touch, the feel of him pressed against her had been so amazingly intense, so incredibly intimate . . . With simple caresses he'd managed to make her feel more cherished, more wanted, than she'd felt in a long time.

With her ear pressed against his chest, she heard the loud thudding of his heart, felt his body shake, and knew he wasn't faking his reactions.

He'd been as deeply affected by their exchange as she had.

She took a deep breath. It had been so long since anyone, including Warren, had made her feel so needed, had made her burn the way Hawk was.

Had been so long since she'd needed someone as much as she did this man, one she didn't know.

Had been so long since she'd done something to make *herself* feel good.

It had also been a long time that she hadn't worried about who thought what, who expected what of her, who demanded that she act one way or another, proper and ladylike . . . Danita was *tired* of trying to be what others wanted.

For this one time, she was going to be and do what she wanted. And what she wanted was to allow this man to make love to her.

God, was she insane? The thought hit her as soon as the decision was made.

But she wasn't stupid. She was on birth control, but still . . .

He must have read her indecision. Despite the larger than life hard-on pressing so deliciously against her mound, she saw the gentling in his eyes.

"Look, I don't want to hurt you. Neither would I press you to do something you don't want," he said, and she batted away the tears that threatened to fall.

"I can make you feel good . . . both of us feel good, without penetrating you. I promise you," he finished, the desire in his eyes no way lessening, nor the bulge in his pants, yet his hands remained still, his arms anchoring her to his body.

Danita raised her eyes and met Hawk's beautiful liquid black gaze, passion stamped harshly on his chiseled features.

She made up in her mind that she was going to do what her body wanted her to do, and to hell with the rest.

Without saying a word, Danita reached up, pulled his head down and initiated a kiss. Within seconds of her lips touching his, he took over.

With her saddling his lap, he lifted her skirt, shoved it up her thighs, and ran his lean fingers down her naked thighs.

The cool air hit her skin, mingling with his warm hands on her flesh, sending goose bumps washing over her skin.

When she shivered, the smile he gave her before he captured her lips was pure sin. As he kissed her, his nimble fingers were busy massaging and playing with her large, unbound breasts.

He broke their kiss and stared down at her while his fingers manipulated her hard, stiff nipples

"So pretty," he murmured.

Leaning his dark head down, he fastened his mouth around one of her breasts, opening his lips wide, and gave each one open-mouthed, warm, wet kisses.

Danita clamped her legs together when her pussy constricted.

He pulled on her breast, sucking one of her nipples into his mouth, and Danita arched her back sharply.

"God. You're beautiful," he breathed. "Such perfectly sculpted mounds."

He stroked a reverent thumb across one erect bud. "Topped by a sweet cherry-wine chocolate kiss, perfect for my mouth." He laughed huskily before fastening his lips on the dark, delicate erect nipple, suckling it as though it were the sweet chocolate candy he pronounced it to be.

The sight of his dark head taking her nipple deep into his mouth, accompanied by the deep suction hold he held on her, forced a moan from Danita's lips.

She grasped him by the back of the head and drew him closer, deeper into her breasts.

He feasted on her tit, laving her rock-hard nipple with the rough velvet of his tongue in strong laps.

He lifted one globe, and with the flat of his tongue stroked her from beneath the crease of her breast, up and over her nipple, swirling his tongue around her areola before taking her straining bud into his mouth to nurse her.

The ache between her legs grew tauter, and her heart seemed to skip a beat in her chest when she felt a long finger edge aside the lacy hem of her panties, and part her slick folds.

"Oh—oh, God . . ." she panted, squirming in his lap, straining against him.

"So sweet, so wet and sweet," he removed his lips on her

breast to murmur. When he licked his dew-covered fingers, the walls of Danita's pussy clenched and released in response.

He pulled her head down and kissed her, his lips covering hers, and her breath caught when she tasted her own flavor on his tongue.

She nearly wept in relief when he slipped the finger back inside her vagina, pulling her lower body into tight contact with the thick bulge straining the zipper of his jeans.

So caught up in the feeling of him catering to her, the thick bulge pressing so insistently against her pussy, reminded Danita of what she was allowing to happen.

Attention from someone had her half-naked in a stranger's lap, dry fucking him?

Embarrassed, she began to push away from him in earnest.

Hawk felt her withdrawal, even as his fingers remained imbedded inside her tight, wet heat.

He brought the hand cupping her breast up to her face and ran the rough pad of his thumb over the lower rim of her lip.

"We can stop this anytime. I don't want to do anything to you that you don't want done," he said, forcing her to look at him.

The way she worried her bottom lip and the uncertainty in her deep brown beautiful eyes struck him hard.

He'd been attracted to her from the first moment he'd seen her. Besides her physical appeal, there was a light around her, one that he'd been drawn to.

The few times his mother spoke to him, she'd told him of his father and of his Native American heritage and family's beliefs.

The men in his father's family, dating back generations, had been givers. They'd been men who, once they recognized their mate, the one woman for them, spent their lives making sure their woman was well taken care of.

In all things.

Her needs supplanted their own, their wants and desires became theirs. Their happiness at all times, paramount to the man.

When his father had died, his mother may as well have died with him, because so well had her needs been taken care of, their bond so deep, that she no longer wanted to live without him.

But Hawk knew if he told her all that now, she'd probably break her neck to run as fast and as far away from him as humanly possible.

And he had no intention of allowing that to happen.

So, he needed to ease up on her.

Hawk leaned forward and kissed her gently in the corner of her lips. Soft, nibbling kisses, soothing, feather light kisses, from end to end of her sweet lips, before slipping his tongue over her perfect mouth.

He heard her groan when he rained biting kisses down her neck before retracing his slick path, sliding his mouth over to her small shell-shaped ear, and pulling the delicate lobe into his mouth.

"Ummm," she moaned, her head falling to the side to give him better access.

"Your skin is so smooth, so perfect," he murmured before taking her mouth again.

The kiss started out gentle, but when he felt her tongue, hesitant, soft, probe into his mouth, he groaned and deepened the kiss, and his once idle finger, still nestled deep within her pussy, stroked, curving inside her clenching walls.

When she ground her hips against his fingers, his palm, riding him, he released a moan he couldn't hold back as he continued to work her body against his. As she made the sweetest, hottest sex sounds he'd ever heard, Hawk used one hand and pressed the rounded globes of her ass together and brought her into hotter, closer contact with his throbbing cock.

He stabbed his tongue in and out of her mouth, in rhythm

with his finger within her pussy, while his thumb stroked her tight, hot clit.

She feverishly rode his fingers, grinding against him, rolling and thrusting her hips as the inner walls of her vagina clenched his plunging fingers with an intensity that had his balls tighten to the point of pain.

"Damn!"

Danita heard the expletive as though from a faraway distance, so caught up was she in the incredulous sensation of his talented fingers fucking her. When he withdrew his hand, she broke the kiss and cried out in distress.

"No—please," she begged, her breath coming out in strangled gasps as she blindly reached down to prevent him from ending the pleasure, not giving a damn that she was begging.

"It's okay," he breathed against her.

He brought both of his hands to her waist, ripped her panties away, and dragged her closer to his thick erection, moving her in tight humps against his throbbing cock.

Danita shut her eyes tightly, grabbed onto his shoulders and gloriously gave in to the ride, bucking her hips, and reveling in the feel of riding him. When he fastened his mouth back on her breast, sucking like a babe on a tit, her body tightened, and she felt the orgasm unfurl low in her belly and ripple throughout her body.

She grasped his dark head as the orgasm took over. She yelled out as her release hit, and within moments she felt his body shudder against hers. He grasped her hips tighter, grinding her against the rough denim, and pulled heavily on her tender breasts as he fucked her in short tight thrusts.

Danita went up in flames as her pussy clenched, and her cum flowed heavily as the orgasm completely unfurled. He gave several more grinds against her before he shouted, released her breast, and ground harshly against her.

When the last shuddering contraction left her body, when

her body recovered from the back-to-back releases, weak, yet feeling blissful, she allowed her head to rest on his chest, listening to the steady harsh thud of his heart.

"Thank you," he whispered, and gathered her close. Danita's heart beat strongly at his quiet words.

In the quiet, deserted diner, sitting in the lap of a stranger, Danita felt cherished for the first time in her life.

28

"Hi, Sinclair, is Warren available? I was supposed to meet him here for lunch," Danita asked the polished woman sitting behind the glass and chrome desk.

The woman paused, and glanced away from the oversize monitor to Danita, standing in front of her. Her subtle once-over raked Danita from head to toe.

"Is he expecting you?" the woman asked. Despite the pleasantness of her tone, Danita picked up on the undercurrents of disdain running beneath it.

From the first moment she'd met Warren's assistant, she'd noticed the woman's chilly attitude toward her. At first she'd put it down to the woman just having a reserved personality, however, when she began to notice how warm she was with most others who entered the office, Danita suspected it was personal.

And when Warren had no knowledge of messages she'd left for him with his assistant, Danita's suspicions had become fact.

When she'd mentioned it to Warren, he'd blown it off, telling her that Sinclair had been with him since he'd opened his practice, and he "seriously doubted" Sinclair would do something so unprofessional as to not give him his messages. The way he'd stated it, along with the expression on his face, made Danita feel as though she'd accused the woman of high treason, so she'd dropped the subject.

However, when it happened again, Danita confronted her, and called her out to her face. Later that day Warren had called her, all but pronouncing Danita a liar and petty for accusing his assistant of withholding his messages.

Irritated, Danita let it go, but had told Larissa about it, thoroughly pissed off. Larissa had, as any good girlfriend would, agreed with Danita, and then warned Danita to watch out for the "trifling bitch." She thought the woman was just jealous that she was seeing Warren.

Danita had eventually shrugged it off when it hadn't occurred again.

"Of course he does, Sinclair. Could you just ring him, and tell him I'm here, please?" she answered.

"No problem, Ms. Adams. I'll let him know that you're here. Please, have a seat." The woman replied, her generous, collagen-injected plump lips lifting slightly to give Danita a tight smile.

Danita smiled in return, and resisted the urge to tug down the hem on her skirt that fanned right above her knees, noting the woman's sharp-eyed gaze running over her, from the top of the neat chignon she'd so carefully crafted that morning, to the new suit she'd bought—one of many new suits picked out by Warren— to the tips of the knock-off Jimmy Choos.

Danita had bought the knock-offs from Sal, her hookup at the Johnson Flea Market on Del Rio Street. With the ridiculous amount of cash she'd shelled out for the suits she'd bought from the exclusive boutique, she definitely needed to watch her budget.

She tugged the hem on the suit, thinking maybe she shouldn't have had it altered. But Lord have mercy, she thought, as much as she'd paid for it, it would have been nice to have it fit her better.

Danita had taken it to her favorite seamstress, Miss Mattie, and although she'd done her magic, making the waist fit to allow the skirt to fall just right over her butt and thighs, Mattie had taken liberties and shortened the hem, telling Danita God didn't give her the legs she'd been blessed with to hide them under some "long-ass grandma skirt."

Although Danita protested, she had been secretly glad Miss Mattie had shortened the hem, agreeing with the woman that below-the-knee skirts really weren't for her.

Danita smiled and thanked Sinclair, turning to walk over to one of the white sectionals to sit down. Out of instinct, she brushed at her clothes before sitting down. But whenever she came to Warren's office—or his condo for that matter—she always felt as though she should have plastic underneath her to prevent herself from soiling the furniture.

Kind of like how her grandmother would have all her furniture covered in plastic so "folks wouldn't mess up her good sofa," Danita thought and giggled.

She swallowed her laughter when Sinclair glanced over at her with one finely arched blond brow, raised in question.

Plastering a smile on her face she shook her head no, and Sinclair smiled slightly back at her.

"I'm sure Mr. Holt will be out shortly. He's with someone important right now," she said, making Danita feel about as significant as a dead flea.

Danita refrained from saying anything, not sure what would fly out of her mouth if she opened it. Instead, she threw a small smile the woman's way in acknowledgement.

When Sinclair went back to her typing, Danita glanced at her watch. She had less than thirty minutes before she was supposed to meet Ms. Washington, one of her housebound clients, for their weekly session.

When her stomach growled again, she subtly placed her palms over her stomach to hide the rumbling sound.

God, she was hungry, and because she'd worked late the night before, and had to go to court on behalf of one of her young clients, she hadn't had time to get any groceries and her fridge was pitifully bare.

When Larissa had suggested they go to Aunt Sadie's for a latte and one of their mouth-watering blueberry turnovers, Danita had made an excuse about not having time, and had returned to the office.

She knew she couldn't fool Larissa for long. It was only a matter of time before the astute opinionated woman caught on to the fact that she was avoiding the diner.

Or more accurately, avoiding the tall, exotic-looking, beautiful busboy who'd worked at the diner.

Danita closed her eyes and took a long deep breath and slowly released it. Memories assailed her of the sexual interlude—strike that—the crazy, out of this world, did this really happen to me, spine tingling, pussy *weeping* in memory it was so good, erotic adventure she'd had a week ago with the busboy at Aunt Sadie's.

After she'd returned to normalcy, or a semblance thereof, she'd realized just what she'd allowed to happen. She felt guilt that she'd had a sexual encounter with someone she didn't know, especially since she was currently in a relationship.

It didn't really matter that the relationship was less than satisfactory, and there were times when she believed her lover was having an affair with his assistant.

Nor that more often than not, her lover had ignored her, put her to the side, or treated her as though she weren't important, particularly when it came to his career and his desire to reach the top. At times she wondered just what he saw in her, why he even bothered to be with her.

But really, none of that mattered. She was the one who'd behaved dishonorably. She could only be responsible for herself.

And although the busboy—Hawk—had made her feel better, not only sexually, but strangely, emotionally, what she'd done was wrong, and the guilt had eaten at her for days.

But . . . he'd made her feel more wanted and *needed* than Warren ever had.

She hadn't felt like that in a long time. And honestly, if she had to be *real* about it, that, more than anything, that feeling he'd given her, that she was *special*, had scared the shit out of her to the point that she'd not returned to the diner.

She shut down her thoughts and her subconscious trying to understand the reasons she'd been avoiding the café and the busboy.

She shook her head to clear her thoughts, and glanced down at her watch.

With a sigh, Danita stood up and gathered her things in preparation for leaving when Warren stepped out of his office, along with a man Danita recognized as one of Warren's wealthier clients, a rancher who owned massive amounts of land throughout San Antonio and Austin.

Even at the distance Danita was from them, she could smell the heady, rich, aromatic smell of the thick, expensive cigar clamped between the large man's mouth.

"Warren, don't know what I'd do without you, my good man!" he said, clapping a meaty hand between Warren's shoulder blades.

"John, it's my pleasure," Warren replied as the two men walked into the room. "I'll have those papers drawn up for you by tomorrow and sent by courier. As soon as the soon-to-be Mrs. Fender signs them, you're all set."

He turned to his assistant. "Sinclair, make sure you send Mr. Fender the necessary documents he needs for the Eastland takeover as well."

As Warren turned back to the large man at his side, he seemed to finally notice Danita. His eyes ran over her, lighting on the shortened hem of her skirt, and his smile slipped, just enough that Danita caught it.

She ignored the instant response, her heart seeming to thump harder, unfortunately not in anticipation of spending time with him, but because she knew he'd have something to say about the alteration.

Danita straightened her back and walked toward Warren, a determined smile on her face.

"Hi, Warren, I was just about to leave. I need to get back to the office. Thought I'd stop by and say hi since I was in your neck of the woods," she said, not wanting to give the impression that she'd been waiting for thirty minutes for him.

"I'm so sorry for keeping Warren from you, little lady. Time just got away from us!" the big man said in his booming voice with a raucous laugh.

"No problem, John, Danita and I didn't have firm plans. She understands business comes first," Warren assured the man, returning his handshake.

"Best get her used to that now, before you sign on the dotted line," the big Texas ranger said, and the two men shared a mutual masculine laughter that instantly put Danita's teeth on edge.

"John, I believe you've met Danita Adams?" Warren more stated then asked.

"Yes, we have met," Danita answered, although Warren hadn't directed his question at her.

"Yes, we have," the rancher agreed, reaching up to remove the ornate Stetson from his head before engulfing her much smaller hand within both of his meaty ones. "Believe it was a few months ago at my engagement party, wasn't it?"

"Yes, it was. I also met your fiancé, Shania, I believe?" Danita answered with a smile, and instantly grimaced when she felt Warren's fingers tighten where they rested on her shoulder.

"Sweetheart, Mr. Fender is no longer engaged to Ms. Clarke."

"Oh, but I thought you were preparing his paperwork for

his prenuptial agreement," Danita answered, feeling her face heat with embarrassment at her unintended faux pas as she moved away from Warren's touch.

"That's okay, Ms. Adams. Hell, I get confused myself trying to keep up with my ladies!" The big man laughed with a light-hearted booming laugh, easing some of Danita's embarrassment.

Smiling in relief that she hadn't offended him, she glanced at Warren, and noticed that she hadn't gotten off so easily with him. When she heard a soft cough, she whipped her head around and caught the amusement in Sinclair's sky blue eyes, and clenched her teeth.

"I hope I see you this weekend, Ms. Adams. You can meet the new love of my life at the ranch," the man said, and after bidding them farewell, left the office.

"Sinclair, I'm going out to lunch with Ms. Adams. I should be back in an hour," Warren told his assistant and turned back to Danita, urging her toward the door.

"I'm sorry, Warren, but I've got to get back to the office. I have a client due to arrive in twenty minutes," Danita interrupted, and gently pushed away from him.

"What do you mean, you have to go? We're supposed to be going to lunch," he replied, grasping her under the elbow and turning back to the waiting assistant. "Why don't you go ahead to lunch, Sinclair. I should be back in no time," he said, infusing more warmth in the tone than what he'd directed toward Danita.

"Warren—"

When he continued to try and drag her with him, Danita forced him to stop, becoming angrier with his refusal to listen, particularly with Sinclair's avid attention on them.

"Warren, you're not listening. I told you I can't go to lunch now. I have a client I need to meet with," Danita hated to do this in front of Sinclair, but Warren was, as usual, attempting to bulldoze her into going along with his agenda—and to hell with hers.

"Look, I've apologized for having you wait—"

"No, actually you didn't," Danita replied, at that point completely fed up with Warren and his tendency to not listen to her. "But that's beside the point."

"And the point is?" he asked, clearly irritated with her refusal to go with him. "Fender is one of my premier clients. Surely you don't expect me to tell him my girlfriend is waiting to have lunch with me, and get rid of him?"

Danita hooked her thumb under the strap of her bag, hiking it up her shoulder. "No, I definitely know where your priorities lie, Warren. You've made that abundantly clear," she returned. "The point *is*, just like you, *my* clients are important to me. So, we'll just have to do lunch later this week. I've got to go," she replied, and ignoring the indignant look and flush of anger washing over his face, she turned without a second look, and swiftly walked across the room and left.

29

His long fingers caressed her naked thighs as he positioned her so that she felt his thickness fill her. A sigh of hedonistic delight left Danita's lips and a smile of extreme satisfaction lifted the corners of her mouth when one of his fingers played with her clit as he rode her in long easy glides.

With her legs wrapped around his lean waist, she struggled to get closer to the source of her pleasure. When one hand lifted her buttocks high, so that his strokes penetrated her deeper, she moistened her dry lips, her heartbeat loud and heavy as it thud against her chest.

"Dr. Adams, your client is here."

Danita hastily moved her hands away from her aching breasts and spun around in her chair, feeling her cheeks flush, startled when Larissa poked her head in the door of her office.

"Yes, uh, give me a minute, Larissa. I need to close out this file," she said, giving her assistant a strained smile, and running her hands over her hair, making sure it was still neatly coiffed in the low bun.

"Are you okay?" Larissa's questioning eyes ran over Danita,

and she felt her cheeks burn hotter at the curious expression on her assistant's face.

"Yes, I'm fine, just give me a minute," she replied, giving her a strained smile, quickly placing her small, square glasses on her nose.

"Okay, just buzz me when you're ready. It's your juvie case, the one the court sent you." Larissa glanced down at the clipboard and finished, "Her name is Merissa LittleJohn. She's also here with Mr. Wikvaya, her lawyer," she reminded Danita. When Danita murmured an assent, assuring her she'd be able to see them soon, Larissa turned and closed the door behind her.

Blowing out a breath from pursed lips, Danita quickly removed her compact from her purse and peered into the mirror. Making a moue of disgust at her reflection, she quickly ran the sponge over her face, refreshing her powder before snapping the lid closed and placing the compact back into her purse.

God, she was a wreck.

It was bad enough she couldn't close her eyes at night without conjuring up images of the man she'd shared the one-time hot sexual interlude with. Now, at work, he was invading her day, her mind either reliving the experience in heated detail, or fantasizing what else he could do to her, with her.

It had been two weeks, and the dreams and thoughts weren't going away. If anything, they were increasing, her daydreams and fantasies had her in a state of constant arousal.

After leaving Warren's office, she'd also been avoiding his calls, and had made sure to be "busy" whenever he left a message saying he'd be coming by her condo.

She knew it was only a matter of time before she needed to come to some decision about not only her relationship with Warren, but about other things as well. Things she had shelved to the back of her mind, things that were keeping her up late at night, or interfering with her ability to work.

Things like a tall, leanly muscled man who had made her feel as though she were the most beautiful woman in the world as he'd made sweet love to her.

She buzzed Larissa and asked her to bring her clients inside.

She smiled in welcome when the door opened and a young woman wearing oversize baggy jeans and a jersey entered her office, and instantly the smile slipped from her lips and her heart erratically thumped when the man walking behind her, ushering in the young girl was the same man who'd been filling her nights and days with hot images of the two of them pressed together, his golden naked body intertwined with hers.

"Hawk," she whispered, and leaned down to grip the edge of her desk, preventing herself from falling back down in her chair in astonishment.

Hawk made sure his look of satisfaction was carefully kept away from his face as he ushered Merissa inside Danita's office.

The myriad of expressions crossing her face were telling . . . and very satisfying, ranging from astonishment, to disbelief, to desire, before her animated face shut down. The desire he saw in her dark brown eyes was worth the two weeks of waiting to see her.

He had given her enough time to settle down, knowing she wouldn't come to him.

Neither had he been surprised when he hadn't seen her around the diner. He was rarely there himself, yet he'd stopped by several times just in case she surprised him.

She hadn't.

And two weeks had been enough.

He'd *expected* her to run away. Knew she would be confused about what had happened between them. The red flush lining her deep brown chocolate face was an indication she was not only remembering their encounter, but embarrassed by it.

He'd found out pertinent information from Leila about Danita over the course of the last week.

Danita hadn't given her last name, but Leila had filled him in on information, more than enough.

She'd told him Danita was a psychologist, something he already knew, and practiced in a midtown practice, sharing the small office with one other full-time therapist and her assistant. She'd also volunteered the information that Danita kept several slots opened in her growing practice for those who normally couldn't afford her high fees, offered her services on a sliding scale, or in some cases, pro bono, without pay.

He kept his eyes on hers and his palm lightly on Merissa's shoulder, as he waited for Danita to invite them in.

The two locked gazes. In hers, even from a distance, he read the shock she felt in seeing him in her office. His eyes followed her small tongue when it peaked out and gently swiped across the bow of her upper rim.

"Hello, Mr. Jarred Wikvaya?" she asked, and he read the question. When they'd spoken, he'd not given her his legal name, had only told her his nickname.

The smile that had slipped from her face returned, and although it was more strained looking, Hawk gave her high marks for her quick recovery from his unexpected presence.

His glance ran over her body. Just as she had been in the diner, she was perfectly coifed, head to toe, nothing out of place.

He clenched his fist, his fingers itching to pull the pins from her hair so that he could run his hands through the loosened, thick strands.

"Hello, Mr. Wikvaya," she said, coming from behind her desk to approach them. "And this must be Merissa?"

Hawk noted as she walked toward them that she wore high heels, just as she had before, adding several inches to her petite frame, yet as she stood before him, the top of her head was no higher than his midchest level.

He slid his gaze over the suit that, although conservative,

still clung to her abundant curves. The open jacket revealed a white silk blouse that cupped and molded her plump breasts, and tucked neatly into the small waistband of her skirt. The hem of the suit skirt ended several inches above her well defined knee, allowing him to enjoy the view of her beautiful, bare legs.

"When I made the appointment for Merissa, Dr. Adams, your assistant assured me it was okay for me to join the first session. I hope that's alright with you?"

"Yes, that's fine. I'm sorry. I've had a bit on my mind lately. It slipped my mind, please come in and sit down." She waved a hand to indicate they should come in.

"Thoughts elsewhere?" he asked. Her eyes widened a fraction and her skin flushed.

Danita glanced back over her shoulder, her eyes flying to meet his.

His smile was just a shade *too* neutral, the expression on his handsome face open.

Danita turned and walked toward her desk. As she walked ahead of the pair, she felt a tingle in the back of her neck, and turned her head slightly. In her peripheral vision she saw his burning gaze centered directly on her backside. She resisted the urge to tug on the short skirt and quickly placed her hands to her sides.

"Please, have a seat," she turned and motioned for Hawk and the young girl to sit in the leather seats facing her desk. After they'd taken their seats, she put on her most professional smile, and stoically avoided looking at the slight straining at the front of his otherwise loose slacks as he sat down.

Danita waited as the young girl took a quick glance around her office, her dark eyes lighting on the various black-and-white prints lining the walls.

"So tell me about yourself, Merissa. What brings you to me

204 / *Kimberly Kaye Terry*

today?" she asked with a small smile, and noted the way her dark almond-shaped eyes widened.

Although Hawk was there with her, she made it a point to address the girl though she encompassed them both in her glance. Whenever she had a first-time client come to her, they were often accompanied by a parent, guardian, or counselor. Unlike other therapists she knew, Danita made sure to begin upfront by addressing the client. It helped set the tone for her interactions with the client, one that told them, from the beginning, they were important to her and she was vested in their growth.

"I don't know. Uh, what do you want to know?" the girl replied, squirming in her seat before glancing up at Hawk for guidance. When he gave her a reassuring nod and settled back in his chair, the girl turned back to Danita.

"Anything you want to tell me is fine. I'm easy," she said and wanted to bite her tongue, her cheeks again burning as she uttered the words and glanced at Hawk, who was watching her intently.

Merissa worried her bottom lip, her young face scrunched up, lines furrowing her brow. "Well, I guess I'm here because I got in some trouble," she mumbled, casting her eyes away, and tucking one of her long braids behind her ear.

The young girl went on, in a voice filled with emotion, about how she'd gotten in trouble—pregnant—and had been kicked out of her house by her parents. After losing the pregnancy, her parents still hadn't wanted her back, so she'd ended up on the streets for a time before social services had intervened.

Apparently in the nick of time, as Danita glanced over the court documents. Merissa had gotten caught up with a local gang doing petty crimes, but ones that if left unchecked, would more than likely escalate into the type of trouble that would land her in jail.

She didn't want to interrupt, didn't want to stop her from expressing herself, allowing the girl to speak the words that had obviously been on her mind for a long time.

Hawk too remained silent, the only testimony to his feelings was the clenching in his jaw. She looked down and saw his hands fisting on top of his thighs.

When Merissa had finished, tears running down her small face, Danita leaned forward and handed her a Kleenex.

She swiped down her face, quickly wiping away her tears, her narrow chest heaving, moving up and down until she calmed down.

"I'm sorry," she mumbled the apology. "Guess you didn't expect to hear all that," she laughed a humorless laugh and hiccupped softly. "Your office is cool. I like all the pictures."

Danita could see she was nervous even though she did her best to appear sophisticated.

"Thank you. Most of it is from a new artist I found at the flea market downtown," Danita replied, smiling softly, mentioning an older part of town frequented by artists and patrons alike.

"I go there a lot! I find all kinds of cool stuff there," the young girl replied, her tears now gone, her eyes sparkling, a smile lifting the corners of her wide mouth.

"I practically live there on my time off," Danita laughed. "It's a great place to go, plenty of art, nice little cafés, and I love the Caridad Boutique."

"You go there? Man, with all your money, you can afford to buy whatever you want," the young girl replied, running an assessing eye over Danita.

"Most of the furniture in my office as well as my home is from Caridads," Danita replied, easily.

"I work part-time at Warton," she said, mentioning another popular vintage boutique that specialized in the same type of eclectic items found at Caridads. "We have some nice things there, too. You could come by and ask for me. I could show you some of the stuff we get before it goes out on the floor, if you'd like," she said shyly. "We're going to be at the Indian Festival this weekend. I have some of my own artwork that's going to be for sale. If you'd like, you could come by. There's going to be local crafts and artists. Lots of food, too. Mr. Wikvaya is going to be there," she supplied. "Maybe you two could come by together. You're coming, too, aren't you, Hawk?" she said, and glanced up at Hawk.

Throughout the conversation, Danita had carefully kept her attention solely on the girl, concentrating on the session and blocking out the sensual man who sat quietly by her side.

"I'd like that, Merissa. Although I'm sure Mr. Wikvaya probably has plans to go with someone else," she said hastily, hoping it was true.

"No, actually I don't. I'd love to take you . . . to the fair," he said, the look in his eyes hot, sending a message directly to Danita, one the young girl completely missed. "It's this Saturday. Starts at noon. I'll pick you up around eleven.

It's a date," he said, one corner of his sensual mouth lifting in a smile, the dimple in his lean cheek flashing.

He said it as though it was a done deal, and Danita felt cornered, not sure how to get out of the "date" in front of the girl.

"Well, then. I guess it is," she said, feeling the muscles in her face twitch as she tried to smile.

Hawk lifted his wrist and glanced at the sturdy black watch he wore. "I think it's time for us to go," he said, and both he and Merissa rose from their seats.

"It was nice meeting you," Merissa said, and shyly offered her hand as Danita walked around the desk to escort them to the door. "I'll come back next week to see you, right?" she asked, the earnestness in her eye strong.

"Definitely. Before you leave, make sure you schedule your appointment with my assistant."

"Yes, ma'am," she said and with a lightness to her step, one completely different than the one she came in with, she began to walk out the door.

"Merissa, you go ahead and talk to Ms. Jones and make your appointment for the same time next week. I want to talk with Dr. Adams," Hawk murmured, and the unsettling in Danita's stomach grew.

"Okay," she said with an upbeat smile and skipped out the door. As soon as she left, Hawk closed the door.

Danita immediately moved to walk away when he caught her shoulder.

"You didn't have to avoid me, Danita," he murmured, moving his hands down her arms.

"What makes you think I was avoiding you?" she asked, hearing the breathless quality in her own voice. She cleared her throat. "I've been busy. That's all."

"Too busy to come to a place you visit daily?"

"How would you know—"

"I asked Leila. She said you're a regular."

"Like I said, I've been busy. I usually am this time of year. This is the time that I see an increase in my client load. After the holidays, people get depressed. I also have taken on more court cases, and—"

Her ramblings were cut off when his lips slanted over hers. Turning her body, he pressed himself closer to her, and pulled her closer. With a moan of surrender, Danita eased her hands up his chest and wrapped her arms around his neck, standing on tiptoe to reach him better.

With a muffled groan he turned her body toward the wall and pressed her against the door, his hands moving down the line of her back to cup her bottom and lift her closer to the thick bulge in his pants.

After long drugging kisses, Danita broke the mood, and moved away from him.

"I can't do this," she murmured, closing her eyes as she kept her back to him.

He was silent for so long, she wondered if he was still there. Turning, she saw that he stood in the same position, his dark gaze on hers. Expecting a rebuttal, she waited for his reply, her heart beating crazily in her chest.

"I'll pick you up here at your office, Saturday, at eleven AM," he said, and with one final look, left her office. When the door closed behind him, she released the pent-up breath of air within her.

30

Hmm. Yes. Just like that . . .

For long moments nothing was heard in the room but harsh groans and soft whimpering moans of pleasure as the two bodies writhed against the other.

"Do you like that, Danita? Am I making you feel good? Tell me . . . talk to me. Do I make you feel better than he does?"

"Oh, God. Yes. Yessss." her response turned to a groan of delight when he widened her legs and allowed the broad head of his dick to slip between the slick lips of her pussy.

"Time to get out of that bed, girlfriend! Rise and shine, give God the glory, glory! Oh, shit, let me stop playing around before a lightening bolt strikes! I know most of you nasty heffas wanna give that dick you were riding *all last night* the glory, glory, so, no, chicas . . . Carmelicious is most certainly *not* mad atcha! If the yum yum was good, then the yum yum was *good* . . . and you'd best to give it some *praisin'*!"

Danita groaned and rolled over in bed, turning down the volume on her clock radio as Carmelicious's voice poured from the small speakers and into her bedroom.

She threw an arm over her eyes to shield them from the sun shining brightly through the thick wood blinds in her bedroom. She opened one eye and looked at the time. Seven o'clock.

"Oh, God!"

She'd gotten all of three hours of sleep.

With a deep sigh she rose from the mattress, but when her muscles creaked out a protest, she slumped back down against the bars of her headboard and closed her eyes, listening to Carmelicious.

"The question of the day is, 'Is your kitty free to roam the city?' That's right ladies, is your kitty free to roam the city?! I can already hear the moans and protestations from our male listeners, but listen up, sometimes a girl's gotta think."

Danita's eyes flew open at Carmelicious's words, and she choked out a rusty morning-sounding laugh. "Oh, please, Carmelicious. Girl, not today!" She laughed and leaned over to turn up the volume on the radio before laying back on her side, facing the radio, resting on her bent arm with one hand cupping her chin to listen.

"You have either been playing it cool with your man, letting him set the pace for the relationship, or you're with some man who is completely ignoring you. Either way, it's time to get yours, ladies! And as my girl Beyoncé sang, sometimes you gotta go to the back of that closet and pull out that freakum dress. Damn, I wish I'd had thought of that one . . . anyway"— the DJ released a deep-throated chuckle before continuing—" could be that the man you thought you wanted—or the man everyone thought you should be happy you *have*—is not the man for you, and it's time to move on! Any way you wanna look at it, understand one thing, ladies . . . emancipation day is here! Let your kitty be free to roam the city! It's your life, and last time I checked, we only go 'round this lifetime once. Make sure you make the best of it, ladies."

Danita flopped back down on the bed, Carmelicious's latest

sage words of advice spinning in her head, as the shock DJ promised to be back after the commercial break.

"Is my kitty free to roam the city?" she questioned out loud and laughed lightly. "God, what am I going to do?" she murmured and forced herself to get out of bed, thoughts of Warren on her mind as she stumbled groggily toward the bathroom, stripping out of her thin nightgown and panties as she went.

Deciding a soothing bath was in order, Danita walked to the oversize tub, letting the water wash over her hands until it was the right temperature before plugging the drain and filling the tub.

She tossed in some bath salts, scented bubbles, and a few drops of her favorite essential oils from the chrome basket she kept filled with her bath essentials, and gazed with unseeing eyes at the frothing water, with absentminded attention as she sat on the wide edge of the tub.

She'd been avoiding Warren, much like she had been avoiding Hawk, and something had to give. She was becoming a nervous wreck.

When she'd been unable to avoid Larissa's questions any longe, finally, yesterday, she'd broken down and told her what had happened.

"Oh, my—are you serious? You did it with that busboy from Aunt Sadie's?" Larisa nearly screeched the words but Danita had hushed her, frantically looking around the restaurant to see if anyone had heard her friend's incredulous reaction before turning back to her.

"Yes, and please lower your voice. I don't want everybody and their mother to know!"

"My bad," Larissa apologized, lowering her voice to comic levels, her face scrunched up, brows lowered, and eyes so rounded they nearly bucked out of their sockets in amazement.

"When did this all happen and *why* are you just now telling me?"

Danita sighed and took a bite of her muffin, chewing thoughtfully before swallowing.

"Yuck. These are nothing like Aunt Sadie's," she groused in disgust before taking a drink of tea. She looked up and Larissa had one of her brows raised, an impatient look on her face.

"Girl, don't make me hurt you . . ." she warned, giving Danita a look that promised a serious beat down if she didn't hurry up and tell her what had happened. Danita laughed.

"Larissa, I don't know what the hell I'm going to do," she said, and proceeded to fill her friend in on what had happened between her and Hawk.

"Oh, Lord," was all Larissa could say for long moments, her chin propped in her hand as she listened in rabid attention as Danita spoke.

"And when he walked into my office looking *too* fine wearing business casual clothes, briefcase in hand . . . you just don't know, Larissa. I nearly had a stroke!"

"I bet you did! Uh, uh, uh, uh," Larissa commiserated with her, caught up in the drama. "During your, uh, interactions . . ." Larissa said, trying to phrase it in a diplomatic way.

Danita just rolled her eyes. "Go on, say what it was . . ."

"Wellll . . ." Larissa dragged out the word, "I'm trying to be as diplomatic as I can." She laughed, and some of Danita's tension eased. "Anyway, my question is, why didn't he tell you he wasn't a busboy? I mean, it sounds like you two did a *little* bit of talking before you got down with it, right?"

"I don't know. He kept the conversation mainly on me. He didn't really talk about himself at all. He didn't bring it up there or at the meeting, but I plan on asking him."

"So, what are you going to do?" her friend asked after a small lull in the conversation.

"I don't know. I really don't know." Danita took another fortifying drink of the strong black pekoe tea.

"Well, you've got to do something."

"Uh, yeah. I know that." Danita rolled her eyes and blew out a frustrated breath.

"Things haven't been all that great with Warren and me. I know, I know," she interrupted Larissa before she could speak when she opened her mouth. "He's perfect. You, my family, and everyone else have told me that," she said, slumping down in her chair. "But, well, I don't know that he's perfect for me."

"I wasn't going to say that. I know the brother is prime. You know that, everyone knows that, hell, Warren knows that more than all of us combined," she said, pulling a reluctant laugh out of Danita. Like many eligible, successful men, Warren had an ego the size to match, and was used to women throwing themselves at him.

"But, you know, Warren really isn't the type of man to chase a woman, you know what I mean? Hell, a man like that is used to beating women off with an ugly stick, as my momma used to say. He sure in hell doesn't need to chase a woman. You gotta go to him if you want to be with him. But you, my friend, need to decide what it is *you* want first."

Her friend's last words ringing in her ear, Danita refocused her attention on the tub, and she turned off the tap when she realized the tub was filled to near capacity.

She sunk down into the fragrant bubble-filled water, the heat and silky smoothness instantly helping to ease the constriction in the bunched, tensed muscles in her shoulders. She considered her assistant's words.

Yes, she knew she had to come to a decision.

Easier said than done, Danita thought, and sunk her body lower in the tub and closed her eyes.

31

Danita smiled as she strolled along the busy blocked-off streets with Hawk before they stopped at one of the festively decorated food booths.

"I definitely have middle child syndrome. In fact, I'm often asked how I am always so . . . so . . . ."

"Cheerful?" he supplied, and when he tucked one of her fly-away strands of hair away from her face and behind her ear, and her skin tingled from the light touch of his hand.

"Not exactly. I guess even tempered is a better word. Not too excited, but not too quiet. Pretty easygoing, a go-with-the-flow type of girl," she said, and thanked the vendor who handed her the tall frothy blue stick of candy.

"And is that who you are? An easy go-with-the-flow type of person?"

Danita had just taken a healthy bite of the cotton candy when he asked his question.

"I guess. At least I like to think so," she replied carefully. After he paid for the cotton candy, they continued their leisurely stroll.

"Are you having a good time?" Hawk asked, looking down at Danita.

"I can't believe I've never been to this festival before," Danita enthused, and Hawk smiled down at her as she delicately bit into the sweet, sticky candy, swirling it around her mouth before swallowing.

"This is the fifth year we've had it. Each year it grows in attendance." He smiled, and as she smiled back at him, he reached down and lightly thumbed away a bit of the sticky candy from the corner of her lip.

With his gaze locked with hers, he licked his thumb. Her apple cheeks blossomed instantly, the red flush visible beneath her deep brown skin.

"We?" she questioned, breaking the connection and glancing away. He placed his hand at the small of her back and maneuvered her around a pair of giggling teens.

"Yes. The unified tribe I belong to began this five years ago. In the beginning we planned for it to be solely a Native American type of festival, but later we thought it would be better if we included other cultures."

"What tribe do you belong to?" she asked with genuine interest in her voice.

"Actually, my mother was Cherokee, my father was Hopi. He grew up on the Hopi reservation in southwest Arizona."

Before she could speak, a young boy wearing a tank top with a white T-shirt beneath and a pair of shorts that hung so low, Danita thought they'd fall to his ankles, came up to them dribbling a basketball.

"Hey Mr. Wikvaya! Come on over and ball with us! We've been waiting for you. They set up a court and we're about to play teams." The young man had barely finished when his eyes moved toward Danita. He cupped the ball beneath one arm, the other hoisted the waistband of his shorts.

"Oh snap, Mr. Wik! I didn't know you were here with someone," he said, his gaze roaming over Danita appreciatively. Danita felt like crossing her arms over her chest as the young boy's gaze seemed stuck straight on her tits.

"Maybe some other time, Tony," Hawk replied, and wrapped his arm around Danita's waist.

Surprised, she glanced up at him. He had an easy grin on his face as he spoke to the boy, and after several minutes of small talk, Hawk reminded the young man of some meeting they had scheduled for the following week. With a wave, the boy ran off.

"That was one of my clients," he answered her unasked question.

"How long have you practiced law?" she asked, and when he guided her to a roped-off area filled with chairs, she waited as he pulled her chair back for her and gratefully sat down, her feet aching from the day of walking.

He sat down across from her, close, so close she smelled his unique, rich scent reach out and envelop her in its embrace.

"For six years. I graduated from law school eight years ago, but didn't actually go into practice until several years later," he told her.

"Why? What made you put it off?" She knew she was probably being nosy, asking so many questions, but she wanted to know about him, wanted to learn more about him, as he'd strangely been reticent about sharing any personal information.

"Hmmm . . . I suppose I wasn't quite sure practicing law was what I wanted to do. At least not criminal law, which is what I studied. I took a few years off from law, came back home, and started working with a few teen outreach programs."

"Is that when you decided you wanted to work in juvenile defense?" she hazarded a guess.

He smiled at her, a somber look in his eyes. "Yes. I empathized with them, understood their motivations. A hell of a lot more than I did those of the upscale members of society, who committed crimes so heinous it made me ill. Especially as many of those crimes were committed against social misfits, the ones no one wanted to believe, or even hear their side of the story."

The look of raw emotion on his face burned bright and intense before he shut down his expression and turned to her, placing his arm around her shoulder, and pulled her close.

She wanted to know what had placed that look of pain in his eyes, wanted to know what secret pain he held hidden.

Danita wanted to ask him more, but let it drop.

Throughout the day, as he had before during their time at the diner, he'd asked her questions about herself, and before she'd realized it, she'd once again opened up to him, telling him things she'd never told a man, small things that no one really had pulled out of her, particularly on such short acquaintance.

There was something about Hawk that seemed to make her feel safe, comfortable.

She glanced up into his dark, handsome face and felt the tingles of awareness and lust flood her.

Well, not entirely safe, she thought.

But for all of that, Danita was beginning to feel uneasy that he hadn't told her anything of substance about himself. Every time she thought he would, he would shut down, retreat.

After she polished off the last of the sweet confection, they continued to walk.

"Are you getting cold?" he murmured, bringing her closer to his warm body.

Danita didn't respond, simply sighed and snuggled deeper into his hold.

As the sun began to settle, the night air was much cooler than the warmer afternoon. Although that had nothing to do with the chill bumps running over her body, and more to do with him and his effect on her body . . . and soul.

When she showed interest in one of the festively decorated,

brightly lit booths showcasing a beautiful variety of turquoise jewelry and ornately designed dream catchers, they stopped.

Danita reached up and touched one, fingering the delicate design.

"Do you like this?" he asked.

"Yes, it's beautiful," she murmured, fingering the delicate dream catcher.

"Do you know what it's for?" he asked, removing it from its hanging. He withdrew his wallet from the back of his well-worn Levi's, removed several bills, and handed them to the vendor.

"No," she admitted and laughed. "Except that Larissa has one hanging on her rearview mirror in her car."

The woman handed Hawk his purchase in a small bag, and he grinned down at Danita.

"A lot of people do that." He guided her away from the booth. "This is for you," he said, presenting her with the small bag. Danita thanked him and dug into the bag so she could admire her gift.

"Actually, it is exactly what it is named. A dream catcher. There are a few legends about the dream catcher . . ." As he began to speak, they moved toward the large platform where a band was setting up their instruments for the night.

"It's believed the origin of the dream catcher is from the Chippewa tribe. They were made as charms to protect the young from nightmares. Legend says the dream catcher will catch all dreams. The bad ones get caught in the dream catcher's webbing and disappear in the morning."

He stood behind her as he spoke, his long fingers covering hers as she lightly caressed the dream catcher.

"The good dreams find their way to the center of the dream catcher . . ." he continued, pulling her close against his warm body and leaning down to speak in her ear so that she could hear him above the sound of the musicians tuning up.

He guided her hands to the middle of the ornate dream catcher. "They float down the feather. So the dream catcher is thought to be a filter which allows only the pleasant dreams to get through."

By the time he'd finished, Danita felt warm and content as she leaned against his hard body, hyperaware of his chest pressed against her back, and the thickness under his jeans pressed against her lower back.

"Do you have any dreams that need to be caught, Danita?" His lips pressed down her neck, sending tingles over her body. "Any dreams that scare you, make you wake up in the middle of the night, sweat pouring down your face, down your body?" he asked.

One hand lightly grasped her around the neck before trailing down between the V of her shirt, tracing down her breasts before resting on her stomach, pulling her even closer to his body.

"Yes," Danita breathed, caught up in the web he and the dream catcher had seemed to weave around her.

"Tell me," he urged.

Danita thought of her most recent dream, her secret fantasy, and shivered. In the fantasy, Hawk was making love to her, satisfying her completely, when a second man entered the dark room. Together the two men catered to her, making love to every part of her body until she was left weak and satisfied.

She moaned, closing her eyes. In the cover of darkness, Hawk lifted her blouse and captured one of her breasts, palming the soft mound and fingering her distended nipple until it spiked in a stiff, painful peak.

When she felt his hand cup her mound beneath the skirt she was wearing, Danita gasped, her eyes flying open.

"Hawk," she moaned, moving her breasts so that he could hold her closer.

"Ssh, no one knows what we're doing. Just enjoy," he whispered the hot words low in her ear.

After she nervously glanced around, and saw the growing audience laughing and beginning to sway to the music, no one paying them attention, Danita's head fell back on his chest and her eyes fluttered shut.

While the band played, Danita allowed the soulful music to pour over her, and she enjoyed the biting kisses Hawk was raining down her neck as his hands massaged and manipulated her breasts. Each pull on her nipples seemed to stimulate her all over her body, the walls of her pussy clenched and released with each pull on her rock hard nipples.

While the band belted out the soulful music, Danita gave in to what Hawk was doing to her body, enjoying the feel once again, of allowing him to cater to her.

32

"I had a great time, Hawk. Thanks. It was exactly what I needed," Danita said, meaning every word.

She hadn't laughed or just . . . relaxed in so long, it felt like a much needed breath of fresh air to her starving spirit. She laughed at her melodramatic mental phrasing.

"What?" Hawk asked, smiling down at her, and she realized she'd laughed out loud.

"Oh, nothing," she grinned up at him. "Just thinking about the day is all. I wish it didn't have to end," she said. As soon as she said the words she felt his dark eyes on her as they stood on the landing of her covered porch in front of her door.

"Who says it has to end now?" His hand came up and he ran the callused pad of his thumb just beneath her bottom lip. He leaned down and captured her lips with his in a soft kiss. His tongue slipped between her lips and lapped across, before he opened his mouth and grasped her fuller bottom rim between his and then slowly released it.

He placed sweet, nibbling kisses down her throat before returning to her lips, only to kiss and bite them, corner to corner, before laving his tongue down her neck and back up again. Danita made urgent sounds of demands, trying desperately to catch his lips with hers, to stop his teasing caresses.

He released a small deep laugh when she grabbed onto his head, tunneled her fingers within his silky strands, and pulled him down to her mouth.

All teasing left and the kiss turned into an explosion of want, lust, and need, so potent in its intensity it left Danita breathless. Her fingers tightened in his hair and when he pushed at her, shoving her against her door so that their bodies were flush against each other, it still wasn't enough. It wasn't nearly close enough.

His mouth opened and he devoured her.

He shoved one leg between her jean-clad thighs and rotated his hips, grinding against the part of her that now painfully ached, desperately needing his touch. Danita widened her legs against his muscular leg, riding it as liquid heat poured from her, washing her clit.

Her skin was itchy, hot, making her feel as though a fire was raging throughout her body.

When he pressed her against the wall, pressed his body tight against hers, Danita hiked up her leg and wrapped it around his waist.

He ground against her, and she could feel the thick engorged outline of his shaft as it pushed against her mound. Feverish, she rolled her hips and torso against the thick bulge, as her tongue fiercely dueled with his, locked in a hot tangled battle.

She shoved her hand in his hair, dislodging the leather band he'd secured it with, and tunneled her fingers in the thick strands.

Hawk broke the kiss, his chest heaving, his thin nostrils flaring widely as he took deep breaths of air. As their gazes locked, his eyes darkened with lust and passion so that they appeared as sooty black as his hair.

"Unless you want it to," he said, his voice barely above a deep murmur.

It took Danita a few minutes before her brain unfogged and she realized what he was saying. He was finishing the end of the sentence he'd started before the toe-curling, tongue-lashing, pussy-pounding kiss.

Drop kicking the ball solely into Danita's court.

"Would you like some tea, or coffee, or maybe something to eat?" Danita opened cabinets with shaky hands, searching for the coffee filters she knew good and well she'd bought when out shopping the week before.

As she searched for the M.I.A. filters, she told herself the churning in her gut was because of the ridiculous amount of candy and food she'd eaten at the festival and *not* because of the beautiful, golden man staring at her through a pair of the darkest, sexiest eyes she'd ever seen, leaning against her counter.

Or because of the kiss they shared on her porch, making out like two randy teenagers.

She stopped and leaned both hands on the counter, and blew out a frustrated breath of air.

"Damn, I know they're here somewhere."

"Danita?"

She turned to face him. "Yes?"

"I'm not thirsty. At least not for anything in your cabinets. Come here." The corner of his sensual wide mouth lifted as he held a hand out to her.

Watching him warily, she pushed herself away from the counter and walked toward him. When she stood in front of him, he framed her face with the palms of his hands.

"You don't have anything to be nervous about with me. Not now, not ever. I promise you," he said.

Emotion swamped her at his simple words.

Oh, God.

She was turning into one big massive crybaby because of this man. But all it took was some small phrasing, a particular way of saying something that completely turned her inside out.

"You know that, don't you?" he questioned, running his thumbs over her cheeks as he stared down at her.

She closed her eyes again, shutting out the sight of his beautiful, earnest face, his eyes so solemn, so dark, staring at her with an intensity that stole the breath from her starving lungs.

She'd known him for such a short time. Couldn't even give a name to what their relationship was. She didn't know anything about him, his life, his aspirations, his dreams . . . all of those things that her mother, friends, and others had indicated were the *mandatory* things one should know about a man before becoming emotionally invested in him.

Yet she didn't think he would ever hurt her. She opened her eyes and looked at him. She *knew* he wouldn't hurt her.

"I know," she coughed, and cleared her throat when the words emerged sounding garbled.

"Do you want me to make love to you?" he asked.

Simple. Direct.

Danita stared at him, her emotions all over the place, her mind still trying to come to grips with what she felt for this man.

One thing for certain, she wanted him. Wanted him to fulfill the promise of his earlier lovemaking. Wanted to know what it would be like to allow him to fulfill the heated promise in his dark, sensual eyes.

"Yes," she said, and taking him by the hand, she led him to her bedroom.

33

Once in the bedroom, Hawk turned her around to face him, holding her loosely in his arms.

"Nice and slow, Dani, everything will be nice . . . and slow." The promise in his dark eyes heated her body, yet chills ran over her skin and she shivered as though cold.

Her lips stretched into a nervous smile, her heart clenching at the nickname he'd given her. No one had ever shortened her name. It was such a frivolous thing to do, yet somehow endearing to her.

He kept his eyes on hers as he began to strip the clothes from her body. She raised her arms as he lifted her blouse over her head, much as a child would for a parent. But there was nothing fatherly about what he was doing to her body, the way he was making her feel. The cool air from her ceiling fan rushed over her bared arms and she shivered.

"I'll warm you up in no time," he promised before deftly unclipping the front closure of her bra.

Her aching breasts tumbled free and Hawk stopped, his hot gaze staring at her breasts. He licked his lips and leaned down, placed a hand under one of the heavy orbs and lifted it to his open mouth.

Danita arched into his mouth as he nursed one sensitive tit with his mouth, and pulled and massaged the other with his hand, sharply tugging on her distended nipple until shudders racked her body. When her pussy clenched, her body tightening with each pull of his mouth, Danita cried out sharply.

He inserted his thumbs into the top of her capris, and ran them along the sides, caressing her before returning to the center to unsnap them.

With methodical precision he unzipped her and laid the flaps of the jeans to the side. Without removing them he brushed his long fingers over the satin of her panties and eased his fingers between her legs, cupping the warmth of her mound. Her female wetness now flowed, pooling in her panties.

Danita moaned and bowed her back, arching herself into his palm.

Delicious tendrils of heat and anticipation coursed through her when he moaned, obviously enjoying the feel of her, before removing his hand.

He pulled her capris down the length of her legs, and lifted her legs so she could step out.

"Oooh," she cried when he grabbed both sides of her hips and brought her lower body flush with his face.

Through the silk of her panties he brushed the side of his face back and forth against the tight, springy curls protecting her mound, rubbing his nose at the center of her heat. Danita grabbed his head and pulled him tighter against her aching core.

One of his long fingers pulled at the side elastic of her panties, peeling it away so that her vagina was exposed. Again he rubbed his nose in and around her, but this time, as he'd moved her panties to the side, he nudged her vaginal lips aside with the end of his nose and inhaled her scent.

"You smell so good," he murmured against the side of her thigh before his tongue snaked out and licked her pussy.

"Oh, Hawk, what are you doing—" Danita's words clogged in her throat when he again separated the lips of her vagina and nibbled and suckled the slick inner lips.

She grabbed onto both sides of his head, her fingers tunneling through the thick silky strands of his hair, inching closer to his plunging tongue.

She felt more than heard his rumbling laugh against her folds, but didn't care. There ought to be a law against what he was doing to her, Danita thought as she rolled her hips against his mouth.

When he hollowed his tongue and curled it around her clit, her knees buckled.

"So good." His words were muffled within her saturated folds.

His hands steadied her, gripping tightly into the flesh of her hips as he slammed his tongue in and out of her core, the only sound in the room her soft mewling cries and the greedy, wet sound of him lapping her cream.

Danita's body was on fire, aching and trembling.

As he licked and suckled her fat clit, engorged and pulsing, Hawk's erection grew painful within the confines of his jeans. Maintaining a steady hand on her hip, he swiftly unsnapped the closure of his jeans and shoved them away, lifting his erection out of his shorts in one move.

When he curled his tongue around her clit, he felt her body tense and in frantic movements, she bucked against his mouth, her fingers painful in his hair as she brought her hips closer and his face tight against her.

Ravenous for her, he shoved the capris from her body and tore her panties away as he continued to feast on her sweet honey.

"Yes . . . yes . . ." she panted.

He lifted his head from the nectar between her thighs to see

228 / Kimberly Kaye Terry

her beautiful face, washed in pleasure, and felt a dew of his own cum on the palm of his hand. Urgent to feel her, he regretfully rose from between her legs, lifting her into his arms, ignoring her cry of distress.

"No!" she cried out the denial.

"Ssh, it's okay. I'm not leaving you," he promised in a low, intimate tone, placing her on the bed.

Taking only enough time to completely rid her of her remaining clothes, pull his jeans and shirt away from his body, Hawk lay back on top of her and quickly made his way down her body.

Spreading her legs, he lifted them and placed them over his shoulders. He then used both hands to palm the generous mounds of her buttocks, lifting her away from the mattress, her vagina back in close contact with his hungry mouth. She released a sweet sounding moan, grinding against him, her cries increasing in earnest as his lips, tongue, and teeth dug back into her sweet, hot core.

As he ate and nibbled her, he inserted a finger inside her vagina, withdrawing her sticky cream. Keeping his mouth busy, he hoisted her legs higher onto his shoulders, her plump ass high, and used his hands to separate her cheeks. He inserted an oiled finger into the little rosy hole of her anus in careful increments.

"Oh . . . oh . . . yes," she mewled, squirming around his fingers, her fingers clutching the floral quilt on her bed.

Her feminine cream was an aphrodisiac to Hawk, the more he ate, the more he wanted to eat, devour, as he eagerly mouthed her and swallowed her honey.

Once her body accustomed to his finger, he eased another inside her and began to move in and out in a steady rhythm until he felt her body begin to quiver, the legs thrown over his shoulder shake, and her head toss frantically back and forth on the pillow.

"Let go," he encouraged her, using his head to widen her legs.

He shoved his tongue as deep as he could within her throbbing, milking walls, used the thumb of one hand to rub her pulsing fat clit, and twisted his fingers imbedded in her ass in short, quick turns.

She broke.

Screaming, her body completely lifting from the bed, she came.

"Yesss!" she screamed.

Danita completely lifted from the bed as her body jerked, her hips slamming against his fingers and mouth. She shuddered, screamed, and pulled at his head, begging him to stop, but Hawk held on until she lay weak back against the mattress.

34

"That feels good," Danita murmured contentedly with her body curled around Hawk's after he turned her around to face him. "What a perfect day. Absolutely perfect."

She moved her head to the side, giving him better access to the nape of her neck, where his lean yet strong fingers were buried within her hair, massaging it.

Hawk's laugh was husky. "It's about to get a whole lot better." The promise in his eyes made her breath catch, and heady anticipation unfurled in the pit of her stomach.

He flipped their bodies so that she lay supine beneath him as his body blanketed hers. As he looked down at her, the long thick strands of his hair fell forward and provided an intimate blanket, enveloping them in their own private sensual cocoon.

"Is that a threat?" she purred, the corners of her lips tugging into an easy smile as she wrapped her arms around him, the tips of her nails scoring the back of his neck before delving within the thick mass of his hair.

He leaned down and captured her lips within his, drawing out her lower rim before releasing it just as slowly.

"No, just a promise of what's to come."

Danita closed her eyes as his tongue snaked down her chin, circling it before drawing it into his mouth. Thinking he'd continue on his journey, she was surprised when he drew her chin completely into his mouth and began to pull on it, as though he was suckling a breast.

She was even more surprised when her body sharply responded to the unusual caress, particularly when his teeth grazed her chin in a biting caress that made her clit throb in tandem.

"God! What . . . why?" she stuttered and gasped, drawing her knees up, and planting her feet on the mattress as her body tilted forward. "How does that . . . why does that feel good?" she asked breathlessly.

He chuckled. "You'd be amazed at what body parts can be sexual hot spots . . . with the right man."

Her head fell back on the pillow when he continued his sensual tonguing down the line of her throat before stopping at the crest of one breast.

"Hmmm . . . yes," he drawled, and through half-closed eyes Danita watched as he lifted one of her breasts carefully, as though it were fine crystal and he was afraid it would break if he wasn't careful.

Her breath came out in even pants, as she waited for him to take it into his mouth.

"Beautiful. Like a mound of chocolate cream with a perfect cherry on top," he murmured before drawing her breast deep into his mouth. His words and hot mouth made Danita cry out in pleasure.

His hungry mouth suckled and milked her until Danita's body trembled and her vagina wept with each hot pull of his mouth on her.

"Hawk . . . please." The words were wrenched from her, her body in desperate need of more.

"What do you want, Danita?" Hawk bit down on her engorged nipple and washed the biting caress with his tongue.

"Anything, everything ... whatever you want to give me," Danita cried out, not caring how desperate she sounded in her need. "I ache ..."

"Here?" he asked, one hand trailing down her body to cup her warm naked mound.

"Yes!" she cried, arching into his palm.

One finger slid between her wet folds while the other pinched her nipples.

God, she wanted more. The one finger he had in her wasn't enough.

Danita begged for more, widening her knees and bucking against him as he fingered her. Hawk lay on top of her and buried his head between her breasts, adding another finger and another until Danita began to weep in open need.

When he withdrew his fingers she felt deserted, painfully so, until she felt him guide the broad head of his penis over her clit in teasing strokes.

"Do you want it, Danita ... do you want *me*?" he asked.

She heard a curious longing in the question that in her state of sexual euphoria she was unable to discern the meaning of. "Yes, please ..." she panted, but despite her need to have his thickness inside her, and her current state of hypersexual need, she knew she'd heard a plea in the question.

Almost as though he was ... begging ... her to accept more than his cock, this act.

She took both hands and framed his lean, beautifully sculpted cheeks, bringing his face down to hers. She took his sensual mouth, just as she wanted him to take her, and shoved her tongue deep inside his mouth. She swept inside his mouth, boldly mimicking with her tongue what she wanted him to do to her with the stiff shaft that was teasing her pulsing clit.

With a harsh groan, he lifted her hips away from the mattress and plowed deep into her vagina in a stroke so powerful and deep, it drove her toward the head of the bed, bumping against the headboard.

"Yes," she hissed.

This was what she needed. His hard-driving shaft plowing into her was what she'd been craving since she'd first gotten a taste of his lovemaking weeks ago.

Yet for all her lust, her crazed desire to feel him rock her, her walls clamped down tight on his shaft, and a feminine instinct prevented his marauding cock from coming any further into her.

"Let me all the way in," he grunted, and with her eyes wide, breath coming out in strangled gasps, she stared into his lean, chiseled face, and his intense cognac-colored eyes bore down into her, as though he could see into her very soul.

They stared at one another, their gazes locked in a battle as old as man, before she whimpered and relaxed. He reached between them and spread the lips of her vagina wide, and Danita moaned harshly when she felt him slide the rest of the way home.

The pressure began to build, mounting as he fed her all of him. She moved restless beneath him, and he clamped his strong fingers on her hips to anchor her down to the bed. His dick was so hard and slick as it moved within her, sliding into her warmth, and Danita wet her dry lips. He raised her hips higher as he filled her, until she was flowing with his thickness.

Once in, once she felt the broad bulbous end of his penis tap against her soft inner spot, she blew out several panting breaths and shut her eyes. He rested his forehead against hers and groaned, clutching the flesh of her hips as he lay immobile inside her with her impaled on his shaft.

"So good. So tight . . . so good," he rasped. "Is it good for you . . . ?" He bit the words out between clenched teeth, his breath fanning the hairs on her hairline.

"Yes." She barely was able to choke out the words past the constriction in her throat. "Yes, yes, yes . . . now, move. Please," she panted.

He laughed low and began to move in strong glides deep into her, rocking into her body with a strength that stole her breath away. Instinctually, she gripped his wrist.

"Oh, wait, please . . ." she begged when one of his strokes hit one of her hot spots in a place where few had ever been able to find, much less tap with just the right amount of pressure that had her biting the inside of her cheek to prevent a scream from releasing.

"Oh, yes . . . ummm, yes!" she screamed, unable to stop herself when he continued his light rhythmic taps against her spot, the pressure that began when he first began to make love to her now reaching to a feverish pitch.

Hawk grabbed both of her hands within one of his, forcing her arms up, anchoring them above her head, forcing her breasts to slap against each other. With her gaze melded with his, unable to look away, she felt him insert his free hand between them.

Expecting—needing—for him to seek out her thick, throbbing clit, she drew in a deep breath when, after anointing his fingers with her own cream, she felt three fingers rest against her bottom before slowly easing inside.

In rhythm he stroked inside her vagina as his fingers pressed in and out of her ass. The exquisite pleasure of both sent flames of need arcing through her body until she thought she'd explode.

His movements became slower, more controlled, his strokes shallow. Her body pressed up, meeting his, demanding that he take her over the edge, only to return to those strong hard plunges that plowed into her, making her weep in sexual agony.

He alternated between shallow thrusts that nearly took him out of her, the broad end of his cock resting at the lips of her vagina, to hard, deep plunges that pressed her body deep into the mattress and her head against the headboard.

Then he pressed his remaining fingers deep into her clenching bottom, slashed his lips over hers and shoved his tongue deep, groaning into her mouth as he fucked her in tight, hard strokes with both cock and hand.

She shattered.

Her body lifted from the bed, she frantically clutched at him, her hand twining in his long hair, and yelled. Her cum was so fierce, it bordered on pain. Stars broke out behind her tightly closed lids, her neck muscles strained as she grimaced against the intensity of her release, her heart literally felt as though it would explode out of her chest.

The inner muscles of her pussy constricted to the point of pain, hollowing out her stomach. She automatically held her breath as she released her body harshly until the last shuddering spasm left her body. When he gently eased his fingers from her anus, their connection now was his driving cock in her pussy. Danita fell back in exhaustion and closed her eyes, allowing him to fuck her until she felt his body tense.

His arms shook, braced on either side of her body, and his cock swelled to near painful proportions inside her milking walls as he continued to rock inside her.

When a low, almost humming sound came from him and she felt his body tremble violently around her, Danita's eyes flew open.

In sensual awe she took in the sight of the beautiful man above her, long hair cascading down his back, his high cheeks prominent, his sensual mouth opened as he roared like the primitive warrior he appeared in that moment, and seconds later she felt his cum splashing hot and thick within her womb.

He fell down on top of her, his sweat and the sound of his thudding heart, mingling, embracing, and intertwining with her as their bodies simultaneously released.

* * *

"Where's your bathroom?" he asked.

Slightly disoriented and shaky after her tumultuous release, Danita slowly opened her eyes, unsure how long she'd slept this time.

It could have been seconds, minutes, or longer. She had no idea, simply knew that her body was beyond replete and her limbs felt like mush.

She moved one weak arm and pointed toward the double doors that led to her bathroom.

After he'd come the first time, he'd lain behind her, pulled her body close against his, and thrown his arm possessively over her waist.

Her body had been boneless and sated after their lovemaking, yet when she'd felt his cock nudge against her bottom she willingly turned in his arms.

He'd flipped her body and within moments had her wet, deliciously so, and with easy lazy glides he'd directed her body toward another earth-shattering release.

"It's been a long day. Why don't you let me take care of you," he said, and nodding limply, not sure what she was agreeing to, Danita's head fell back on his shoulder. He lifted her and strode toward the bathroom.

Danita lay back against Hawk. Her head resting on his chest, lolled to the side with a blissful smile on her face as he ran a soapy wash towel over her.

He circled her breasts with the towel, paying close attention to her nipples, erect and throbbing.

Her tub was large and sat directly beneath the skylight she'd had placed in her bathroom which allowed the starlit sky to illuminate the room. When she'd had it installed she never imagined she would share the beautiful night sky and romantic atmosphere with a man.

She'd once had thoughts of inviting Warren to a special bath, had even gone so far as to set up the atmosphere with wine, candles, and an empty silver platter, hoping he'd want her to be the main dish.

Not only has she not been the meal of his choice, he'd declined and instead gone to a business dinner in hopes of wooing some new client or other.

She sighed and leaned further back into Hawk's warm, wet embrace.

Warren.

Danita thought of the message she'd left on his voicemail, saying they needed to talk. She had been finally ready to admit they had little to nothing in common, and after having been on the receiving end of Hawk's attentive lovemaking, both in and out of the bed, little doubt had been left in her mind about her future with Warren.

When he'd finally returned her call, sounding more put out that she had canceled accompanying him to his client's prenuptial party, than that she didn't want to see him anymore, she'd ended things with him.

"What's on your mind?" Hawk asked, as though he could read her inner thoughts.

Danita sighed and leaned further into his body as he stroked her breast with the soapy towel, the contrast in smooth and rough heightening the pleasure to her sensitive nipples. Because of his attentive lovemaking earlier, her breasts were hypersensitive, and she groaned when he ran the soapy towel around them, pinching her nipples with his fingers beneath the towel.

"Nothing of importance," she dismissed and settled deeper into his embrace. "Hawk, how long have you known Leila?" As soon as she asked the question though, his hands stilled, fractionally, before his caresses continued. She waited for him to respond, and when he said nothing, she grew impatient.

Despite how good his cleansing was, she felt she wasn't going to allow him or her libido to distract her. Throughout the day she'd realized that whenever she asked him about himself, he would give little detail before he would deftly turn the subject to something else, usually about her, smoothly avoiding answering any real questions about himself.

"Is there a particular reason you don't talk about yourself to me?" She cut right to the heart of the problem.

"Well?" she prodded, when again, he said nothing.

She felt him sigh behind her, and watched him dip the towel into the bath suds and gather more water before squeezing it over her stomach, allowing the warm water to trickle down between her breasts and the center line of her torso before disappearing beneath the frothy bubbles that camouflaged her mons.

When he wrapped the towel around his hand and stroked down her body, the intent clear that he was heading for her vagina, Danita raised a hand to still him, preventing him from going any further.

"*Well?*"

"There isn't much to tell," he finally answered.

"Earlier today at the fair, you said you owed Leila's great-aunt a debt. Is that why you help her at the restaurant? Is it your way of repaying this debt?" she questioned, and before she could stop herself, asked, "Or is it just an excuse to be around Leila?" She knew she'd gotten to him when the hand she held tightened a fraction.

When Leila had been confused about her feelings for Brandan, she'd mentioned to Danita her odd relationship with Hawk. Although she hadn't come out and said it, and at the time, Danita hadn't known Hawk, Danita felt there was more to their relationship than Leila had disclosed.

"Leila is like a sister to me. There is nothing going on between us other than a lifelong friendship," he said with a small bite that surprised her. He didn't speak for a while after that, and returned to running the towel over her body.

When he did, his words surprised her. "Aunt Sadie picked me off the streets. Literally. I was turning tricks, and if it hadn't been for her . . . well, there is no telling where I would have ended up."

Her breath caught in her throat and her mouth fell open. Of all the things he could have told her, she never expected to hear this.

"What? I . . ." she broke off, completely thrown, unsure what to say.

"I don't like to talk about it. It's a part of my past, and something I don't want to revisit." He put an end to the conversation, and Danita wanted to weep in a curious blend of frustration and compassion.

"Hawk . . . please," she began, only to have him cut her off by turning her around to straddle him, and pulling her head down to slant his mouth on hers.

After long, desperate-feeling kisses, kisses that felt more than passionate, Danita kissed him back, wrapping her arms around him. He kissed her, saying more with his whole being, his kisses, than he was able to say with words.

"Please, Dani . . . I don't want to talk about it." He spoke the words against her mouth, his forehead resting against hers.

She wrapped her arms around him and held on, giving him the only comfort she knew he'd accept.

"Thank you." As he spoke, he silently dictated to her to open her legs for him by nudging at them, and she obeyed.

"Are you sore here?" he asked, and ran the towel over her mound down the line of her leg where pussy and thigh met, and back between the crease of her sore fat clit.

"Umm . . . yes," she admitted, yet her pussy clamped on to the lean finger and milked it, her ass rolling against his hardened thickness pressing against the small of her back.

Despite the vigorous sexual activity over the last hour, she still wanted him.

"God, what is wrong with me?" she said aloud, and laughed reluctantly.

"What do you mean?" he asked, continuing his hot, thorough washing.

"I've always enjoyed sex. But I don't know if I've ever loved it so much that despite being sore I want more. And I've *never wanted, uh...*" she hesitated, and when he filled in the words she ducked her head, suddenly embarrassed. "Yeah. *That,*" she reiterated, and groaned when he lined the towel with his finger, soaped it up, and inserted it into her anus.

"But it felt good, you enjoyed it," he said in confidence.

She couldn't deny the truth of his words. Instead of answering, she lay against him and allowed him to minister to her.

"What other fantasies do you have? Ones you've never shared... ones you never thought could possibly happen, but the one you ache to have fulfilled?" he asked, slowly running a clean sponge over her body, the water slowly trickling down the line of her breasts, and Danita closed her eyes, enjoying the attention.

"Hmmm. I don't know," she hedged, although the fantasy she dreamed of, the one she *knew* she'd absolutely never have fulfilled, suddenly burned in her mind. The same one she'd thought of at the fair. The one of Hawk and an unknown man making love to her, both at the same time.

"Tell me..." His low, husky voice encouraged her to share her most illicit sexual fantasy.

After she shared it with him, she felt odd, wondering if he would think less of her for sharing the forbidden fantasy she'd long dreamed about, yet never had the nerve to try and have fulfilled.

She turned around, trying to gauge his reaction. But he said nothing, instead smiled at her, ran a lightly roughened thumb down her cheek, and leaned down to kiss her.

"You think I'm a freak, don't you?" She laughed nervously.

"No."

He turned her around fully, and placed her legs around his lean hips.

"What I think is you are a woman who deserves to have every one of her fantasies fulfilled," he said with a promise in his eyes that was suddenly frightening to her, considering what her fantasy had been.

He lifted her body and slowly impaled her, pressing deep into her welcoming warmth, and soon Danita got caught up in the rapture of his incredible lovemaking and all thoughts of what she'd shared with him were forgotten.

35

"Oh, I'm sorry, I didn't know you were in here," Danita said, walking into the bedroom and seeing Gregory, Hawk's ex-roommate in the room.

"I thought you left. Excuse me," she murmured, forcing her eyes away from the low-slung towel wrapped around his lean waist.

Confused as to the reasons for Gregory's state of undress, she forced her gaze away from his hard, shower-wet body and dewy chest, turning to go.

She'd come over to Hawk's apartment after he'd invited her over for dinner. His ex-roommate was there, and the two of them had been hauling a piece of heavy furniture from one of the rooms into a truck as she'd come in.

Hawk had introduced them, and when the other man had smiled at her, his light gray eyes ran over hers subtly, yet she'd easily picked up a sexual interest in his gaze.

He was similar height to Hawk, yet broader. His body reminded her of Leila's husband's, with his thick, muscled thighs bulging around the loose fitting shorts he wore, and the muscles on his chest straining against the plain white T-shirt. She'd stared at him, unable to look away when she caught the thick bulge straining his shorts.

But she looked away when she saw he'd noticed, a small smile flitting across his sensual lips.

Now, as she turned to leave, her hand on the doorknob, Gregory's next words halted her before she could leave.

"No, it's no problem. In fact, Hawk invited me," he answered.

Danita spun around to face him, a question forming on her lips to ask what he meant when Hawk opened the door and walked inside.

"It's okay, Danita, I invited Gregory."

Hawk walked over, the heat from his body blanketing her back. She automatically leaned back, resting her back against his chest.

Turning around she looked up at him, confused. He leaned down and kissed her, whispering against the corner of her mouth,

"It's all for you, sweetheart. Everything I do will be for you," he said.

"What's going on, Hawk?" she asked, breaking away, her eyes frantically watching his while her heart beat wildly against her chest.

Without answering he quickly divested her of her clothing before shucking his jeans and pulling his shirt over his head, tossing them all in the corner of the room. When he turned her around, her eyes widened in alarm, her heart racing when Gregory stood before her, the towel no longer hiding his rigid cock from her eyes.

Swallowing, easing back until she was as close to Hawk as she could be, she gripped his forearms, her nails sinking into his skin as she frantically sought to get away from Gregory approaching her. Her body shook as the clarity of what Hawk intended to have happen came crashing down on her.

"Hawk, no! I don't want this! I—"

Her words were cut off when Hawk moved her face around and claimed her lips, at the same time that Gregory knelt down in front of her. His fingers separated the lips of her vagina and he stroked into her core in one hot, long swipe. She cried out against Hawk's mouth, bucking her hips against the marauding tongue stroking her, but firm fingers held her still as his foreign tongue continued to eat her.

Despite her denial, the feel of Gregory's tongue against her soaking pussy, swirling and laving her clit, as Hawk handled her breasts, toying and plucking at her extended nipples, was as overwhelming in its affect on her mind and body as it was intense. She reared her body away from Gregory's insistent tongue sliding over her pussy, swallowing the cream that now flowed so thickly from her body.

"Close your eyes and pretend it's me between your thighs, Danita," he whispered, and Danita allowed her eyes to flutter close as Gregory added his fingers and inserted two inside her tightening, slick core, his tongue continuing to lave her vaginal lips, gliding over her hood, before taking her extended, tight, blood-filled clit into his mouth.

She gasped, and helpless, unable to stop her body from enjoying what he was doing to her, rolled her hips and widened her stance to give him better access. The slight stubble of his cheeks rubbing against her inner thigh added to the erotic feeling, and when he plunged three of his thick fingers deep into her core and tapped against her inner spot she broke the kiss with Hawk and ground against Gregory's face, her inner walls clamping down on his fingers, milking them as her orgasm began to unfurl.

When she felt her body tighten, she tossed her head back and forth against Hawk's hard chest, no longer thinking of right and wrong, her body taut, ready to explode. The tingling sensation unfurling in her belly rushed through her until she broke. She released a loud keening wail as she came, and her body shook violently from the intensity of her release, sweat running in rivulets between her breasts.

Hawk laid soft kisses along her throat as Gregory continued to feather his hot tongue over the lips of her vagina, stroking between her lips in feather like touches until her body calmed.

As soon as the last shuddering waves left, she turned around in Hawk's embrace and buried her face against his chest. It was a long moment before she was able to move her head and stare up at him, her mind in a chaotic whirl, her emotions all over the place, afraid of what she'd allowed to happen, dismayed at how good it felt to allow Gregory to do what he did.

Tears stung the back of her eyes, and her throat was clogged.

With her breath coming out in gasps, her chest heaving, she looked into his eyes, searching for an answer in his dark gaze, an answer she knew couldn't come from him. An answer she alone had the answer to.

"We can stop this now. We don't have to go any further with it. It's up to you, sweetheart," he murmured, wrapping her in his arms.

Hawk stared down at the woman he knew without a doubt was his. A woman he'd known was his from the moment he'd met her.

He wrapped his arms around her, tightening his hold, and lay his head on top of her soft curls. The feelings she aroused in him should have scared him, they were so intense, so powerful they seemed unreal. She shared herself with him, her goals in life, her fears, and told him things he knew she'd never shared with another he knew.

She was his.

She belonged to him, whether she knew it or not, and the thought that after the lovemaking they shared, she'd want another had made him see red. But he knew that he was the last man she'd ever be with. She hadn't admitted her love, but he knew it was there. She'd had the fantasy of being with another, and *he* had been the one to fulfill it. He wanted her to have no doubts that she was his, and if it took allowing her fantasy to be fulfilled to do so, so be it.

He would do anything it took to claim her.

But just once.

"But, it will never happen again, Danita. I will not tolerate another man touching you. Ever," he said, lifting her face, wiping the tears from her eyes. "You are mine," he said, waiting for her response.

She closed her eyes, and unable to speak for long moments, rested her cheek against his heart. She felt Hawk's heart beating as strongly and loudly as hers against her naked face. He wiped the lone tear that had escaped out of the corner of her eyes with the roughened pad of thumb, and the look in his dark eyes was so intense, so filled with . . . God, *love,* Danita wanted to run away from the power of its intensity.

What she'd allowed to happen—what she'd longed to happen in her fantasies—he'd given to her. What would he think of her, that she'd enjoyed another man's mouth on her and wanted to know—just once—what it would feel like to have two men make love to her at the same time?

"Why?" She needed to know why he'd brought another into their lovemaking. She had to know his reasoning for allowing such a thing to happen. If he cared for her as much as his eyes, his words, his actions had shown over the last weeks of their relationship, why would he allow this—invite another man to share her?

"It's for you sweetheart. Everything I do will now and always will be for you. No one else." The look of an emotion she refused to name shone so brightly in his eyes, it forced Danita to turn her head away, unable to accept what she saw.

"But you have to be the one to say you want this. Only you,

Danita," he said, his thumbs caressing each side of her face gently.

Taking a deep breath, her heart racing loudly to her own ears, she mutely nodded her head in assent and lay her head back down on his chest.

Hawk gently cradled her in his arms and carried her the small distance to the bed where he lay her down. Turning away from her, he opened the side drawer and withdrew a prophylactic, and sheathed his thick erection before lying down beside her.

Danita felt the mattress dip behind her and knew that Gregory had joined them on the bed. Goose bumps feathered across her naked body and she fought the desire to cover herself with her arms, to hide her body from the hot gaze she felt searing her back.

Licking her lips, she looked up at Hawk, the only lumination coming from the slow burning candles in the room. The vanilla scent from the candles, and their low light, added an overall erotic feeling to the room.

She ran her gaze over Hawk's beautifully sculpted features, from his soulful eyes, down his prominent nose, to his chiseled sensual lips, and felt the knotted muscles in her body begin to relax, to lose some of the tension, his presence soothing her overwrought nerves, calming the frantic pulsing of her heart.

He pulled her close to his warm welcoming body, and before he claimed her lips with his own, murmured, "Relax, sweetheart. You can trust me. Always."

After delivering soft kisses over her lips, he stroked his tongue deep inside her mouth, while one hand delved down between her slick core.

She moaned into his mouth, while gyrating her body against his hand, losing herself in him. When she felt a second pair of hands lightly touch her back in feather like touches, she tensed.

Hawk released her lips. "Relax, sweetheart. I'll take care of you," he promised.

Taking a calming breath, Danita nodded her head and wrapped her leg around Hawk's lean hips and in earnest, moved against his fingers as they plunged in easy glides in and out of her, her cream now flowing over his hand and sliding down her perineum, the sensitive seam separating her vagina and her anus, moaning in delight at the feel of his plunging fingers.

When Hawk withdrew his dew-covered fingers, she felt Gregory's large hands separate the cheeks of her buttocks, massaging, squeezing the globes, before one of his fingers, buried between her ass cheeks and slick with some type of lubricant, circled her anus, ringing her hole in careful tight circles. She shut her eyes and grit her teeth when she felt a small, slick object ease into her, accompanied by a gush of gel filling her anus.

Giving her no time to react, Hawk began to inch his shaft inside her vagina. Simultaneously, she felt the bulbous knob of Gregory's cock press against her opening, and instantly clenched up, tightening against both invasions.

Although Hawk had introduced her to this method of lovemaking and she'd enjoyed it, the thought of a man she didn't know performing this act on her was one that filled her with anxiety.

With her muscles tightening, she bucked her hips away from Gregory, and impaled herself on Hawk's thick cock in one hard thrust, rubbing her pelvis against his groin. The hot action elicited a tight groan from his clenched lips. As he stroked inside of her, his hands ran over her body.

"Accept him, Danita. This is for you," Hawk insisted, softly, stroking a hand along the side of her body before resting it at the curvature of her waist.

With a moan of acceptance, her body and mind having a tug of war of denial versus hot anticipation, her body won. Danita relaxed her muscles and allowed Gregory passage, accepting his careful strokes until he was deeply imbedded inside her.

For long moments the trio didn't move, each enjoying the sensation of being inside the other, bodies slightly shifting to accommodate the other.

And then Hawk began to move. His fingers dug into the smooth swell of her hip as he dragged his cock in and out of her wet core. She leaned closer to him and pressed her mouth against his, her lips eagerly opening when she felt the tip of his tongue nudge them until he stroked into her mouth with his tongue.

She whimpered against Hawk's mouth when she felt Gregory's hand glide over her body. He cupped one of her breasts in his hand, flicking a thumb over her nipple until it spiked, painfully pressing against his palm.

Although her mind was still battling against what she was doing, her body began to undulate, skewering Hawk's cock before gliding off enough to grind her buttocks on Gregory's shaft. Sandwiched between the two men, blood rushing to her head, her body on fire, she undulated back and forth, driving her hips forward and then back, riding Hawk's shaft, then rolling her hips against Gregory's strokes as he penetrated her deeply from behind. Her body and limbs trembled violently as her delicious forbidden fantasy blazed to life, the sheer eroticism of two men making love to her sending both mind and body into heated overdrive.

When Hawk released her lips, he leaned his dark head down and captured one of her breasts in his mouth, grazing his teeth over her erect nipple. At the same time Gregory moved his fingers from her waist to her stomach, his fingers trailing down to her mons before toggling her clit.

Danita cried out against the onslaught of sensations on her body and grasped Hawk by the back of his head, pulled off the band from his ponytail and tunneled her fingers through the thick, silky strands, her head tossing on the satin-covered pillow, lost in the sensual web the two men had snared her within.

She hiked her leg higher, wrapping it more securely around Hawk, hooking her foot around the outer cheek of one of his buttocks. Back and forth she rolled her hips between them, glorying in the exquisite feel of two large bodies covering her, front and back, of two men caressing her body, catering to her with dual sets of hands, lips, and cocks. Two thick shafts stuffing her to the brim as they ministered to her every need, while driving her to the ultimate satisfaction, driving her to a mind-shattering release she felt hovering, just out of reach. The walls of her pussy sucked and milked Hawk's hard driving cock, while she maintained a suction grip on Gregory's cock, impaling her from the back until a rush of euphoria swamped her.

She came in hard pulsing waves, her body shaking, accepting Hawk's powerful corkscrew thrusts while Gregory's short tight thrust from behind shoved her completely over the edge. Her eyes tightly closed, the muscles in her face contracted along with every muscle in her body. Her toes curled, her body arched sharply, she took desperate gasps of air deep into her lungs, and her body shook violently as the orgasm tore through her.

Hawk swallowed her screams, pulled her on top of him, and Gregory's athletic body deftly moved with them, never losing contact. With her on top of Hawk, he kept the kiss going, and she felt Gregory nudge her legs until both of them straddled either side of Hawk's long stretched out legs.

Gripping her hips, he continued to deliver the short, shallow thrusts into her ass as Hawk crushed her pelvis against his, angling her, grinding her cunt on his cock. His powerful thrusts banged deliciously at her inner spot, as her clit ground against the wiry hairs around his shaft.

When a second orgasm hit, she nearly blacked out. She tore her mouth away from Hawk's and screamed as the orgasm raced over her body. On and on the pleasure spiraled, and her throat became hoarse as she wailed her release.

Her boneless body, completely depleted, fell on top of Hawk. She heard Gregory's guttural shout of pleasure before his hands grabbed her hips, and he plunged into her several more times, until she felt his body spasm and felt his release. His groans of pleasure mingled with Hawk's, as he, too, issued several quick thrusts in succession before he grasped her tightly, grinding into her before she felt his body shake as he came.

Harsh sighs and breaths were the only things heard in the dark room. When Gregory pulled away from her, she couldn't move, and remained lying on top of Hawk's heavy chest.

The bedsprings creaked out a protest, and when Danita heard movement in the dim room, she opened her eyes, seeking out the source of the sound.

She could barely make out Gregory's large form as he stepped into his jeans and shrugged his T-shirt over his body. Minutes later Danita heard the door to the bedroom open and close.

Her eyelids fluttered closed as Hawk nestled her closer to his body, drawing the light sheet over their cooling bodies.

Before she fell into a deep sleep, she felt Hawk's hand caress the top of her head. Then he pressed a tender kiss on her face.

"I love you, Danita," he whispered against the damp curls framing her temple.

36

"Tony, have you thought about your plans after you're released from the Ranch?" Hawk asked, mentioning the name of the outreach program that helped young men transition from juvenile hall to a life in the community. "Have you thought about what we talked about last week?"

The young man sitting across from Hawk with his body hunched down, his long legs encased in baggy jeans stretched out in front of him, tugged on his baseball cap, pulling down the rim even further to shade his eyes.

Hank had represented Tony in court, and had convinced the judge to place him in the Ranch, a place known for helping boys like Tony get their act together. It hadn't been easy getting the boy into the place, and he'd had to call in a lot of favors and do some heavy petitioning on Tony's behalf.

He hoped the young man would take advantage of the situation, and not squander the opportunity.

"Sit up." Hawk issued the command without raising his voice, yet the young man immediately obeyed.

"Yeah, I been thinking. Just not too sure 'bout it yet," he an-

swered. Then he removed his hat, setting it in his lap as he fid-
dled with the brim, looking down at the cap and not at Hawk.

Hawk saw himself fifteen years ago in Tony, and he ran a
hand over his long hair, pulling it away from his face.

He'd been the one to represent Tony in court when the
young man had been involved in a robbery at a convenience
store. Tony had been in the backseat of a car, passed out drunk,
when a couple of his friends decided to rob the store, unbeknownst to him.

In all honesty, though, Hawk knew that while Tony hadn't
known what his friends had planned, and had woken as they
sped away from the scene, had he been awake, it was more than
likely he would have followed along with them.

He saw kids like Tony every day in court. Came across kids
like Tony every day in the poor neighborhood where he kept
his small law practice, which was also the same neighborhood
he'd grown up in, and after graduating from Harvard Law
School, had returned and chosen to live in.

And like the boy in front of him, Hawk had been a young
man no one believed in. He'd been involved in drugs, hustling,
and pulling off petty crimes. Had Aunt Sadie not helped him,
he would have ended up another street casualty.

Aunt Sadie had literally pulled him back from the precipice
of a certain bleak future. And so he could do no more than give
back, to help those who were a mirror of the young man he'd
once been, and devote his career to steering as many as he could
from the same future he'd once faced.

"What's not to be sure about? Look, you have this opportunity to make something of your life, and not end up just another thug looking for the next gig. Opportunities don't come
this way all the time."

"Yeah, yeah, I know," Tony mumbled, avoiding Hawk's eyes.
"Like I said, I just don't know yet," he replied.

"It sure will beat the hell out of where you'll end up if you keep going the same way you're going now." Hawk heard the grim tone in his voice, but it still didn't seem to be sinking in with Tony that if he continued on his current path of self-destruction, he would end up either in and out of prison, or worse, dead.

But he held back from yelling at him, or worse, lifting him up and trying to knock some sense into the boy's head. Both methods would result in the same reaction from Tony.

He'd shut down on Hawk, tune him out, and the progress they'd made together would be ruined. He ran a frustrated hand over his hair.

It wasn't too late for him to get on the right path. He was a good kid. Had family support, parents who, although they worked long hours, were doing their best to raise him. Unlike Hawk, who, if Aunt Sadie hadn't come into his life, there was no telling how he would have turned out.

"I know what it's like, Tony, hanging out with the wrong crowd, trying to fit in. I've been there—".

"Man, you don't know what it's like," the young man mumbled, interrupting Hawk, his jaw clenched, nostrils flaring, a light flush underscoring his deep brown skin.

"Listen, Tony," Hawk started, and sat forward in his chair, clasping his hands together. "Not too long ago, I was just like you . . ."

". . . getting in trouble, a real player, I thought I was. Always getting into situations I had no damn business being in. Skipping school, doing drugs, yeah, Tony, I was a lot like you."

Danita inched closer to the partially closed door, unashamedly listening in on Hawk and the boy's conversation. She'd come to break it off with him, confusion and depression settling over her as she made the decision, but it was one she felt she had to make.

She had already been with one man who didn't share himself, not his complete self with her, though they were worlds apart in their treatment of her. Hawk made her feel special . . . loved, but she wondered if he would be able to open up about himself, bring her into his world so that she would be able to fully invest her emotions in him. Unless he could, there was no point in continuing their relationship.

She listened with tears in her eyes as Hawk outlined the grim choices the boy faced if he didn't get it together, didn't straighten up his act.

The words he spoke came from the heart. Danita didn't have to be in the room to see his face, to know the truth. It was all in his voice, the emotion stark, plain to hear.

By the end, when Hawk had finished, there was a long silence. She heard the scraping of chairs and rustling noises that alerted her that the meeting was over, yet she remained glued to the spot.

When the door opened and Hawk came out, his arm around the young man's narrow shoulders, they locked gazes.

———

37

"Hey," she said, feeling shy for no other reason than she felt vulnerable, embarrassed, and angry. Embarrassed she had been caught, obviously listening to his conversation with the boy, and angry over his refusal to share with her what he gave to the young man so willingly.

And vulnerable because she'd allowed—willingly allowed—him to fulfill a fantasy of hers. That she'd, in a way, exposed herself to him.

"You weren't going to leave without seeing me, were you?" he asked, his astute penetrating gaze seeing straight through her.

Danita resisted the urge to cross her arms over her chest as though to protect herself from his all-knowing eyes.

Tony startled them both when he spoke. "Hey Mr. Wik, I'll catch you later." He spoke into the silence, curiously looking back and forth between Hawk and Danita.

Hawk turned away from Danita and smiled slightly at the young man.

"Okay, we'll pick up where we left off. And don't forget

what I said. I'll be checking in with your parole officer this week," he warned the boy.

With what seemed to be relief, Tony hitched his backpack over one thin shoulder, nodded to Hawk, and murmured a good-bye to Danita before quietly leaving them alone.

"Yes, I mean no, I mean . . ." Danita clamped her mouth shut.

"Come in," he said, and Danita followed him into his office.

He closed the door behind them, and immediately went to take Danita into his arms.

She shoved away from him, holding up a hand. He then noticed the note that she held clutched in her fist, and glanced from her to it, a question in his dark eyes.

"For me?" he asked, indicating with a nod of his head the note she had clutched in her fist.

Danita licked dry lips. "I didn't want to interrupt your session . . ." She broke off when he pried the note from her hand. He scanned the contents, a small tic in his jaw the only indication of his emotions.

"So, you're leaving me, too?" he asked, and turned away from her. He walked over to the bay window in the corner of the large, open office.

"No. Yes. I don't know," she said, her confusion giving her a headache, as she still couldn't sort out her feelings for him.

He turned back to her. "Make up your mind, Danita. Either you want me or you don't."

She sighed.

"I do want you. That's what makes this so damn hard."

He said nothing, simply looked at her.

"But I just ended a relationship where I was always left in the dark as to what was going on."

"And you think this is what I'm doing? Leaving you in the dark about my feelings? What else do I need to do to . . ."

"Stop right there." Danita saw the way the conversation was going. "I never said that."

"No? Then what is it Dani?" he pleaded.

She walked toward him, taking his outstretched hands, and he guided her to one of the large chairs in the room.

She succumbed, allowing him to sit her in his lap, and for her head to rest on his chest.

"I want you to let *me* get inside. I want you to share yourself with me. I want to give you pleasure, I want you to receive what I have to give openly. God, I don't even know how to explain it." She felt like weeping in pure frustration.

He stroked a hand down her hair and pulled her closer, and she felt the hard ridge beneath his slacks nudge against her buttocks.

He laughed. "You don't think you give me pleasure, Dani? Nothing could be further from the truth."

"Yes, but you are always the one to give pleasure. Selfless pleasure. Mind-blowing selfless pleasure." She laughed without humor, feeling exposed and raw. "Please . . . let me be the one to give you pleasure," she begged.

Danita noted the confusion on his face and slowly eased away from his lap. He reached out to stop her but she ignored him.

She lay between his legs and with her eyes trained on his, unfastened his slacks and reached her hand inside his boxers to lift out his thickened shaft.

"Allow me to be the one you let get close to you, the one nestled as tightly in your heart as you are in mine," she whispered, running her hands down his hardening length to cup his warm scrotal sac before maneuvering the shorts down and away. She rasped her thumb over the tiny eye at the end of his cock, and wiped away his moisture before she licked it off her thumb.

"Danita . . . what are you . . ." he stopped, inhaling a deep breath when she leaned down, opened her mouth wide, and engulfed him.

He leaned down and tried to pull her wet, tight mouth from around his shaft, but Danita kept herself steady.

She eased her mouth up and down the length of his dick, swirling her tongue around the plump, round knob, and gently licked the tiny slit in the center that wept a small bead of his seed before opening her mouth wide and sliding it over his erection until the end bumped the back of her throat.

"Danita . . ." he panted.

Danita glanced up and smiled around his thickness. His head was thrown back as he groaned, and the cords in his neck starkly stood out against the golden hue of his skin.

"Shit!" he grunted. The expletive was as unexpected as it was raw, coming from Hawk.

He grabbed both sides of her head, tunneled his fingers in her curls and twisted his hips, and she felt his dick bump the back of her throat.

Danita was entranced with the almost animallike sounds of pleasure he uttered, and the feel of his hot, hard shaft cradled in her mouth.

Danita grasped his cock, ringing him with her hands in counterclockwise motions as she deep throated him, taking as much of his length as she could in her mouth. Helpless, he grasped her by the hair and pumped shallow thrusts into her mouth. His strong, lean body began to shake as his orgasm hit.

Her eyes fluttered closed as his hot, sweet cum filled her mouth and eased down her throat. When he pushed her away, seconds after coming, his face was set in taut lines, and she knew it had nothing to do with overwhelming joy after the mind-numbing blow job she'd just given him.

The first blow job, mind-blowing or otherwise, she'd given to any man.

38

"Why did you do that?"

Danita slowly rose from her crouched position between his legs, straightened her clothing, and searched for the hair clip he'd pulled off her hair.

She gave up, knowing that she had more important things to do than search for the missing ornament.

Tucking her loosened hair behind her ears, she pulled her bottom lip into her mouth and glanced at Hawk worriedly.

As soon as she rose, he got up from his chair, zipped his slacks, and turned away from her. He now faced the window in the far corner of the room.

But damn, she was tired of him, in his own way, calling the shots. She wanted to get to know him. Longed to know why after going to such a prestigious college he chose to live in the same impoverished neighborhood he'd grown up in. Why he hadn't accepted the offer to practice with the high level law firm he'd interned with.

He continued to stare out the window into the pitch dark night. The silence in the room grew until Danita couldn't take it any longer.

"Hawk?"

His body jerked at the sound of her voice, as if he'd forgotten she was there. He turned his head slightly toward her, yet didn't look at her. Although he said nothing more, remained still and quiet, his body language spoke volumes.

She licked dry lips and hesitantly began to walk toward him. When she was less than a foot away she stopped. She reached a hand out to touch him, but allowed her hand to fall at her side when he turned back to face the window.

"Why don't you talk to me?"

"Don't you care about me? Don't I make you feel special? Haven't I proved how much I care about you by now? Isn't that good enough? Aren't *I* good enough?" The tic in his lean jaw was the only emotion on his face.

"Of course you are! That's not what I'm saying, damn! What's wrong with you? I just want to get to know *you*, Hawk. Really know you. I love that you want to know everything about me. I love how you make me feel when you're making love to me, when you hold my hand and just listen to me talk about my dreams, my goals, my aspirations . . . but, what about you? In the last weeks, I swear I've told you things I've never told anyone, shared with you things I never even admitted to myself!" She stopped, closed her eyes, and took a deep breath before continuing.

"But whenever I try to learn anything about you, when I ask you to share yourself with me, you either flip the script or clam up and won't tell me anything!" When he turned around to face the mirror, Danita felt the overwhelming urge to grab his thick ponytail and force him back around to face her.

He was shutting her out.

Again.

And she was getting damn tired of it.

She didn't think he'd answer it took him so long to speak. Danita blew out a frustrated breath and turned, needing to get away from him. Before she could move he turned to face her. His beautiful soulful eyes, filled with pain, stole her breath.

"It's not that easy," he said, gripping the flesh of her upper arm tightly.

"What's not so easy? Just talk to me, Hawk. Let me in, let me get the chance to know you as well as you've gotten to know me. Just talk to me," she begged without shame.

When he simply stared at her, Danita reached out and touched his face, running her fingers down the side of his smooth cheek.

He captured her hand and brought it to his lips, placing a warm kiss in the center.

One corner of his sensual, wide mouth lifted. He laced his hand with hers and walked her over to the big chair in the corner and sat down, placing her in his lap.

She lay in his lap, and although she was uncertain about him, or them as a couple, she couldn't help enjoying the reassuring thud of the sound of his heart against her ear.

"Hawk, can I ask you something?"

"Yes,"

"About the, uh . . ." her voice trailed off, unsure how to broach the subject.

"About Gregory joining us in our lovemaking?"

As usual, he seemed to know what was on her mind without her voicing it.

"Yeah . . . that."

He sighed. "It was something you wanted, something you fantasized about. I wanted to be the one to gift you with your fantasy."

"Do you always give women their fantasy?" she intuitively knew this was not only an important question, but the answer would give her better insight into what made him tick, why he on the one hand was the most attentive lover she'd ever had, while at the same time he was strangely closed off.

"I grew up on the Hopi Reservation in northeast Arizona. My family farmed, as many other families did on the reservation. My father died before I was born. My mother left when I was a kid. Said she couldn't handle raising a kid on her own. Didn't want a kid hanging around reminding her what a mess she'd made of her life."

Although he hadn't answered her question, Danita wanted desperately to turn around in his arms and soothe him, kiss him, do anything to take away the pain she heard in his voice.

Yet she remained still, simply feathering her fingers along his arms exposed by the pushed-up sleeves of his shirt.

"There was a young girl whose mother was a teacher, and after school she and her mother would come to the reservation. She was quite a bit older than me. I was only fourteen at the time. She was nineteen.

"She was so exciting to me, with her tattoos and wild ways, and she seemed to have what I wanted. Freedom. When she decided to leave her hometown that neighbored the reservation, I begged her to take me. She did.

"There wasn't anything I wouldn't do for her, and she knew it.

"When we first moved to Texas, we had a little money but it didn't last. So when she said we needed to hustle to get money, I willingly did it. I had no plans to go back to the reservation. There was nothing there for me.

"She met a few friends, and they would come to the motel we stayed at and . . . party with us.

"By party you mean—"

"The usual fare. Drugs. Sex. I was only fifteen, had only been with one woman, so I admit the attention I got was so new, so different. Damn, once she saw how much her new 'friends' were digging me, she decided it was time for me to earn my keep."

Danita was unable to prevent the sharp inhale of breath that resonated loudly in the room. Then she felt him smile against her hair.

"It's okay. It was a long time ago. And I did what I had to do to survive. The money we earned was good. Got even better when we were invited to parties where women—and men—paid top dollar for the type of services I'd become so good at," he laughed without humor and Danita wanted to cry.

It was a long time before he spoke, and Danita felt the shame radiating off him in waves. If she could, she'd go back in time to kick the woman's free-loving ass for manipulating a young boy in such a horrible way.

"Whenever I brought up the subject that I no longer wanted to prostitute, she'd get angry. Accuse me of not loving her. Cry and say that if I loved her, I would want to take care of her."

"Just like your mother."

Danita didn't realize she'd spoken out loud until he sighed and said, "Yeah, I guess so."

"I could see where your life, the way you grew up, made it hard for you to open up."

"I never really examined the whys of it. I guess that's a good enough reason as any," he murmured, stroking the top of her head. "I think this need I have to please, at any cost to myself, is part of it as well."

Danita was content to lie against him and hear the reassuring rhythmic thud of his heartbeat against her ear.

He placed two fingers beneath her chin and angled her face toward him so he could see her. "Where does all of this leave us?" he asked, and Danita heard a note of uncertainty in his voice, and her heart softened.

She reached a hand up and stroked his face, her thumb running over his sensual lips. "If you think anything you've said changes my feelings about you, you don't know me as well as you seem to think you do," she said, gently stroking her thumb over his beautiful, sensual mouth.

He opened his mouth and captured her finger in it, pulling the digit into its warmth, and suckling it before releasing it.

He pulled her toward him and they exchanged a long, leisurely kiss before she pulled away reluctantly. "But—" she began, placing a hand on his chest when he started to pull her back. "If this relationship is going to work, you've got to trust me. You've got to trust me enough to know that I'm not like the women in your past. Nor am I one to shy away from the truth. I'm a big girl. You can push me sometimes, fight with me, state your own opinions, but most of all, just let me in. That's all I ask. Do you think that's something you can handle? I want it all. Because if not, this isn't going to work. And I don't want a portion of you. I want all of you. The good and the bad. If you don't think you can handle sharing yourself, all of you, then this isn't going to work for me."

He looked at her, really looked at her. The intensity of his stare felt as though he was trying to look into her very soul. Danita felt her stomach clench the longer he stared at her, considering her words.

He framed her face. "I do want to share it all with you, Dani. I've never wanted, never trusted that I could do that with another person. But I want it. With you. I'll try my best to do what it takes to show you how much you mean to me."

Tears were in her eyes, and she rapidly opened and closed her lids, batting them away.

The smile that broke out across his lean, handsome face, the warmth in his eyes with a promise of what was to come warmed her heart and eased away any lingering feelings of doubt.

The things he told her about himself, things she knew he rarely shared with anyone else, explained so much. She drew away from him and cupped each side of his face within the palms of her hands.

"Thank you," she said and leaned up to kiss him. Even as she felt tears run unchecked from her own eyes, she thumbed away at the lone tear in the corner of his.

One side of his sensual mouth hitched upward as he placed a hand over hers. "What do you need to thank me for?" he asked, huskily, emotion deepening his voice.

"For loving me. For sharing yourself, all of you, with me."

"None of my history makes you think twice about committing to me? Makes you doubt whether you want to be with me for the long haul, Dani?" His voice was tight, but the deep emotion she saw in his expression was anything but.

"Is that what you want? The long haul?" she asked and caught her breath, waiting for his answer.

"I do," he answered simply.

Before she could answer, he went on, "Because if you say yes, you're saying yes to the whole package," he murmured, his eyes darting over her face, the love in his eyes bright, nearly blinding. "No turning back."

Danita carefully considered his words, thought over what her life had been like without him. In the few months of their relationship he'd come to mean more to her than anyone. She was tired of looking for what was missing in her life, tired of playing second. Tired of giving all she had to give and not getting anything back in return.

She smiled around the mist of tears in her eyes. Doubt, insecurities and fear of what might or might not happen fell off like the useless baggage they were as she saw a future of love and acceptance in his eyes.

"No turning back," she finally agreed, a small smile playing around the corner of he mouth.

When he pulled her close, she willingly went into his arms and wrapped her arms around his neck, embracing him as tightly as he was embracing her, secure in the love he had for her, the love they shared, and more than ready to begin their journey of discovery of one another, together.